# Gerwyn's Problems

Ken James

Ken James



ISBN 978-0-9928690-4-5

Published in the United Kingdom in 2014 by
Cambria Books, Wales, United Kingdom

CHAPTERS

Ken James

# One

You've been up since eight o'clock, Jonathan, it is now eight thirty and you've not said a word to me since you rose,' complained Lynwen, as she paced back and forth nursing her pet Pekinese whose, nose was in the air sniffing the aroma of burnt toast. 'You've poured your own coffee, made your own breakfast, slammed the door a few times and given an occasional grunt. Do tell me if I have upset you in any way.'

'You have a gift for ruining everything whenever you present yourself within my circle of influential friends and colleagues. The talents you possess aren't the kind I would have wished for in a dutiful wife.'

'Would it overtax your patience if I asked you what the hell you are talking about? What on earth have I ruined? What terrible deed have I done to bring on this bout of pouting?'

'I am not pouting. I am, however, extremely disgusted with your behaviour. These past two years we've been married I have continually had to remind you an Engineer's wife should exercise decorum. You act like a randy teenager.'

'What do you mean by that remark?' she demanded, placing her Pekinese on the settee and adjusting the neckline of her pink-laced nightdress, her morning appearance making her look a little more than her twenty five years.

'If you don't know now you never will.'

'If I knew what you were talking about I'd hardly be asking you to explain. For God's sake spit it out.'

Jonathan Pallet spun around sharply, his brown eyes staring hard at her. He wanted to shout abuse at her, but when he was in such emotional states he stammered badly. Instead he turned away from her, picked up his tie from the sideboard and began to adjust it around his neck in front of the wall mirror, focussing hard on the knot.

'Last night was four hours of embarrassment and quite insufferable,' he snapped. 'I remained sober and cringed every minute of my humiliation.'

'The trouble with you is you're stuffy, petty and over sensitive.'

'Forget it. Do yourself a favour and get dressed, or go back to bed, you look awful.'

'Thank you very much.'

'Your eyes have turned colour; the flirty blue has changed to blotchy-red.'

She turned around, her face flushed with anger. 'Go and take your beaky stuck-up nose and your podgy face into work and get out of my sight.'

He tried to keep calm. 'Have a look in the mirror, my beauty. You may just see the black roots of your blonde hair.'

'Don't say that! You know my hair is naturally blonde. Anyway, with your beer pot and stoop, you're beginning to look like an old man.'

Jonathan reached for his jacket. 'Because I am three years your senior, you seem to make this little difference an excuse to look for a younger man.'

She sat on the settee, trying to remember last night, 'What do you mean by that remark?' she asked tentatively, picking up her whining dog again.

'That kid you were seducing last night, he must have been in his teens.'

'So that's your problem. You're feeling jealous because I danced with Mike last night.'

'Mike? You were very familiar with Mike last night.'

'Bloody hell,' she fumed, dropping the dog on the settee, 'You're getting all moody over a dance.'

'I am not moody, nor am I jealous, I merely expect a wife of mine to consider the circumstances. I felt enormously embarrassed, and that's putting it mildly.'

'How do you think I felt sitting around all night while you prattled on endlessly about bonus schemes and cutting costs with that...that bore?'

'That bore, as you call him, was an influential colleague who was interested in my ideas. You should've given a little support instead of cuddling up to that teenager every time an opportunity presented itself.'

'He is not a teenager, he's twenty one, and I was not cuddling up to him.'

'Don't lie. Of course you were. You took advantage of every slow dance.'

'He kept asking me for dances. You weren't interested.'

'Of course he kept asking you, you pushed yourself into him so tightly you nearly squeezed the breath out of him.'

'The days of sitting by your husband's side smiling and nodding like a donkey went out when Henry the VIII died. Just because you want to act the Brain of Britain, doesn't mean I have to listen to that bullshit.'

Jonathan made a violent move towards her, grabbed her by the shoulders and shook her aggressively, his heart pounding with anger.

'Let me go!  Let me go!'

'Listen you bitch, do you think I'm a complete idiot? Were my eyes deceiving me when I saw you kissing him? Did you think because you were in the middle of the dance floor I couldn't see you? Did you think I didn't miss the pair of you when you both disappeared the same time? You don't just lie to me, you lie to yourself. Worse still, you believe yourself.'

'Go to hell!  Go to hell!'

'That might be an idea, I'd probably get more loyalty there.'

Jonathan threw her back on the settee causing the Pekinese

to scurry off, and then stormed out.

* * *

I'll phone in sick, thought Gerwyn in the early morning darkness of his bedroom. He'd taken fifteen minutes to persuade his lethargic body to get out of bed, during which time he'd lain on his back, blankets up to his nose, listening to the December wind howling, and the torrential rain bombarding his window panes. He sat huddled on his bed pondering the decision, his five-foot frame made to look smaller by his wilting head and his overspread shoulders. He crossed his arms over his vested chest and shivered. I can't do a full day's work on a few hours sleep. I should have a cushy job by this in life. A job where I could take a day off without them ringing me up asking how long I'm going to be ill. Shall I phone in sick?  'No no,' he whispered in the darkness. 'It's too soon to be sick again.'

Switching the light on, he dressed, disconnected the battery and bell from the alarm clock and sighed heavily. He slumped along the landing and into his fourteen-year-old daughter's bedroom. Ceris's body half rose instinctively, her long fair hair fell over her blue eyes, the distinctive colouring of her father.

'What do you want dad?'

'I've reset the alarm clock for you love. Eight o'clock OK?'

'Yes. What's the time now?'

'Quarter past six, you've got a couple of hours yet.'

'Have you taken that bell off the clock?'

'Yes love.'

'I was having a nightmare when that went off. I thought I was in hospital having an operation without anaesthetic.'

'Sorry love.' He tilted his head, 'I always use my battery and bell when your mother's not here.'

'How is she?'

'She's fine; it was her appendix, Ceris. But don't worry, she going to be all right.'

'Will she be there long?'

8

'For as long as it takes I suppose. I've got to go now. Make sure David gets up won't you, love?'

'Don't I always?' She lay back on her pillow.

Gerwyn made his way downstairs as images of past years floated through his mind: he was pulling in cables, wiring oily machines, carrying ladders, bursting his brains fault-finding on broken appliances, mending greasy cookers and never being promoted or making enough money.

He had a slow methodical wash as he mentally grumbled about the past, from the membrane-drying cement dust on the building sites blocking his nostrils, to the masonry drills dead-stopping and wrenching his wrists; from the oily factory floors, to the old wooden ladders slipping splinters into his hands. Thinking and pondering in self-pity, he was half conscious of what he was doing, he suddenly found himself driving his Ford Escort through the factory gates. I'll have to stop these mental excursions; they'll get me in trouble one day. Don't remember driving up the main road.

He parked his car, and then battled against the strong winds making his way across the concrete parking area; his head bent forward, his hands clenched tightly in his parka pockets. He charged the swing doors with his shoulder and entered the fluorescent brilliance of the factory. The clocking-in clock snapped at his card, then he inspected the time and realised he was four minutes late. Shylock will dock me for that.

He made his way through the huge machine shop looking contemptuously at the army of motley machines spread out in disorderly rows. The leaking compressed air hissed at him, dissipating the petrol blue haze hanging in the air after the nightshift. He quickly passed through, crossed the concrete yard and entered the electrical workshop where he was greeted by Steve, the shop steward, who was sorting his tools on the steel bench.

* * *

Jonathan was driving his Vauxhall Astra at an alarming speed. His storming out of the house after his quarrel with Lynwen had left him in a careless and irresponsible mood. Speeding down the long and winding road to town, he was oblivious to everything. He had driven up from the low land where he lived, surmounted the hilltop, then put his foot hard down on the accelerator, frenzied, as though he were pressing his foot on the throat of his wife. He joined the traffic on the busy A-Road, but his speed did not diminish, for he could not clear his mind of his cheating wife. He had finally concluded she was treacherous, thick-skinned and numb to the pain she was causing him.

He thought of the past events he had taken her to in the hope that she would be an asset to his ambitions and impress the influential people he associated with. But each picture he saw of her was one of leading on a member of the opposite sex; looking deep into a young man's eyes, dancing close in an erotic manner, laughing at juvenile jokes, having her bottom slapped, dallying, trifling, toying and always wearing provocative, revealing clothes.

His face was crimson with rage, his knuckles white as he gripped the wheel with vice-like hands. But worse, was when she denied all knowledge of her antics and lies would roll off her tongue as smooth and pure as a gentle stream meandering through woodland. He could not break down her pretentious innocence because she believed the lies she told. 'Yes,' he whispered to himself, 'She believes herself when all around her knows it's all a fabrication of the truth.' He'd had enough of the lying bitch...

A scream of brakes and a high pitched prolonged horn brought him back to his driving as he stretched his neck in a nervous reaction. He relaxed his foot off the accelerator and slowed to a reasonable speed as he approached the outskirts of town. He smirked unconsciously as he thought of her hearing the news of an accident he might have been involved in. She'd like that; get killed pranging the car. Maybe that's why she winds me up in the morning. Have me drive off in a rage. She'd be free. She could enjoy herself with her young studs and my insurance.

He smiled to himself. I'll have to be as cunning as her, he thought as he drove his car in to the car park at Flint's Component Factory.

* * *

'Morning, happy,' Steve said, his tall, six-foot figure towering, his long brown hair touching his shoulders.

'I don't find anything good about it to be honest, Steve,' moaned Gerwyn.

'I didn't say it was good, I merely said it was morning.'

'This place depresses me.'

'What? This comfy electrical shop with its festooning cables hanging on the walls, and the boxes of fluorescent tubes, the oily benches and post war drilling machine? Be grateful you're not on a building site.'

'I don't just mean the electrical shop, I mean the whole factory. It's prison for a day.'

'You went out last night and dunked your head in a beer barrel didn't you? And now you can't cope with the hangover.'

'That would be something. No, I've been up most of the night with the missus. She'd been suffering stomach pains for hours so I called the doctor. He booked her into hospital straight away; it was acute appendix. They operated immediately. I couldn't leave her until she came back from the operating theatre, could I? When she did come back she didn't know who I was.'

'Is she all right?'

'When I left she was dazed. I expect she's sitting up and enjoying bacon and eggs now.'

'Don't sound so envious.'

'Nothing seems to be going right lately. I feel all knotted up inside.'

Steve closed the lid of his toolbox and sat down. 'You should have rung in sick.'

'I did think of it but a picture of Shylock crossed my mind.'

Steve stood up and put his arm around Gerwyn's shoulder, dwarfing him. 'The wife's all right so cheer up.'

'Yea, I suppose you're right. There are times, though, when I feel I'll only be happy when I've retired. Yes, come to think of it, I'll be happy when I reach sixty five.'

'Another five years you'll be happy then.'

'I'm only forty. I don't look sixty do I?'

'Let's have a look,' said Steve with mischievous eyes, placing his heavy hands on Gerwyn's shoulders. 'At a closer look I would say you look younger, about fifty five.'

Gerwyn's face dropped, but then he could see the glint in Steve's eye, 'Do you think I'd look younger if I wore my hair at shoulder length like you? I know your hair is dark and mine is a bit grey, but maybe I could use a bit of colouring.'

'You want to be sixty five but look thirty five is it? I'll take you over the valley to some of the hot spots; I'd fix you up with a nice little blonde.'

'You're married!'

'So what, she goes her way, I go mine.'

'That sounds like aggro. I want to be contented like the old boys. I see them sitting there on park benches, smoking their pipes and smirking; kids grown up, mortgage paid, nest egg in the bank, that's freedom.'

'You're a space traveller. Those guys are sitting on the bench because they've nowhere else to go, probably been told to bugger off out by those caring for them. A lot of those old boys on the benches are lonely. What have you got to worry about? Nothing.'

Gerwyn gave it some thought, 'Maybe not. My two oldest will look after themselves while Hilary's in hospital, and Allison will go to Hillary's sister in the other street. But the cost of living has caught up with me, that's the problem. I've got the mortgage to pay, my car is on hire purchase, and there are a few other things to pay for. Three kids can be expensive.'

Steve shook his head. 'You've got a good job which brings in a regular wage.'

'I know you're right Steve, but that doesn't solve my problems. I just need a little extra cash to maintain things. I asked Shylock for some overtime last week, but according to him there's none going.'

'You asked for overtime? We spend years fighting for a shorter week and you go and ask for overtime!'

'In reality,' moaned Gerwyn, 'we still work the same number of hours, but now the extra hours are called overtime.'

'But it's not compulsory. Anyway, if you want to earn some more money you'll have to do what the rest of us do: work shifts.'

Gerwyn's pale face went a shade paler. 'I couldn't work shifts. It wouldn't agree with my constitution. It would upset me.' He went to his steel locker and pulled out his blue boiler suit. Placing it carefully on the radiator to warm, he turned round and leaned back on the heater.

Steve looked through his work cards he'd collected from the job tray, disgruntled at what Jonathan Pallet had left for him. Gerwyn's staring eyes were transfixed to the floor as he went into a semi trance, his lifeless hair sticking out limply. Occasionally he'd pucker his lips as though some doubtful thought had crossed his mind: 'I could never come to this place at night. I've seen those machine operators in the morning after working a nightshift; they're like zombies.'

'If you want to earn the same money as shift workers, that's what you've got to do. You can't work days regular and expect the same money as those zombies.'

'And then there would be two afternoon shifts, two day shifts, two off and start all over again,' he moaned--'How do you cope, Steve?'

'I don't. I opt out of reality. After six shifts my head is like an oil drum full of manic bees.  My muscles are lumps of soggy dough, but my resistance is low, so a couple of pints and I'm pissed.'

'I heard it takes years off your life Steve.'

'You've got to die sometime.'

'God I could never do it.--Christmas is only three weeks away. I'd rather go without a present than earn extra money working shifts.'

Steve gave him a hard look, 'You do all right moonlighting.'

'Repairing Christmas tree lights? Thank-you jobs, they are.'

'How long have you been here, Gerwyn?'

'Just over two years.'

Steve puckered his lips, 'You're entitled to apply for grade eight status.'

'I thought you had to have special qualifications for that grade.'

'You need to satisfy a list of requirements, that's all. The main requirement is service. You have to be employed by the company for at least two years and be able to do the job. You satisfy those requirements. It means eight pounds a week more.'

'Eight pounds more?' Gerwyn placed his hands together and shuffled up to Steve. 'Do you think Shylock would give me the grade, Steve? I don't think he likes me a lot.'

'He doesn't like anybody. Besides, you do the same work as the rest of the sparks here, and that includes grade eight work.'

'I don't really know what grade eight work is, Steve; I just do what Shylock tells me. It's never been explained to me. I'm sorry, Steve, maybe I should have taken more interest.'

'Stop apologising. That's the trouble with you, you're always sorry and showing a lack of confidence.'

'I don't like a lot of aggro Steve. You know how tight Shylock is. He can get very upset where money is concerned. You'd think he was paying the money from his own Building Society account.'

'He's no problem. You're entitled to grade eight. If he refuses,

I'll take him through the grievance procedure.'

Gerwyn grimaced, and his brow furrowed. He went quiet for a few minutes, and then looked plaintively at his shop steward.

'I think the very sight of me upsets him Steve,' he said, tilting his head to his right shoulder. 'I don't want to get into his bad books.'

'You don't need the cash badly then, do you?'

'I do, Steve. It's just that, well, It would sound better coming from you' He tilted his head a little more.

Steve straightened his back and placed his hands on his hips, 'Now wait a minute Gerwyn, the procedure specifically states the first move in any grievance must come from the individual. You'll have to see Pallet yourself first.'

'But I haven't got a grievance Steve, I've got a problem.'

'You've got a problem all right. Now listen, if you want promotion, you'll have to make the first move.'

'Yes, I suppose you're right, I'll see him tomorrow.'

'Tomorrow? What's the matter with today? Just don't ask him first thing in the morning.  He's always in a foul mood in the mornings.'

Gerwyn was looking at Steve, but he didn't seem to be taking it all in.

'He smirks at me, Steve, and accuses me with those dark eyes of his. He twists his lips and drains the confidence from me, and then he stands, towering over me, making me feel like a midget; I'm only five feet but he's over six.'

'Are you sixteen ounces? He does those things deliberately to intimidate you.'

'He succeeds.'

'He's just a man like you and me.'

'He's not like me, Steve.'

Steve glanced at his mate who's face had added lines around the eyes. 'Gerwyn, you all right?'

'I'm fine, Steve. Do you think we could go to the canteen for a

cup of tea?'
   'Come on, we'll have one before I start this lot Shylock left for me.'

# Two

Been given a light job for the morning, Gerwyn?' Joked the fork-lift driver in the despatch department, stopping his truck to have a quip at Gerwyn. 'Careful you don't fall off that stepladder, those light bulbs can prove heavy at times.'

'Good boy Colin, I can always rely on you for an original joke,' replied Gerwyn, his five-foot figure stretching to reach the light fitting.

'You sparks are top paid men, and all you do is change bloody bulbs. Doesn't exactly stretch the power of thought, does it.'

'This is just a fill-in-in job while our better halves have a lie-in.'

'Whenever I see an electrician he's changing bulbs.'

'It's not exactly a technical department down here, is it?' A monkey could be trained for this place, a clean area with a couple of dozen female packers on the production line. Your missus washes your overalls once a year, does she?'

'I'll swap you pay packets any day.'

Gerwyn looked at Colin sitting in his forklift truck and asked plaintively, 'Will you drive me up to the electrical shop, Colin? I'm a couple of 60 watt lamps short.'

'You must be joking; you should have brought more with you.'

Gerwyn slowly got down off the ladder. 'Listen, I had to carry a box of 60 watt lamps, four five-foot fluorescent tubes, two eight-foot tubes, tools and a step-ladder. I'm like a pack mule about the place.'

'Don't let the job get you down, Gerwyn, just because you are too short. Get it? Two short? Bulbs I mean.'

Gerwyn ignored the reference to his height and picked up the boxes of spent lamps, fluorescent tubes, the step ladder and his toolbox. With everything hanging on him precariously, he walked off.

'Never mind, Gerwyn, the exercise will do you good.'

'Your cholesterol is congealing sitting in that fork-lift all day' Gerwyn said quietly. 'I hope it's got a dead-man's handle; you'll run some poor girl over one day when you snuff it.'

He pushed through the large rubber swing doors, spreading his legs to prevent the doors from rebounding on him, but they sprang back knocking the spent tubes out of his grip and exploding. After he had cleared up most of the broken glass, he passed through the assembly department, nodding to the busy girls sitting at the rumbling conveyor. They wolf-whistled him as he knew they would. He made the long trek through the despatch yard, past the loading bay and across the road. He continued through the assembly shop, up steep concrete steps and around the main machine shop before reaching the electrical workshop. He was surprised to find the production foreman inside looking impatient, his hands gripping the collar of his white overall coat, tight around his thick-set stature. His craggy face was stern but lit up when he saw Gerwyn.

'Gerwyn, the automatic is on the blink; the production line will be held up if we don't get it going soon,' he said in a cockney accent.

'Sorry, my work-load's all sorted for the early morning period down the despatch department,' he said, throwing the used bulbs in a big steel bin.

'Never mind the bloody despatch department, this takes priority. Steve's on another priority job, so that leaves you.'

'The foreman down despatch has been chasing Shylock for days to get these lighting jobs done,' he said, nervously as he reached for a new box of lamps from a shelf.

'Leave the despatch foreman to me, I've marked the

requisition form with a bold 'Urgent'.  I want this job done now!'

'You might be able to sort the despatch foreman out, but what about Shylock?'

'I'll sort Shy...Jonathan out.--Do you call him Shylock to his face?'

'Don't be ridiculous, I call him Jonathan. He doesn't call me Mr Freeman.'

'Never mind, never mind. Come on.'

Gerwyn conceded, 'I'll collect some testing gear and follow you over,' he sighed.

After collecting what he thought he might need for the job, Gerwyn walked across to the big machine shop. As he entered he was hit by the deafening roar of two hundred machines, blanking out all verbal communication; from the thudding of the presses to the rattling of the automatics, the rumbling of the milling machines to the screeching of the high-speed drills and the droning of countless gearboxes. Such ear-splitting noise inspired the workforce to lip- read. The oily, hazy atmosphere always depressed Gerwyn so much that he tried to breath as shallow as possible not to pollute his lungs. He nodded to many of the sickly-looking operators painted by the oxygen-starved ambience, before arriving at the complicated Maindy Auto'. His face was not a happy sight.

'Come on, Gerwyn,' shouted the foreman, 'production is suffering.'

Gerwyn looked at the massive complicated machine, its large separate control cabinet looking depressingly formidable. It housed the electronics and electrics, all neatly compacted in sections of relays, printed circuit boards contactors and hundreds of metres of different coloured wiring. Snaking along the floor from cabinet to the machine was the grey elephant-trunk-like harness packed with wires which pulsed the messages to the control box. The machine was dead and awaiting the technical skills of Gerwyn to bring it back to life.  He climbed up on to the platform of the machine where the operator stood at the control consul.

'You'd better tell me exactly what the symptoms are,' he yelled, trying to raise his voice above the din.

'It stops half way through the cycle,' the operator screamed back. 'I've got to get up on the control platform and start it up all over again.'

Gerwyn shook his head and made his way down the steps and around the back to the control panel. He took out a grubby electrical drawing, unfolded it, until his arms became inadequate then placed it on the floor and studied. He tested everything he could in the panel carrying out all the simple obvious checks in hope it might be a sticky contactor or faulty solenoid.. He came to the conclusion the trouble was in the bowels of the machine itself, where lay oil-proof control limit switches.

He needed help from a machine-tool fitter to strip the machine. Firstly, he had to justify calling out a fitter by proving where the fault lay.  He spent another half hour removing cover plates and protective steel cladding which caused the usual cutting of fingers and getting oiled up. He got through the trauma by swearing and hitting the machine with his hammer.

Shining his torch inside the belly of the big machine he could see a limit switch arm hanging limply at the side of a steaming cog wheel near hydraulic pipes. His heart gave a skip, for not only had he located the fault, it was not an electrical fault but a mechanical one. It was a specially designed striker-bracket made from tempered steel and had a complicated geometrical shape.

'Any luck Gerwyn?' shouted the foreman, who had made several visits to the machine, and asked the same question each time.

'Yea, it's not an electrical fault, it's a mechanical one,' he yelled above the din. 'You'll have to fetch a fitter.'

The foreman looked at Gerwyn suspiciously, 'And after he's spent an hour on it, he'll tell me it's an electrical fault.'

'No, no. You bring him over and I'll show him what the

trouble is. It's definitely a fitter's fault and possibly a toolmaker needed.'

'That's the production figures down the chute. Do you think it can be done today?'

'You'll have to see the boffins for that answer.'

'Balls to this, I'm putting it in the hands of the Production Manager.'

Gerwyn shrugged his shoulders, 'I wish I could do more.' He packed his tools into his plastic toolbox.--An angler's accessory box which held all the tools and paraphernalia an electrician carries. It hung insecurely on a plastic handle. Gerwyn gave a sigh of relief and made his way back to the electrical workshop, his head buzzing from the noise. Maybe the right moment to approach Jonathan Pallet for upgrading crossed his mind. He looked at the bloody piece of paper towel wrapped around his finger secured by black insulation tape. I look good, he thought. Found the fault on the Maindy Auto and I'm all greased up plus an injured finger. I hope sniggering Sid isn't there. As he crossed from the machine shop to the electrical workshop he noticed Jonathan's car in the side car park. Good, he thought, he's in.

Unable to knock Jonathan Pallet's door because his hands were full of tools and testing gear, he nudged the handle of the door down with his elbow and pushed his way in.

'Morning Jonathan,' he said softly, his eyes alternating from Jonathan to Sidney. 'Good morning Sidney,' he added to the mechanical engineer.

They both mumbled, morning, as they continued writing at their respective desks, not bothering to look up at the intruder. The room was only six feet wide, ten feet long and eight feet high. Having two facing desks, three steel cabinets and a number of shelves stacked with technical books and catalogues, it only left room for two plastic chairs pushed up against the wall. Gerwyn shuffled against the chairs and stood in the only available space near Sidney Soper. Eventually their writing came to an end and Jonathan Pallet looked up, surprised at the grimy appearance of Gerwyn.

'Fall down a hole or something, Gerwyn?'

Gerwyn gave a half-hearted chuckle at the old joke. 'I've been busy on the new Maindy Auto; an hour I've been working on it and when I found the fault, it was a mechanical problem.'

Sidney Soper looked up from his writing and peered over his spectacles. An enigmatic grin came to his saliva-shining lips, and his brown eyes gleamed at Gerwyn with accusation.

'It's always a mechanical problem when an electrician can't get things going,' he drawled.

'No honest now,' defended Gerwyn. 'An interior striker arm for A51 limit switch has snapped and a new one will have to be made.'

'I'll send a fitter along to sort it out,' sneered Sidney, then returned to his paperwork.

Gerwyn squared his shoulders, 'As I'm here Shyl... Jonathan, I wonder if you've got five minutes, I want to ask you something.'

Jonathan stared at him for a few seconds, not answering the little man. 'Yes? Well?'

Gerwyn tilted his head to the left, and then placed his toolbox and testing gear on the floor giving him more time to think. He looked at Jonathan trying to find the right words, clasping his hands together, twisting them. Jonathan looked him up and down with contempt, furtively glanced at his colleague sitting opposite, and then rolled his eyes up into his head.

'Uh...I've been thinking,' began Gerwyn.

'Congratulations,' snapped the engineer.

Sidney peered over his glasses and grinned.

'I mean, well, I've been here now for over two years and....'

'Congratulations and celebrations'

The mechanical engineer took off his glasses and chuckled, then replaced them.

'Let me work this out Gerwyn,' said Jonathan, 'You've been thinking, and you've been here for two years. Does that mean you've been thinking for two years?'

Sidney removed his glasses again and chuckled, 'I think you'll have to inform the shop steward about that, Jonathan,' he said.

'To hell with you,' snapped Gerwyn, the humiliation angering him. 'You're like a couple of school kids.' He picked up his tools.

'Don't be touchy, Gerwyn,' said Jonathan. 'Get to the point and tell me what you want.'

He replaced his tools on the floor. 'I've been told I'm entitled to be made up to grade eight, he said boldly. 'I've been here two years,'

'You've been told. Maybe I should have been told. Who's authorising such a promotion, may I ask?'

'Well, it, sort of came up in conversation,' he said, wiping the palms of his hands on the legs of his overalls.

'It sort of came up in conversation, Sid,' repeated Jonathan. 'Let me envisage the scene. I see you sitting down sipping a well-earned cup of tea--Let us say, you're with your shop steward--when suddenly, out of the blue the S/S says, "You've been here two years, Gerwyn, ask Jonathan for a rise. "

Gerwyn bowed his head slightly, 'Something like that,' he said, glad to have the negotiations in motion. 'I work on a lot of grade eight jobs, I think. Take the Maindy I've just been working on.'

'There are grade eight jobs are there? As opposed to grade seven, you mean?'

'You must admit some jobs are more complicated than others.'

'They are all electrical jobs in a competent electrician's day. You really should not be so naive as to be set up by the more experienced electricians. We require at this establishment what we term as grades six, seven, and eight craftsmen. The number we require is, of course, decided by the Senior Engineer. Not, as you have been led to believe, by the bloody shop steward. Now, The Senior Engineer, in all his wisdom, has allotted us five grade eight electricians and two grade seven. If we start asking him to revise those numbers, he may carry out an investigation into our requirements and decide we are over manned. However, if a grade eight craftsman should terminate his employment with us in the future, you may apply for the post. Until such time you will have to wait, is that perfectly understood?'

'I see,' said Gerwyn, sighing loudly. 'Does that mean I should only do grade seven work until I get a grade eight post comes along?'

'If you wish to be a grade eight in the future, you will need to be prepared for it when, and if, you are called for the duty, However, I will bring your eagerness for the post to the attention of the Chief Engineer the next time I see him, I'm sure he will be impressed.'

'I'd appreciate that, Jonathan, I could write to him if you're busy.'

'You wouldn't go over my head, would you Gerwyn? Listen!' growled Jonathan, changing his tone, 'I have a job here for you, it's a yearly maintenance on the Air Conditioning Plants for the office block; plant room I to 8. Take it and get on with it,' he said handing Gerwyn a white card.

'I haven't finished the El weekly down at despatch yet.'

'Why? It doesn't take long.'

'I had a lot of extras to do. When I came up here for more bulbs the production foreman nabbed me for the Maindy job.'

Sidney looked up from his writing and grinned again. 'There's nothing like a few extras to stretch the job.'

'If you don't believe me ask the despatch foreman.'

'Well hurry up and finish the despatch job first,' said Jonathan. 'And make sure you write a report on all the extra work you've claimed to have done. Then do the air conditioning.'

'I thought this air conditioning job was worth more than four hours, Jonathan,' queried Gerwyn nervously, reading the card.

'You're confusing it with another Plant job,' his engineer replied curtly. 'Just get on with it and stop whinging.'

'I don't think so Jonathan. I did plant rooms I to 8 the last time it came up, I'm sure the time was four and a half hours.'

'I've just taken the official time out of the Time and Study book. Don't argue. Just get on with it Gerwyn.'

Dejectedly, Gerwyn picked up his toolbox and testing equipment and left the office, leaving Jonathan and Sidney smiling with satisfaction. Sidney took off his glasses and shook his head in mock disapproval. 'You're a swine Pallet,' he said, grinning through his large protruding teeth. 'You've cut another half hour off that job.'

'The boffins in Time and Study are too soft.'

Gerwyn walked across the concrete yard to the spring-loaded doors which led to the machine shop. He attempted to push his way through but the doors swung back on him, knocking his toolbox and breaking it away from its flimsy handle. The box flew back into the concrete yard crashing to the ground and bursting open. The contents spilled everywhere sending fuses flying, washers gyrating, tiny bulbs bursting and an uncountable number of small nuts and bolts going in all directions. He would not have felt so bad had Sian, the attractive young secretary from the office, not been passing at the time of his mishap.

'Why did you do that, Gerwyn?' She joked, trying not to notice his embarrassment.

'Sian, I'm having a bad day, love.'

'Let me help you,' she said, as she sat on her heels and began to pick up the pieces, tucking her clerical file under her arm.

'Thank you Sian, love.'

'Anytime Gerwyn, anytime.'

'I love the way you said that, Sian,' he said, admiring the twenty one-year-old's perfect shape beneath her skin-tight jeans, and pink top which was even tighter than her jeans.

'Now, now, Gerwyn, I'm picking up your tools not you.'

'You're a perfect pick-me-up Sian, I'm feeling better already.'

'There, that's the lot.'

'Thank you Sian, I really appreciate your help, honestly.'

'That's OK,' she said, giving him a wink and a mischievous grin. 'You're quite cheeky sometimes, you know.'

'Best part of the morning,' he said, as he watched her go, his eyes following her until she disappeared into Jonathan Pallet's office.

# Three

Gerwyn's wife was sitting up in bed in the eight-bed ward chatting to the patients. They were all waiting for their visitors to arrive. Hilary was a small boned lady with a thin face and a slight figure. Her pale green eyes had lost their sparkle after the ordeal of her appendix operation and her mousy-coloured hair had no sheen, but she smiled with a spirited determination. All the ladies were in bed and wore respectable attire as the ward Sister demanded at visiting times. The tops of the lockers were neat and tidy; plastic jugs full of water and a plastic beaker ready for use.

As the visitors passed the second bay in which Gerwyn's wife waited, she noticed a man carrying a portable television. Hilary looked expectantly to the entrance waiting for the appearance of her husband. A middle-aged couple came in, and then came an elderly lady appearing confused and flustered, looking around the room. She threw her arms in the air triumphantly when she recognised the lady she had come to visit. A group of five came in and spread themselves to various beds; but no Gerwyn. Hilary pretended she didn't mind and busied herself straightening the bedclothes, gently caressing and flattening the creases. Soon the short figure of Gerwyn appeared, flushed and breathless. He made his way to his wife and gave her a peck on the cheek.

'How are you feeling, love?' he asked automatically.

'I'm all right. Trust you to be last in. Where are the children?'

'I thought it best not to bring them this evening. I didn't know whether you'd be up to it. It's high up here. This is the 6th floor.'

He pulled up a plastic chair and sat at her side.

'The children could have come,' she said, disappointingly.'

'There's plenty of time for them to visit. How are you?'

'I'm all right, I told you. I'm feeling a bit sore that's all. I didn't sleep very well. There's an eighty-five year-old lady in one of the cubicles wailing all night and calling for her mother.'

'Her mother still alive?'

'Of course not; the old dear is confused.'

'I'm sorry to hear that, love. Maybe you'll have a better night tonight. I haven't had a very good day myself.'

'I expect it's been worse than mine,' said Hilary with irony.

'Well the bonus is down for one thing. I've been very busy in work. I went to see Shylock for a--'

'Shylock?'

'I've mentioned him before, Jonathan Pallet, my boss.'

'Oh him. He seemed quite nice when I met him at the Christmas do.'

'He's not as nice as you think. I went to see him for a rise.'

'You're lying to me, Gerwyn.'

'I did, honest.'

'Good God, What got into you? Don't tell me: Valium.'

'I'm not a junkie—I've asked to be promoted to grade eight.'

'Grade eight? You're all electricians. You're not a basket of eggs to be graded.'

'You don't understand. There are different skills and crafts required from each man.'

'What did he say?'

'He turned me down.'

'Why is that? You're as good as any of them. Fight for your rights.'

'I don't know, love. He says I can't have grade eight, so that's it.'

'Has anybody else got grade eight?'

'They all have except me and Ronnie.'

'Well then, go and see your union. Don't let them take advantage of you. I know you; half- hearted, that's you.'

'You don't understand, Hilary, it's a little more complicated than that. Maybe I can make a few quid some other way.'

'You'll have to stop going out for a drink so often.'

'You mean I should go out once a fortnight instead of once a week?'

'You go out more often than that.'

'I don't really. I go on a hobble now and again, but that's no fun.'

'Don't say hobble, private jobs, you mean. Hobble means to walk with a limp.'

'That's how I feel after doing them. You want to try crawling around in some attic for a couple of hours.'

'Did you think of bringing in my portable TV? I wanted to watch Coronation Street tonight.  It's nearly time for it.'

'That's what I meant when I said I've had a bad day; I was turned down for upgrading, upset my toolbox spilling the contents all over the place, squashed until I nearly suffocated in the lift on the way up here, then the lift got stuck between floors, and when I walked into the ward with the TV in my hand, the staff nurse took it off me to have the plug checked for safety. That's the procedure here, so it seems.'

'Did you tell her you are a qualified electrician?'

'She has to stick to the procedure, hasn't she?'

'I wish she was as quick with the portable telephone that's not working. I wanted to phone you this morning to tell you I need a clean nightie, but I couldn't.'

'Do you think I should go to church, love?' Gerwyn asked earnestly.

'What on earth for?' retorted Hilary.

'It might change my luck.'

'There's something wrong with you Gerwyn, you're going floppy in the head. It's those Valiums you're taking. You'll have to stop relying on them; they're taking all the fluid away from your brain. You'll have brain damage if you carry on.'

'Don't talk daft. I only take one now and again, and don't talk so loud, I don't want it broadcast throughout the hospital. I have one occasionally, that's all.'

'Occasionally! You walk around the house like the Hunchback of Notre Dame deafened by the bells.'

'You're in a funny mood...You look nice and comfortable lying there--looks cosy.'

'What are you trying to say now?'

'Well you look nice and settled and comfortable: you've got your drinks at you're side, chocolates...and fruit. You're doing OK that's all I'm saying.'

'Well good God. You're jealous!'

'Don't be daft, of course I'm not.'

'I'm not here to enjoy it. I've had my appendix out. I've been ill.'

'I know, love, I know. I didn't mean...Just calm down.' Gerwyn looked round furtively hoping nobody overheard the conversation, but was disappointed to see one middle-aged lady looking his way. She was distracted however, by a young man entering the ward carrying a portable television. His mop of black hair almost hid his brown eyes as he scanned the room. He wore a pair of denim jeans and a grey, short-sleeved shirt. Gerwyn recognised the television he was carrying.

'Who does this TV belong to?' called the young man loudly. 'Anybody here?'

Gerwyn cleared his throat and put his hand up like a schoolchild wanting to leave the room. The young man nodded and brought the television over, placing it on the trolley-table at the foot of the bed.

'It's all yours,' he said cheerfully. 'You can use it now. I've put a 3 amp fuse in the plug. The 13 amp in there was a bit much.'

'I've been meaning to change that,' said Gerwyn, half smiling. 'You a spark, then?' he asked, then felt a fool.

'I was when I started here four years ago, but with these new flexibility agreements, I now range from a Domestic Assistant to an Electronics Engineer. Oh well, happy viewing. Got to go,' he said, and left.

'That's the kind of job I should have, really. Nice clean job with nice clean conditions. A youngster like that should be out on the building sites wiring houses or in a factory mending machines.'

'Why didn't you put a 3 amp fuse in that plug?'

'I didn't have a 3 amp at the time.'

She gave him a suspicious look. 'Plug it in for me and tune it to Coronation Street, I've missed half of it already.'

Gerwyn obeyed. He placed it on the bedside locker, tuned it in to the required programme and sat back. He looked around the ward inspecting the occupant of each bed. Then he examined the visitors at each bed. Everybody seemed to have something to talk about. He folded his arms and then he unfolded them and folded them again.

'Talk to me,' she said.

'I thought you wanted to listen to the television, love.'

'I don't want people to think I'm addicted to the thing.'

'Shall I just make motions with my mouth?'

'Don't be stupid, you'll look ridiculous.'

I only said that to have something to say.'

'What? Oh. Well, just say something, as long as it makes sense.'

Gerwyn looked around the room again and smiled half-heartedly at nobody in particular. His eyes wandered beyond the entrance of the ward and into the corridor where he caught a glimpse of a young nurse passing. She gave him a big smile, her blue eyes sparkling in the fluorescent light. 'I wouldn't mind having a straight simple heart attack,' he whispered, turning his head to his wife. 'Just a slight one. That nurse could come and give me a bed bath. You wouldn't mind that love, would you?' But his quietness was lost in the other conversations going on in the ward.

'What? What are you mumbling about Gerwyn?'

'I was just telling myself this is not a bad hospital if there's not a lot wrong with you. You're treated like a lord. Not a worry in the world. All you have to do is sit back and be served on. Bacon and egg for breakfast, cup of tea anytime you want it.'

'What on earth are you rambling on about?'

'You asked me to say something, love. Oh I see, the adverts are on.'

'Yes the adverts are on. What were you saying about the hospital?'

'I was saying, providing there isn't a lot wrong with you, being in hospital can be like a little holiday.'

'You can come in anytime you like without having anything wrong with you.'

Gerwyn sat up and stared at his wife, then smiled broadly. 'Can you, love? That sounds promising.'

'Of course you can. After having three kids, you are entitled to have a vasectomy. And the sooner you have it the better.'

Gerwyn clamped his legs together, then looked around the room to see if anyone noticed his sudden change of expression and movement.

'What did you want to say that for? You're always bringing that subject up; you know I could never undergo that sort of operation.'

Gerwyn said very little after that. He was very much relieved when the pretty nurse appeared again and shouted, time, bringing the visiting to a close.

'I've got to go now, love,' he said quickly, as he leaned over and gave her a farewell peck on the cheek. 'See you tomorrow.'

'Ta ta, love, don't forget my nightie, will you?' Then she turned back to the portable TV.

# Four

Jonathan, have you got five minutes to spare for your favourite shop steward?' asked Steve, opening the door of the Engineer's Office and pushing his tall figure half through.

'I take it you're here officially as a shop steward and not as an electrician?'

'I've got Gerwyn with me, it's about his upgrading. He qualifies for grade eight now.'

'You are very tiresome at times, Steve. I have already told Gerwyn that there are no vacancies for grade eight electricians at present.'

'Fair enough,' said Steve, puckering his thick lips and shaking his shock of brown hair. 'I want to make it official. You are saying in effect, there is no grade eight work for Gerwyn.'

'I didn't say that. What I am endeavouring to make clear is that the allocation for grade eight craftsmen at this factory is filled.'

'It means exactly the same thing,' remarked Steve, still not fully into the room. 'What you are saying is that the existing grade eight men are coping quite well without the help of Gerwyn, yet he fills in for us on many occasions when required. He is working on grade eight all the time. I will have to take the matter through the grievance procedure.'

'Steve, you'd better come in and we'll discuss it,' relented Jonathan, showing annoyance to Sidney, sitting opposite him.

Steve walked in confidently, followed by the insecure Gerwyn. Gerwyn looked at his boss apologetically, but the disgruntled engineer returned a disgusted expression. Steve sat down but Gerwyn remained standing, nervously, his head tilted slightly to the right. He glanced at Sidney and found him peering over his glasses at him.

'Now,' began Jonathan, there is no way we can give Gerwyn grade eight status. The number of personnel required does not justify another grade eight electrician. It's as simple as that. As I told Gerwyn, I would love to help him, but my hands are tied.'

'Fair enough, if your hands are tied we can arrive at a, failure-to-agree situation, and carry it on to the next stage of the grievance procedure. I must ask you officially, at this point in time, to arrange a meeting with Mr, Crabbe and myself.'

'I don't see any point in troubling the senior engineer.'

'Are you refusing to arrange a meeting with me and Fred Crabbe?'

'I'm not refusing anything. As far as I am concerned there is no vacancy for a grade eight electrician, unless, of course, you know more about my job than I do. Perhaps management has advised you about this job and omitted to inform me,' he said, sarcastically. 'Unless, of course,  you are creating a job? Now, please, I'm busy,'

'Don't start talking about jobs being created,' Steve snapped.

'Calm down, Steve, we don't want to say things we may regret.'

'I'm calm enough, it's you who's changing the subject. The fact is that you want Gerwyn to carry out grade eight work but you're only prepared to pay him grade seven wages.'

'What Gerwyn is entitled to is the wage he agreed to, and accepted, when first he started here.  The Contract of Employment is honoured.'

'The Contract of Employment states that he will be employed as a grade seven electrician on a day shift regular basis. You are asking him to carry out work that is outside that contract. Therefore, you pay him the wage outside that contract. We will have to come to a failure-to-agree.'

'Alright, let us suppose you take the matter on to the next

stage and meet with Fred Crabbe, the first question he will ask you is, has the man got the necessary qualifications which warrant grade eight status?'

'Only one qualification is needed: That he's capable of doing the job and has been doing the job competently for the past two years. You have authorised him to do Grade 8. You have no grounds to turn him down.'

'A candidate has to satisfy all the qualifications as laid down in the company manual. And there is no doubt about that.' said Jonathan, raising his voice indignantly. 'You really should know all about that as an experienced shop steward.'

Gerwyn's head tilted a little more, and Sidney's self-satisfied expression had been lost in the pretence that he was more interested in his paperwork than the conversation. But now there was a crease creeping up on Sidney's lip giving him away, and a cold sweat beginning to shine on the face of Gerwyn.

'He's been here two years I agree,' continued the engineer, 'but that's all I do know. Is he prepared to do small jobs of other trades? Can he supervise if necessary? Can he read electrical drawings? Has he served an electrical apprenticeship? There are many conditions he has to satisfy you know.'

'Don't talk ridiculous, of course he can satisfy all those conditions. If you don't know that by now you must be completely out of touch with your workforce.'

'If you'll excuse me,' said Sidney, getting up and making for the door, 'I must make a visit while you sort yourselves out.'

'Excuse me,' said Gerwyn, slowly rubbing his hands together, 'but if it's going to cause a lot of bother...'

'Hold it, Gerwyn,' said Steve. 'Our engineer is adopting a work-to-rule attitude.'

'Another condition I would like to bring to your notice,' said Jonathan, showing an air of triumph. 'Gerwyn needs to be in possession of his final City & Guilds. Did he obtain his final?'

Both shop steward and engineer looked at Gerwyn

simultaneously. Gerwyn straightened his head and nodded with little resolution, again rubbing his hands nervously.

'I've got my Part 1.'

'The conditions laid down in the company manual specifically ask for Parts I and 2. So you see, Steve, he cannot satisfy all the conditions.' Jonathan smirked, waiting.

Steve stared at his boss, thinking. 'You know as well as I do that if your eyes are the right colour the conditions are overlooked. There are, and you can't deny it, craftsmen working here who have been upgraded without having passed their final City & Guilds.'

'Management have tightened up on that slack practice, and I haven't the power to overrule.'

'Your recommendation will go a long way for Gerwyn's upgrading, you know that.'

'My hands are tied, sorry, I'm not going to argue anymore.'

Steve stood and glared at the engineer. Then he looked at Gerwyn who had tilted his head again and was taking interest in the service manuals, books and catalogues on the shelves. Steve took another dark look at his boss but controlled his anger. Jonathan sat smugly displaying an air of satisfaction.

'Right,' failure-to-agree, status quo exists,' Steve said. 'You are deliberately obstructive in this case, so you force me to take it on to the next stage of the procedure. As you are not prepared to arrange a meeting with myself and the Senior Engineer, I'll make the arrangements.'

'I didn't say I would refuse to arrange a meeting. However, I think it would be inconvenient at the moment because I am extremely busy.'

'That's all right, I can pick up a phone.'

'I'm not refusing, I will arrange it when I have time.'

'Sorry, can't wait for pigs to fly, might take some time in evolution. Come on, Gerwyn.'

Steve walked out, Gerwyn followed, sheepishly, casting an embarrassing glance at his stony boss, but Jonathan was busy dialling a number on the telephone.

Jonathan looked up, ensuring that the two had left and the door closed, 'Hello, Fred? Steve is on his way up with the whinger. He's after a grade eight position; I've already turned him down. Just for your information he hasn't got his Part 2 City & Guilds.'

'Couldn't you have handled it?' came the sardonic tones of Crabbe. 'Good god, do I have to sort out all your problems?'

'I tried my best to prevent him from taking it further. You know what Steve is like when he can't have his own way.'

'I know what the pair of you are like when you get together, you're like a couple of squabbling teenagers. It's just another major incident over a triviality. Leave it with me! I'll sort it out!'

'I'd appreciate your support on this particular case, Fred.'

'Yes yes. You've got my full and unequivocal bloody support. Just keep the man away from my office in future.' He slammed the phone down.

'Thank you Fred,' said Jonathan to a purring telephone, and he continued writing.

* * *

The works canteen at Flints Component Factory was full to capacity at lunchtime. All of its four-foot square, red veneered-topped tables which took up the large floor area were occupied by the manual workers, office workers and middle management. Gwyn, who was scanning the crowd for any mates who maybe dining, had resigned himself to eating alone on the small stage at the far corner of the canteen. He was holding his steaming dinner on a brown plastic tray among the hubbub of numerous conversations. He began moving away from the self-service counter towards the stage when he saw Gerwyn sitting alone at a wall shelf where there was a spare stool.

'On a fantasy trip, Gerwyn,' he shouted to his mate, unbalancing him on his stool.

'I wish you wouldn't do that, Gwyn. My nerves are very

sensitive today.'

'Your nerves haven't had a day off for some time.'

'I feel tired, Gwyn.'

'That's unusual for you, you're normally knackered.'

'Where've you been all morning? You've got a better hideout than Lord Lucan.'

Gwyn raised his hand and ran it through his sandy, greying hair, his pale blue eyes inspecting his dinner which he had placed on the wall shelf, 'It hasn't been an average morning, pal-- They shouldn't make me pay for this dinner; they should give it me for being so conscientious. What have you had to eat?' he asked, observing Gerwyn's empty plate.

'Same as you, hot-pot and chips. The dinner's not too bad, but the pudding was a bit heavy.'

'You didn't leave any for the sheep out the back, I notice,' said Gwyn, referring to the animals that came down from the sparse grasslands of slag hills at the back of the factory.

'I never waste anything I pay for.'

'Mmm, Average, I suppose,' said Gwyn, pushing a fork-full of hot-pot in his mouth.

Gerwyn looked at him wolfing it down, 'I'm going for a cup of tea, do you want one?'

Gwyn nodded. 'Milk, no sugar.'

When Gerwyn returned with two teas he found Gwyn sitting at a table which had become vacant so he sat there.

'This is better, my back was breaking on that stool,' he said, placing the cups on the table. 'You enjoyed that, didn't take long to get that down you.'

'The food isn't that bad,' said Gwyn, contradicting his earlier remark. 'There's a lot of unjustified moaning about this place. The prices are average, too.'

Gwyn was an average man. He was average height, average build, average appetite and gave average work rate. He looked upon his wage as being average and he claimed to be an average drinker. In his middle fifties, he was the most experienced electrician at Flint's Components.

'How's the wife, Gerwyn?' he asked, remembering Hilary's operation.

'She's gaining slowly, Gwyn. She's not strong enough to do the housework though. She was hoping to find a part time job somewhere, but there's no chance of that now.--What shift is Steve working, do you know?'

'Let me see now...I'm days, Byron's afternoons...Peter?...He's off on his rest days...so Steve is nights. Why? Problems?'

'Not really. I just wanted to know if he'd had a meeting with Fred Crabbe about my grade eight. We saw Shylock last week. We were going to take it to Fred straight away, but he couldn't be found.'

'He was pre-warned I expect.'

'Pre-warned?'

'Well aye, the first thing Shylock does after a meeting with Steve is telephone Fred. Fred prefers to disappear than argue it out with Steve.'

'It's a bit sly of Jonathan.'

'Jonathan is quite above average in the devious department. Fred is the same, but the champion of them all is Sid. Sid is above, above average. You'll be given the run-around for a few months. Do what I did, use the internal telephones to do the walking for you. Give Fred a ring, he doesn't know who's calling until he answers and then it's too late. Mind that's no guarantee either. I've called him in the past and he's told me quite enthusiastically to come up and see him straight away. When I knocked on his office door, he had disappeared. Later he will apologise and tell you he was called away on an emergency.'

'Maybe it will be better if I leave it all to Steve.'

'Do it yourself, it will be much quicker in the long run. And if they keep avoiding you, write a letter to the Personnel Department asking for an interview, that'll shift them. The engineers of today don't have the integrity they had when I was an apprentice. Today, all they want to do is pass the buck.'

'You know them well, Gwyn. I wish I knew them as well as you.'

'They won't pull the wool over my eyes.'

'I've had a few jobs in my time. I can't seem to stick a job for more than five years, I always think the next job is going to be better.'

'There's no next job now; not with three million unemployed. There's a dark cloud of an unemployed workforce waiting to pour a deluge of cheap labour on you. The unemployed will take anything that's going at any wage structure.'

'Maybe you're right, perhaps I'd better not pester them for upgrading.'

'Don't be daft. The only reason they don't want to give it to you is because they can spend it on themselves. If the engineers can save a few pounds at your expense they can spend it on some useless gadget for them to play with. They think nothing of spending a couple of grand on a sophisticated testing instrument, and then lose interest when the novelty has worn off.'

Gerwyn was shocked, 'Don't somebody check up on them?'

'They're a law unto themselves, mun. A bunch of selfish bastards, they are. If one of them walked into my local one night, I'd take him out the back and give him a good kicking.'

Gerwyn hadn't heard Gwyn talk like that before. He sipped his tea and let the conversation drop.

They finished their tea and made their way back to the electrical workshop. They walked through the hissing machine shop, hands in pockets, Gwyn whistling, Gerwyn quiet and thoughtful.

'I was called to a neighbour's house, once,' Gerwyn said, emerging from his reverie.'

'Was you indeed,' said Gwyn. 'Now that's exciting.'

'He had a socket on the landing that wasn't working,' continued Gerwyn, ignoring his mate's satire. 'I did the usual checking: fuses, testing for power etc. Then I took the socket off the skirting board and found it hadn't been wired.'

Gwyn stopped and grabbed Gerwyn's shoulders, 'Even more exciting.'

Gerwyn shook his head despondently. 'This guy said he'd bought it in Woolworth's, fixed it to the skirting board and it never worked. He didn't realise it had to be wired. That's the type of thing that happens to me, see.'

'Was he a bit...you know?'

'He looked intelligent. Anyway, I wired it for him. Had a night out on him, I did.'

'Talking about a night out, it will be Christmas soon. I'm looking forward to a few days off.'  Got everything prepared for Christmas?'

'Just about. It was a bit of a push, but we've got things under control now.'

'Here we are, then,' said Gwyn, as they emerged from the machine shop and crossed to the electrical shop. 'Let's look in the work-tray and find the easiest job.'

'Do me a favour, Gwyn, if you see Steve when you change shift, ask him about my grade eight?'

'Yea, if I remember.'

# Five

Fred Crabbe had suggested his office as the venue for the meeting of middle management. The meeting was arranged to discuss the modernising of the factory's major machine shop. His room, situated on the third floor of the administration block, and overlooking the industrial estate road, was not as big as the normal boardroom. However, it was spacious and furnished with a desk, and a long table that could cater for eight people if required.

Fred sat in his usual place, at the centre of the long table, facing the door and flanked by his two Junior Engineers. His dark untidy hair was long enough to curl up under his collar. His tie, pulled to the side a little, had a grimy shine to it and was creased in places where creases should not be. His brown eyes were agitated, continually moving from one object to another, but always returning to the gentleman at the head of the table: the building superintendent. He was busily pulling out papers and files from his briefcase; his quick, busy-like movements, his ruddy complexion, his meticulous pin-striped suit, starched white collar and knotted tie together with his occasional pause and quick study of a particular document, kept the members of the meeting waiting.

The building superintendent's foreman, a thick-set man with a grey scrubbing-brush moustache, sat on his direct right hand side and was continually adjusting his rimless glasses and touching his short-cut spiky grey hair.

Fred turned around with an expression of boredom on his face, and inspected the monitor screen of his computer, placed on the shelf behind him.

The gaunt, ashen faced, production manager, sitting opposite Fred, was staring into the boardroom table, his grey eyes showing a vacancy, reflecting tiredness.

'Well gentlemen!' the superintendent suddenly barked, causing the production manager to raise his head, 'I see we are all present. We may as well make a start. We all know the subject for which we have all gathered here today. However, I feel it will do no harm to briefly go over the main points to refresh our memories: The management in all its wisdom has decided that some of our production lines are behind the times and need bringing up to date; this means upgrading and  more efficiency. We require modern equipment, new technology, and higher production. All of which is to make us more competitive.  The plan is to get rid of all our old machines and install robotic technology in their place.'

'Robots,' queried the production manager.

Fred interjected: 'They will be sophisticated hydraulic, electronic, electric units that will have a number of high quality steel limbs.'

'Yes, thank you Fred,' said the building superintendent who had appointed himself chairman.  'It will mean partitioning off half of the main machine shop by building a wall right down its centre; one half will be what is now known as a "Clean Area" for the robots and the other half for the few existing machine we will be keeping.'

'How many of these robotic machines are going to be installed in in the "clean area"' asked Jonathan, with a tone of scepticism.

'At its completion,' said Fred, 'there will be 10 new units which will take up the floor space of the Clean Area.

'Ten!' gasped the production manager, 'But there are a hundred machines in that area at the moment, keeping eighty five operators busy.'

'Let us make one thing clear from the beginning,' asserted the

44

superintendent, 'It is not our job to worry about the workforce or the number of people who may be made redundant. We must be concerned only with the conversion of the factory to ultra-modern requirements,'

'What work does it entail on the mechanical side? asked Sidney Soper. 'I'll have to know what materials to order.'

'Don't go fretting yourself about materials,' said Fred. 'It will be a straight forward job which will only require little assistance from you; the removal of compressed air and coolant tanks for example.  The removal of all the heavy machinery will be carried out at weekends by a contractor who'll tender the lowest quote.'

'Yes weekends will be the most convenient times,' agreed the superintendent, looking at his foreman. 'Darren, our main job will be replacing a false ceiling over the new machine shop to make it dustproof and sterile.'

'No problem,' replied the foreman, confidently.

'I will have to reorganise the whole of the production line,' reminded the production manager. You lot maybe enjoying yourselves with your Meccano and Lego sets, but I will have to maintain a profitable output.'

'We will have to juggle your lines around for a time until we sort it all out,' said Fred. 'I do hope you will have patience with us,' lifting his eyebrows.

'It's going to take a month to five weeks to plan and adjust the lines,' complained the production manager. 'That will require the cooperation of the engineering department.'

'We are always at your disposal,' said Fred, proudly.

'That's when you can find an engineer.'

'That accusation is hurtful,' said Fred—Jonathan ? Sidney?'

There is only one man on shift and two on days regular, as far as I'm concerned,' said Jonathan. 'We utilise them the best we can. There are two hundred machines in that particular shop. On top of that we have plant maintenance schedules. Maybe we should have more men,'

'Or greater efficiency,' quipped the production manager.

'I'm in the same boat,' said Sidney. 'But I'll manage somehow.'

`What is going on? demanded the production manager. 'Are you suggesting we keep up production while you remove the machines?'

'We will endeavour to do a section at a time so that we gradually decrease the production on the old stock as it is transferred to the new installations,' said the superintendent. 'Don't worry, the changeover will be gradual and still productive.'

'Steve, our shop steward, will find the extra work a good support for his argument that we require more electricians,' said Jonathan.

'More electricians?' exploded Fred. 'Out of the question.-- Paul,' said Fred, turning to the building superintendent. 'From what financial fund is this project going to be paid?'

'It's an open cheque; However, it's not going to be abused by individual departments.'

'That's fine by me,' said Fred. 'Not only will we have plant contractors in to move out the old machinery, we'll also have the installation of the new robots installed by contractors.'

'We have an agreement with the unions that all internal installations will be carried out by our own men,' reminded Jonathan.

'You leave Steve and his comrades to me,' said Fred. 'I'll give them a bit of overtime on the weekends, that will keep them quiet.'

'What about the department's finances?' asked Jonathan.

'We can stretch to a little overtime on weekends. We can have our boys carrying out mundane work while the contractors can take responsibility for the main installation.'

'And the production labour force?' asked the production manager. 'You know, those 85 human beings who are going to lose their jobs 'Are they going to be consulted? There will be trouble when they find out.'

'Management are aware of the risks, we'll sort it,' snapped the superintendent

'That kind of contempt causes strikes.'

'It may be a convenient time for them to go on strike. As I have stated, management is aware of the situation.--Right, you now have copies of the plans. I will be grateful if you will begin the work as soon as possible after the Christmas Holidays.' He stood up and closed his briefcase, his sanguine complexion contrasting greatly to that of the production manager who also stood.

'Good day, gentlemen. If I don't see you before the festive holiday, have a very happy Christmas and a joyful New Year.'

He left with mutterings of begrudged seasonal greetings, his foreman and the production manager following him out.

***

Jonathan arrived home from work to find the house cold and miserable. The central heating had been turned off automatic control and none of the gas fires were burning. To make matters worse his wife was not at home and the place looked very untidy. Some of Lynwen's clothing were strewn over the settee along with a pair of her ruby slippers. The Pekinese quickly jumped off the settee and scurried to his basket in the corner. Jonathan switched on the fire in the lounge, then went straight to the kitchen and put the kettle on. Seeing the central heating programmer was in the off position, he switched it on to constant with unnecessary force and a great deal of annoyance. After making himself a cup of tea and getting a biscuit from the barrel he settled down by the fire. He had drunk half his tea when he heard the front door slam and the footsteps of his wife in the hall.

'You're home then,' she said, as she entered and threw her coat across the back of the settee and went to the dog and stroked it. 'How is my little darling, then? Has he been lonely?'

Jonathan glared at her and the dog. 'You're late, aren't you?'

'Bit of a discrepancy in the books. Dean insisted I stay and sort it out.'

'Who?'

'Dean, the Branch Manager; my boss.'

'You always referred to him as Mr...whatsit in the past.'

'Has the kettle boiled?'

'It has, now.'

'Aren't you too hot with that fire blazing away?'

'If I was too hot I'd have turned it down. It's winter, you know. It would make a nice change to come home to a warm house.'

'You`re Mr Efficiency, aren't you? If there's nobody here to appreciate it?' she called back as she went to the kitchen to pour a cup of tea.

'Lynwen, do you see that grey rectangular box on the kitchen wall? It's called a programmer. It was invented to make life easier for people.'

'Jonathan, shut up!  I'm not in the mood for your warped sense of humour or your childish sarcasm. I forgot to set it this morning.'

'You shouldn't switch it off automatic in the first place.'

'Sometimes it gets too warm, so I switch it off,'

'But there is an 'advanced' button especially for such occasions.'

'Oh I don't understand that. Don't make such a fuss over it. It's warm here now.--Anyway, more important is the news I had today.  I learnt that the house next door to us has been sold.'

'Praise the lord. Maybe their central heating will help keep our house warm.'

'There's a problem. It's been sold to a man who is a bit of a cowboy builder. He calls himself a Developer. What's more, he has big plans for the house next door,' said Lynwen returning from the kitchen with a cup of tea and a biscuit,'

'How do you know all this?' asked Jonathan, suspiciously,

'A friend in work told me. He read it in the local press.'

'How did he know our property was near to the property in the press?'

'I don't know.'

'People don't just read the local press and suddenly come across an address and say--Oh this address is next door to Jonathan Pallet.--Do I know this friend of yours? What's his name?'

'Gerald...something.'

'How old is he?'

'I don't know,'

'How old does he look? Stupid!'

'Don't call me stupid.--Middle twenties, I suppose. Why? What's your problem?'

'I had a feeling he wouldn't be decrepit.'

'What do you mean by that?'

'What are these big plans that are mentioned?'

Lynwen grabbed her coat from the back of the settee and produced a newspaper from its pocket. She handed it to Jonathan, folded it at the page where the announcement was printed. She pointed it out, and then sat back sipping her drink miserably. Jonathan snatched it from her and read:

7 Rees Street, Travail, Cwm Morlais.
It is proposed that a double storey
extension be built at the rear of the
above premises.  Anyone wishing
to make an objection should write to
The Chief Clerk, Town Hall, Cwm Morlais.

'You know what that means?' said Lynwen, after she had given Jonathan time to digest the notice. 'It means the existing kitchen next door will be pulled down and a new one twice as high will be erected in its place.'

'I know what it means. It will be like a barrack wall and take away our light.'

'We'll have tunnel vision. All we'll see is the backs of the houses opposite.'

'I know. I'm quite aware of the restrictions it will cause. Who is this cowboy, anyway? I expect you know him,'

'You've got a terrible twisted brain inside that skull of yours.'

'Well? What do you know about him?'

He bought the house for a few thousand because it's in bad repair. Then he got a grant. He employs men who are claiming social benefits. They come cheaply, but he charges top prices.'

'You know it all. I don't mind putting up with a little inconvenience from a neighbour who is earnestly trying to improve his property. But I'm damned if I'm going to be hustled by a cowboy who is going to devalue my house. I'll write a letter while you make a decent meal for a change.'

'Is that a compliment?'

'You can take it any way you like.'

Lynwen reluctantly made her way to the kitchen. Jonathan went to his study and composed a letter to the Chief Clerk, unable to concentrate on the subject; his mind full of Lynwen and her male friends, his imagination running amok and a green monster growing bigger with every picture in his brain. He gritted his teeth and forced himself to write one word at a time; the letter had to be written.

# Six

All the old machines at the south end of the production area at Flint's Components Group factory had been electrically isolated. They were greasy, cold and awkward; some prodigiously muscle-straining, others small and complicated. All looked unnaturally still on the Sunday morning when it had been decided to begin the reorganising of the production lines. The work had started with a great deal of enthusiasm, followed by confusion and inevitable frustration of many workers carrying out different jobs in the same area at the same time.

The eighteen men of different trades taking everything apart made the machine shop look like a scrap metal yard being invaded by automobile enthusiasts looking for spare parts.

The machine-tool fitters were dismantling various parts of machines, the toolmakers were removing expensive moulds from the same machines, and the fork-lift drivers were serving both craftsmen by skilfully removing the parts when required. The pipe fitters were unscrewing compressed air lines, balancing on girders above the busy area. The electricians were on the floor and in the air. Some were on temporary scaffolding disconnecting conduits, while others were removing electrical cabinets that served the bigger machines.

Steve came down the ladder and called to the three other electricians who were working the weekend with him. Sweating and with black oily patches on his face, he hung his hacksaw on the handle of the pipe-vice and looked up at the piece of bus-bar he had been trying to extricate from the long section which was too heavy and dangerous to remove all at once.

'Come on, I've had a gutsful. It's 9.30, anyway. Let's go to the canteen and have a cup of tea while we wait for the brains to arrive. Those engineers couldn't organise a sandcastle competition in the middle of desert.'

Gerwyn, Gwyn and Ronnie rubbed their hands in their blue boilersuits and began to walk down the middle aisle, relieved to hear the shop steward call for a break.

Then Jonathan appeared, wearing jeans, yellow woollen sweater and training shoes. He'd come unnoticed through the door at the far corner of the machine shop.

'Where are you lot going?' he yelled.

Steve muttered something about the timing of Jonathan's arrival. He shook his head at the pregnant stomach of his boss; a characteristic that outshone all others of the man.

'It's 9.30,' Steve shouted back, and continued walking. 'We've been here since seven.'

'Everything all right?' his boss wanted to know.

'As well as can be expected considering the cock-up.'

'What cock-up?' he asked, looking round. 'Is the horizontal bore disconnected?'

Steve stopped walking and turned round. He raised his arm and offered his open palm to the mentioned machine; there were several craftsmen and a fork-lift truck hovering around the huge machine. The production foreman was also there, standing akimbo and being bumped occasionally, as he witnessed his prize machine being cannibalised by the busy workers.

'What do you want me to do?' Steve asked. 'Hang by my ankles from the girders?'

Jonathan scowled at the fitters working on the machine, 'I told Sid to let the electricians disconnect the machine first, then let the fitters follow up.'

'Try telling that to them, and the toolmakers. They want to finish by noon. We'll be lucky if we get away by midnight.'

Jonathan shook his head in disgust as Steve continued to the canteen with his workmates. As they strolled through the loading bay, the massive overhead crane droned on its elevated rails like an aeroplane above them. Gerwyn thought it might be an opportune moment to remind Steve of his upgrading.

'Steve, I've been meaning to ask you about my grade eight situation,' he said, keeping it as private as possible. 'Do you think there's any hope of it coming soon?'

'I mentioned it to Fred Crabbe last week. He said he'd have a meeting with us next Wednesday afternoon at 4.30.'

'I finish work and half past four, Steve.'

'That's the time Fred insisted on. He finishes at five o'clock; convenient for him.'

'I see. It's a pity he couldn't fit it in a four o'clock, though,' suggested the little man, gazing hopefully at Steve.

They continued walking through the north end machine shop, Gerwyn walking faster to keep up with Steve's loping strides, and wanting satisfaction.

'Do you think he'll give me my grading on Wednesday, Steve?'

'I'll take it to Area Office. He doesn't like workforce problems going out of the factory.'

'I don't want to cause a lot of animosity, Steve.'

'You could have fooled me. It's too late, the wheels of friction have been set in motion.'

Gerwyn tilted his head and said to Steve in a sorrowful voice, 'Maybe it's best if I forget the whole idea of being upgraded, Steve.'

'Okay. I'll give Fred a ring and tell him to cancel the meeting.'

Gerwyn went into a stupor, his face paling. Did he hear his shop steward right? Oh god. 'Steve...Steve...don't get me wrong. It's just that I don't want to get you into trouble.'

Steve stopped, his powerful arms gripping Gerwyn's shoulders, 'Now listen, don't mess me about. Do you want grade eight or not? I don't enjoy going into the office and battling up against a brick wall of an engineer who will look at me astonished pretending he had never heard of the request before. You should know their ploys by now: firstly they adopt a hostile attitude to try and frighten you. If that doesn't work, they put their arms around your shoulders and tug at your heart strings, claiming financial difficulties, and when that fails they prolong the negotiations hoping you give up in despair. You need a lot of stamina.'

Gerwyn pulled himself together. 'You're right, Steve. The way I see it, we are working together this morning doing the same kind of work. The only difference is we are being paid different rates of pay. Don't make sense to me, Steve.'

They began walking again, Steve shaking his head. 'You can't go along with that line of argument. We're all doing work this morning which is what we were taught in our basic training. Just don't go working on the electronically controlled machines, the paging system and synchronising the generators—you're not carrying a pager, are you?'

'Well, I don't always carry one. Only if the shift electrician is late or goes early.'

'Bloody hell, Gerwyn, they won't give grade eight when you're doing the work and not getting paid for it.'

'I don't know what to do for the best, sometimes, Steve. Gwyn was late coming in the other morning, and if I didn't answer his bleeper Shylock may have given Byron a verbal warning for not waiting for his relief to arrive. So I did it to cover Byron's back. Shylock loves the disciplinary procedure.'

'Yea, well, I suppose you've got a point. But try not to let Shylock know about it; I mean if you're covering for somebody.' They entered the canteen. Steve pointed. 'See Selwyn over there? He's a grade three semi-skilled man. He'll do anything to have a Sunday overtime shift. They've got him where they want him. He'll never get above grade three.'

Selwyn was organising the weekend rations for the workforce, placing a tray full of hot toast on the stainless steel counter alongside a large aluminium teapot that was steaming from its lidless top. His jet black hair was combed flat and backwards, held there by a large quantity of hair oil which reflected the fluorescent lighting as efficiently as polished ebony. There wasn't a grey hair to be seen on his fifty five year-old head. He was a dapper of a man with a very fine black moustache which seemed to be pencilled on. His neck seemed to have lost its strength, for it had disappeared into his chest, leaving his large head resting between his shoulder blades, and his chisel-like chin irritating his thorax.

'Everything ready?' Steve asked him.

'Just about. Help yourselves.'

'What have we got, Sel?' asked Gwyn. 'Average breakfast of bacon and eggs with a couple of juicy sausages?'

Selwyn laughed, pretentiously. 'You'll have to put up with two toasts and a cup of my specially brewed tea. There's a bucketful of sugar at the side of the mugs,' he added pointing to a carton and a stainless steel bowl belonging to the food mixer.

The four took what they wanted and sat at a nearby table. Selwyn noticed that Steve was hiding his toast with his hands. Steve, unaware Selwyn was creeping up behind him, began to eat his toast.

'You've got three toasts, you thieving git. Put one back,' said Selwyn. Come on now, Steve, be fair.'

'Go away Selwyn, I'm starving. I haven't had any breakfast.'

'That's not my problem. I've counted the number of engineering staff in this morning and I've allocated two toasts per man. Somebody will go without if you don't put it back.'

'Engineering staff? Huh! I heard the production foreman inviting the haulage contractors up for a cuppa and a bite.'

'You're lying!'

'He's telling the truth,' confirmed Gwyn.

'That's it! They can stick the job. I'm not doing it again.'

'Not until the next Sunday double time, is it Sel?' said Gwyn.

'Very funny. They can get the catering staff in next time.'

'They won't do that,' said Steve. 'Not when they can get you on the cheap.'

'I'm not going to put up with the abuse from those who are left out; those toolmakers think they're executive stock.'

Selwyn continued to mumble under his breath as he returned to the counter. He picked up the internal telephone.

'I wish I had a rasher of bacon with that toast,' complained Gwyn, wiping his lips.

'I could have done with a little marmalade with mine,' said Ronnie, his green eyes staring at the empty table, his long red hair hanging to his shoulders.

'I thought working on Sunday was against your religion,' reminded Steve.

'I would much rather attend our prayer meetings. But Jonathan told me if I didn't come in this morning he would have me transferred to another factory, and have a man moved here who wouldn't be so contrary to his wishes.'

'The bastard—sorry Ronnie no disrespect meant. He had no right to make that threat. I'll make sure you won't be victimised because of your beliefs.'

'I'd rather not be the cause of any trouble,' replied Ronnie, raising his eyebrows and shuffling in his seat.

'That's the trouble in this place, nobody wants to be the cause of any trouble. That leaves Shylock with a blank cheque. You should have told me about the problem, Ronnie.'

'It's no problem. I don't want you to think I'm being ungrateful, Steve, but I'd rather look after my own affairs.'

'He's pushing you around. If he gets away with it with you, he'll try it on somebody else. I thought you had strong feeling about the Sabbath. You surprise me at times, Ronnie.'

'My wife and I live locally. If Jonathan carries out his threat and moves me to another district it will cause a great deal of inconvenience and possible hardship on my family. Christ worked on the Sabbath to help those he loved.'

'But what if this is the thin end of the wedge and he insists you work more Sundays?'

Ronnie thought for a moment, and then shrugged his shoulders. 'I will have to cross that bridge when I come to it.'

'It all sounds hypocritical to me,' said Gwyn. 'Could never understand people preaching one thing and practising another.'

'Hypocrisy will be found in many walks of life, Gwyn,' said Ronnie. 'You're not a religious man, I believe?'

'That's right. There's no point in me going to church because I think it's a load of rubbish.  I'd rather not go than be a hypocrite.'

'Where were your children christened, Gwyn?' asked Ronnie. And who do you have to bury your dead? I heard your daughter got married in church last year.'

'Yes...well...the missus wanted them christened...And it's nice to have a church wedding, isn't it? Give them a start in the right direction, sort of thing.'

'So you make use of the church but don't support it? There's no doubt in my mind, Gwyn, that is a form of hypocrisy. And again, there are those people who fornicate and go home to their wives acting innocent and true.'

Steve's toast stuck in his throat and he coughed. Gerwyn looked at him, knowing Ronnie had struck a chord in his shop steward.

'I think you're right,' supported Gerwyn. 'But there are a lot of inconsistencies in religion as well. They reckon in the last world war there were Christians on both sides blessing their bombs and praying their side will win. Would your church support war, Ronnie?'

'I don't know what your idea of church is, Gerwyn, I'm not a member of a religious denomination. I am a Christian; a follower of Jesus Christ. I don't support armed forces or any particular government of society. I was born to pay allegiance to a moral code. I am not going to forfeit my right to Heaven by involving myself with temporary worldly distractions. There are people who think that the only existence in God's Universe is this corrupt globe we call our world. It's not true.'

'So our trade union hasn't got much credit, Ronnie,' said Steve.

'Trade unions are temporal; secular. Nothing to do with the spiritual world of God.' He smiled and turned to Steve. 'I don't know if there are any shop stewards in Heaven, Steve.' He paused. 'I hope so.'

'Ay up! Here comes Shylock,' warned Gwyn, who was facing the door. 'If he goes to Heaven count me out.'

Jonathan came in followed by Sidney and the whole remaining Sunday work-force. The orderly conversation of the electricians was suddenly drowned out by the confused chattering of a dozen different topics as the disorganised queue of workers bided their time waiting their tea and toast. Selwyn was calling Jonathan beckoning him to come to the back of the kitchen. He pleaded for patience while more bread could be issued, but leaving the workforce to serve themselves wasn't the wisest thing to do. The toast was soon gone before half the men were catered for. However, Jonathan had the key to the pantry and issued more bread, but the seeds of bad feeling had been sewn. Eventually, Jonathan came to the table where the electricians sat, carrying a cup of coffee and a piece of toast.

'How long are you lot going to take for break?' he snapped. 'There's work out there.'

'We haven't long sat down,' said Steve. 'We had to wait for the tea and toast to be made, didn't we? Organisation, that's what it's all about.'

'Your cups are empty and your toast is gone. I'm not stupid.'

'We're quick eaters.'

'I'd like you to demonstrate your speed on the Horizontal Borer, now that it's available. I want it all completed by 4.30 this afternoon. No later!'

'I hope your wit goes down better with management,' said Steve. 'I don't like those kinds of jokes, Jonathan.'

'When I joke, I smile. I'm not smiling now.'

'Jonathan, when you were in bed this morning we were labelling hundreds of control cables. Yesterday we disconnected thirty machines and removed about a mile of conduit. We've got another thirty machines to disconnect and there are ten to be repositioned, re-tubed and reconnected ready for start-up in the morning. We'll be here till midnight.'

'I hope it's you're the one who's joking.'

'I'm not smiling either,' retorted Steve. 'Listen, we want a meal at one o'clock and another at six o'clock. If we don't have them we'll either pack it all in or go home for food and come back. Depending on how tired we are, we may even stay home.'

Jonathan became flushed as he read the faces of each man in turn. He'd wanted the responsibility of the reorganisation to be left completely with the contractors, and fought energetically to achieve that end. But when he was forced to have his department play its part, he suddenly showed a great deal of enthusiasm and said he could better it by cutting the work force to four electricians. By such drastic action he'd proved to management that his plan was cheaper.

He was beginning to rue his boast now. He would look a complete fool if the job was not completed by Monday, plus Monday's production will be lost. Fred would give him the evil eye. He knew the four electricians hadn't been shirking by the amount of work completed.

'Listen, Steve, I don't want any complications with start-up in the morning. Our department will be the laughing stock of the factory if production lines are held up.'

'We agreed to come in this morning at seven o'clock instead of the usual eight o'clock, didn't we? We'll also stay and get the job finished, but don't tell me we should finish it by 4.30. That ridiculous statement doesn't help at all. We'll never do it in that time and you know it. You were the one who cut the sparks from seven to four.'

Just then the production manager entered the dining hall and came straight to Jonathan,  his gaunt figure looking as though it could have done with Sunday morning in bed.

'Your wife has been on the phone,' he said to Jonathan. 'She wants you to ring her back as soon as possible. She said 'immediately, ' actually.'

'Couldn't you tell her I was busy, Donald?'

'I did. But she said it was very urgent. She sounded quite upset.'

Jonathan huffed impatiently, then turned to make his way to the phone, ordering his men to get back to work and displaying a great deal displeasure.

'Come on,' said Steve. 'We'd better make a move.'

They made their way back through the machine shops. Gerwyn asked Steve what he thought of religious Ronnie.

'Good spark and he pulls his weight. Shylock gets his pound of flesh.'

'But did you hear what he said about trade unions? He's not a member is he?'

'No. He gives nothing, but asks for nothing either.'

'He reaps all the benefits.'

'You can't expect him to work for a lower wage.'

'You ought to hear him demanding his holidays; and his break times and his protective clothing. He wouldn't have those benefits if the trade unions didn't fight for them?'

'Good thinking, Gerwyn. I suppose he does make use of some things he doesn't contribute to. You believe strongly in unions then, Gerwyn?'

'I'm a staunch supporter, Steve, we need unions and the benefits they fight for.'

Steve looked down at Gerwyn as they hurried along and grinned. 'I'm giving up the shop steward's job next year, Gerwyn, too much hassle, I'll nominate you for it, okay?'

'Uh? I—I  don't really think I'm cut out for that sort of thing, Steve. My nerves won't stand it. Do you think we'll be working till midnight, Steve? I don't mind helping out if you want.'

'Yea okay, Ger.  Let's get stuck in, shall we?'

'I'm with you, Steve, do you know what I find strange about this place, Steve?  No maintenance foremen.'

Steve grinned again, but walked on. 'Shylock got rid of those two long ago. The only decent thing he's ever done. They were dead wood, the pair of them. Always remember, Gerwyn:  A foreman is disliked by management and union in this place. They've got nobody to turn to when they're not wanted.'

'Oh, I'll never be a foreman, Steve. Definitely not.'

Ken James

# Seven

Jonathan burst the door open to his terraced house in a fit of rage and found his wife standing at the rear window, dressed in her long, Lincoln green, dressing gown. She was furtively peeping through the curtains. She didn't turn to greet him, but appeared to be mesmerised by some commotion in the rear garden of the house next door to the left hand side.

'I've been trying to phone you,' he said, curtly. 'Have you left the phone off the hook? It's engaged all the time. What's so damn urgent it can't wait till I finish work?'

'Have a look out there,' she said, without taking her eyes from the scene. 'If the telephone isn't working it's probably because of them out there. If you hadn't come now I was going to get the hell out of here.'

Jonathan flung the curtains wide open, much to Lynwen's annoyance, and was struck dumb by the upheaval outside. The single storey annexed kitchen of next door down, which once stood six feet away across the yard from his kitchen, was there no longer. In its place was a mountain of stones and mortar mixed with wooden laths, slates, rafters, earth, kitchen slates, tiles and countless other pieces of domestic construction material. In the midst of it all was a gigantic JCB excavator listing precariously like a sinking oil rig, and only feet away from the Pallet's kitchen.

'Good god!' How long has this been going on?'

'Just after you left they began the attack. Two of them have gone now. They began with sledge hammers and crowbars, like demented madmen, swinging and banging. I thought our double glazing was going to shatter.'

'Didn't you tell them to stop, woman?'

For the first time since he came in, Lynwen looked at her husband. 'Would you like to go out there with that machine swinging about and the building collapsing all over the place? I'm not bloody superwoman.'

'You could have called to them.'

'I did, from the upstairs window. But when that JCB came bursting through our adjoining garden wall I gave up. One of them laughed at me and said he'd replace anything that was damaged.'

'Replace? Replace? Our double glazing cost thousands of pounds. It's vacuum sealed...high precision...it can't be replaced just like that.'

'The machine has been stuck in the mud for the last twenty minutes. They can't move it.'

Jonathan went into his kitchen and opened the back door. He pushed his head out tentatively, and then proceeded gingerly into his small back yard. Near the silent excavator was a twelve-foot mound of mixed rubble, rocks and timber approximately ten feet from Jonathan's back door. On top of the mound stood a stocky man about thirty years of age standing akimbo; he was about five feet tall and wore jeans torn at the knees. His dirty white tee-shirt emphasised his bulging chest and muscular arms. He looked around his work area with mean grey eyes and a triumphant grin on his dusty rugged face. His tightly curled, fair hair had a blue tinge of mortar dust. He was deliberately avoiding the presence of the astonished Jonathan. He apparently did not feel the coldness of the damp misty morning.

'What the hell are you supposed to be doing?' yelled Jonathan.

He stared at Jonathan with much contempt. 'You mean you can't see? I thought it was obvious,' his rough voice deep in his throat.

'You realise other people are living in this street? Can't you see the danger you're causing?'

'There are other people? Good god, and there's me thinking I'm on a desert island.'

Jonathan kicked at the stones on the concrete of his yard that had over spilled from the demolition. There were lumps of mortar and half sand bricks as well as huge splinters of wood. He inspected his windows closely and scanned the large sheets of glass for damage. Lynwen looked through the glass at him, wide-eyed.

'I realise you are entitled to work on your own land, but there are safe ways of working and there are dangerous ways. You don't seem to be giving me or my property any protection.'

'Look if I damage your property I'll make good. I don't know what you're whinging about.'

'I'm not concerned with you making good. I don't want any damage in the first place.'

Jonathan looked at the big excavator, the driver still in its cabin, his head and shoulders partially blanked out by the reflection of the windscreen, its massive bucket hanging menacingly.

'And where the hell do you think you are going with that thing,' he called to the driver.

He looked at Jonathan apologetically and shook his head; sorry he had taken on the job.

Jonathan looked around again and saw that his gatepost at the end of his yard was leaning out from the garden wall. He looked at the driver and pointed to the post.

'I'm sorry,' the driver said, sincerely. 'I drove as carefully as I could but the ground gave way and the machine tilted and nudged the wall.'

It was then Jonathan noticed that the near end of his stone wall, adorned with a variety of small alpine flowers that had taken years to grow, was dislodged and leaning outward.

'I'll fix that for you,' said the burly builder. 'The machine's okay now. It got stuck for a bit. If you like, I'll pull the old stone wall down and replace it with a nice concrete block wall.'

Jonathan couldn't believe his ears; His lovely stone wall? 'Listen Mr...What's your name?'

The builder sat down on his mound of rubble and leaned his elbows on his knees, cupping his granite chin in his hands. 'Bull. Charlie Bull.' Then he glanced at Lynwen still staring out, and winked at her. She recoiled into the shadows.

An appropriate name, thought Jonathan. 'Listen, Mr Bull, I don't want that wall touched.  One of the features that attracted me to this house was that it had an old fashioned garden with stone walls, upon which there are many rockery flowers. Furthermore, I'd rather you didn't do any more work until you've constructed temporary safety partitions to protect my property from the hazardous methods you use when working.'

Charlie looked at the driver. 'Dew dew. That was a mouthful.' Then he turned to Jonathan.  'Look, mate, that wall is between our gardens which makes it joint ownership.'

'I think you'll find it difficult to split along the middle,' Jonathan replied, smugly.

'Well, I can't make any promises. I'm not concerned with old bloody walls with flowers on them when I'm in full flow. Good, tidy concrete blocks is what I like. I'm excavating for drains, not Roman remains with a knife and fork.' He stood up and pointed at Jonathan. 'And if you want partitions, you build them. I'm not wasting money on bloody partition.'

Jonathan's face turned red. 'The partitions are your responsibility as a....builder. You're the one who's causing the danger.'

'I'm not throwing good money away, mate.'

'Now look, Mr Bull. I have already prevented you from building a double storey extension, and if you can't give me protection, I'll stop you building altogether.'

'What are you on about? This is going to be a double storey extension.'

'No it's not. I've got a letter in my desk from the town's Planning Department. It states quite categorically that your plans have been refused.'

'And I have a letter from the same place stating, quite categorically,' he squeaked, aping Jonathan voice, 'that planning permission has been approved.'

'What?'

'I'm building a double storey extension, mate, with an apex roof.'

'You'd better go and see the council before you waste anymore of your money.'

'The letter I've got in my house is all the assurance I need.'

'But you can't do it,' repeated Jonathan, shaking his head. 'You'll decrease the value of my property; all I'll see from my kitchen is a twenty-foot wall. You just can't do it.'

Charlie lost patience and leaned forward. 'Read my lips. I've got planning permission. Now this JCB is costing me money hanging around doing nothing.' He turned away from Jonathan and shouted to the driver. 'Bank this rubble at one end of the garden and start digging the footings there,' he pointed to edge of Jonathan yard.

'You can't have that monstrous machine so near my property. One slip and the thing will demolish my kitchen.'

'Don't be dull. These drivers are brilliant. They can come within an inch of your window and dig a hole without any problem.'

'Like the garden wall and my gatepost, for example.'

'Bit of bad luck, that. There was nobody here to guide him in. I'm here now.'

'Everybody I've known dig their footings with a pick and shovel when it's so near the property. You're being irresponsible.'

'It takes days to do it that way. You worry too much.'

'I'm warning you, you'd better not touch my property with

that thing.' Then Jonathan turned round and went into the house.

'He doesn't care a damn. He's quite mad,' he told Lynwen.

'They say he's the same wherever he works,' she said.

'I'll go and see the council building inspector tomorrow -- and the environmental department -- and the planning department.'

They both stood at the window watching the machine rock back and fore, its monstrous neck stretching and clanking into the sky, jack-knife and come thundering down into the mounds of rubble, just yards away from their kitchen. Jonathan knew the bucket would come within two feet of his living room window when digging the footings. His eyes turned to the impatient Mr Bull who suddenly jumped up on to Jonathan's yard. He had his back to the window looking down where the footings were being dug out.

'Come on. Hurry up,' he yelled to the driver. I need these footings to be at least six feet deep.'

Jonathan's face went paler as he envisaged a six-foot trench running alongside his yard, just six feet away from his kitchen door. Then he turned sharply.

'I can't stay here all morning,' he said. 'I've got a major job going on at the factory. And that's not going as planned.'

'I hope you're not going to leave me here on my own,' she pleaded.

'What do you expect me to do? Get a shot gun and shoot the bloody idiot? I'm going to work. Lock up and go to Jane's'

As Jonathan was talking, the excavator's motor suddenly roared at a high speed like a pneumatic drill's generator when extra load is asked of it. He looked out of the window and saw the huge metal leg of the machine slowly sink into the soft clay on the section that had been cleared, causing the machine to list dangerously. The bucket of the machine was overhanging Jonathan's yard, the more it tilted the closer it came to his kitchen. He ran out and came face to face with Charlie Bull, who was pulling at the neck of his tee-shirt as though it was too tight.

'Stop!' Jonathan shouted. 'Tell him to stop immediately.'

Charlie raised his arm to Jonathan but kept his eyes on the sinking leg, not attempting to stop the driver but hoping to assure Jonathan that everything was all right.

'The main sewage pipe runs just there,' shouted Jonathan. 'He'll go straight through it.'

'Stop panicking,' said Charlie, but his face was flushing up and his fingers still played with his tee-shirt.

'Stop panicking?' Repeated Jonathan, 'If he breaks the pipe the machine will sink deeper and the bucket will go straight through my kitchen.'

Just then, the leg of the machine caught something solid deep down, it stopped sinking and began to push the machine up straight.

'That's it,' said Charlie, relieved. 'He's got it. Marvellous machine these JCBs. They can get out of anything.'

'He's probably hit the sewage pipe,' said Jonathan, despairingly. 'Do you realise that?'

'I didn't know the sewage pipe was there, did I?'

'If you've fractured that pipe all the sewage from up the street will build up. The sewage, just like water, with find its own level, and where do you think that will appear? In my bloody bathroom, that's where. My house will be like a cesspool!'

'Oh we'll sort it out one way or another.'

Jonathan, frustrated, flabbergasted, frightened and picturing his bathroom full of stinking sewage, turned in a daze and went back in. 'I've heard of cowboy builders,' he said to Lynwen, 'but he doesn't even come up to that level. I'm going back to work. If you see any turds floating about you'd better ring me again.'

'What?'

'Come to think of it, is that telephone working?'

He went and checked. Picked it off the coffee table and held it to his ear. There's nothing wrong with it. Why didn't you answer it?'

Lynwen was staring out of the window. 'I didn't hear it ring.'

Jonathan dropped his arms to his sides as though all strength had gone out of him.

'Lynwen, stay here and keep an eye on the house; especially on the bathroom. Any signs of water rising in the lavatory pan, you must ring me straight away.'

'You're not expecting the lavatory to overflow, are you?'

'I don't know what to expect.'

Lynwen followed him to the front door, and then pulled at his arm as he opened it.

'Jonathan, I'm sorry about last night.'

'You certainly had bloody fun. But then you always do, don't you?'

'You're always getting involved in conversation.'

He turned to her, his eyes cold, his face grave and pale. 'I've got a career, remember? I expect my wife to impress people.-- That is, impress them in a manner befitting an engineer's wife. Who do you think I was talking business with while you were playing about? My District Engineer, my boss.' Do you know what remarked? He said, "I see your wife is enjoying herself."' That's what he said. Very ominous, don't you think?'

'I'm sorry, Jonathan, I really am.'

'Lynwen, you are always embarrassing me in public and apologising to me in private. It's not on Lynwen. It's not on!' He slammed the door behind him.'

# Eight

I may need a few days off, Fred, if the inconsiderate fool persists on bullying his way around my property,' said Jonathan as he paced to and fro in Fred Crabbe's office. He had his sky blue V-neck jumper on, a pale blue shirt and a Canary-yellow tie. His boyish face was red with emotion making him look younger than his twenty five years.

Fred sat at his desk leaning his elbow on its polished surface, his forefinger pressed to his lips. His brown hair was untidy after running his hand through it impatiently. He was like a man who had been up all night, for his chocolate jacket looked crumpled in parts and the knot of his brown tie was getting lost under the collar. He didn't want people knocking on his door giving him problems, especially Jonathan. Jonathan was supposed to be making life easy for him, not complicating things. He could never work out cost-cutting schemes if he had those little people knocking on his door. Only last week the computer had juggled the future shift patterns around in a hundred different ways when the screen suddenly read, twenty pounds savings on each man.  Fred was ecstatic. Then a girl came in from the typing pool and his elbow hit a key as he turned round. He hadn't noticed the screen had cleared until he'd gone over the typist's work. He was furious when he realised he'd lost the complicated calculation. He wanted Jonathan to leave him alone.

'Don't waste your holidays, Jonathan, you have flexible hours, remember. Just come into work for a few hours each day and give the men enough work to keep them covered for the shift; a bit of plant maintenance here and there will keep them happy,' he said with much generosity. *The changeover will be soon.!`*

He got up from his chair and began displaying extravagant gestures by raising his arms in the air and walking around his desk. 'Remember you are an Engineer. Engineers have privileges. Responsibility lies heavy upon us. We need to have breaks now and then. *The damn robots will be here soon.'*

'I don't believe it,' said Jonathan, not hearing the words of Fred, for he had got used to his ham-acting ways. 'I phoned the council on Monday, they said the original letter they'd sent me had a typing error, and should have read 'Approved' and not 'Planning Refused'.'

'You have already told me, Jonathan and I couldn't believe it. Some typing error, that. I couldn't believe it' he repeated louder.

'That bloody cowboy has cracked my yard in half from one end to the other and now it's threatening to slip into the trench he'd dug.'

The more Jonathan talked of the problem the bigger it seemed to grow, which brought on an attack of stammering.

'Whe...when Lynwen goes out to...to hang the clothes on the...the line, she's like a blo...bloody cloak and dag...dagger spy, shuffling along with her ba...ba...back to the wall.'

'Don't put up with it Jonathan. Don't put up with it,' said Fred, giving his junior undying support. 'Just come in for a few hours, man.'

'When I ca...came out of the...the house this mor...morning I neeeerly had my head chopped off, you know.'

'Good heavens above, man!'

'Broken slates flying through the air like an athlete's bloody dis...dis...discuss. Jagged edges. He had somebody riii...ripping off his main roooof and slinging them through the air. No safety shoots! No ba...barriers. The road was liii...littered with broken slates and striiiips of bro...broken wood. School children had to go over to the next street to ge...get to school.'

'He's got to be stopped, Jonathan. And you are the man for the job,' said Fred, stretching his arms, pointing dramatically at

Jonathan like a Shakespearean actor.

Jonathan stopped, for his breathing was heavy. He looked at Fred with a great deal of scepticism. He wasn't sure whether Fred was sending him up or being sincere. Fred, in turn, was looking Jonathan in the eye.

Yesterday I thought his house was on fire,' continued Jonathan, controlling himself.

'Never!'

'Smoke was billowing past my window, thick and black. I went out on the front doorstep and nearly choked.'

'Good god, Jonathan. What next?'

'I'd walked to the middle of the road before I realised it wasn't smoke at all.'

Fred's arms were agitated, his face full of shock. 'What was it, man? What was it?'

'Fu....fu...fuc'

'Jonathan!'

'Du...du...dust! 'Dust. Bla...bla...black...stinking dust, Fred. He had three id...idiots--no masks! No pro...protective clothing-- sitting on the rafters ki...kicking down the lath and pla... plaster ceilings. They'd taken out the front window completely to let the du...dust pour out.'

Just then somebody knocked gently on Fred's door. The door opened and Steve popped his head in. 'It's ten o'clock, Fred. I've got Gerwyn with me for our re-arranged meeting.'

'I haven't forgotten,' said Fred with a generous apology. His plan was foiled. Jonathan had delayed him. Fred had planned to have disappeared before his shop steward arrived. 'Give me five minutes.'

Steve closed the door and he and Gerwyn sat on some chairs outside Fred's office.

Jonathan stared at Fred, his stammering gone. 'What do they want?' he asked, suspiciously.

'Oh...grade eight. Gerwyn's grade eight.'

'He's not still persisting, is he?'

'Have you ever known Steve to give up?'

'I hope you're going to support me this time, Fred.'

Fred sat behind his desk and huffed. 'I've refused him, but you know Steve. He'll take it all the way through the grievance procedure. He won't get it, don't you worry. You've refused him. That's good enough for me. No way will he have it.'

'Pay that little twerp eight quid a week more for doing the same work as he's doing now!'

'Jonathan, you are the best judge. I bow to your supreme gift of character reading.'

Jonathan eyed Fred with scepticism. Fred, in turn, raised his eyebrows, daring Jonathan to doubt him.

Outside the office the two mates sat in their blue boilersuits. Gerwyn was sitting with his hands between his knees gently rocking backwards and fore, staring into the vinyl floor tiles. Steve, his arms folded, his long legs outstretched and his head resting on the wall behind the chair,  was looking up at the ceiling, waiting patiently. The silence was making Gerwyn nervous and he sighed several times.

'Do you think he'll give it to me today, Steve?'

'I don't know. These engineers are a law to themselves. Tell you what though, you'll have your grade eight eventually even if I have to take it to Head Office; they won't like that. Oh boy, they won't like that,' he said, folding his arms behind his head and smiling.

'Well, I think if we fail today, Steve, we ought to forget about it. Don't you think so, Steve?'

Steve sat up straight in the chair and looked at Gerwyn, stony-faced. 'You want to chicken out, do you?'

'I don't want to sound ungrateful, Steve, but I think you've done your best. If Fred can't get it for me, I don't see what else we can do.'

Steve resumed his relaxed position and put his arms behind his head again. 'There's plenty we can do. You worry too much. If you were asking for something which you weren't entitled to I wouldn't be wasting my time. You're entitled to grade eight and you're going to get it.'

'Sid Soper explained to me that our department's financial situation isn't too healthy at the moment.'

'Bullshit! You believed him, did you? He and Jonathan are playing the con-game.'

'It was the day I went to see Jonathan about being a day's pay short.--The day I couldn't get in because of the blizzard, when my car was snowed under. Anyway, Jonathan wasn't there, so I asked Sid's advice on it. He explained that nobody got paid because of our financial difficulties.'

Steve shook his head at his mate. 'You'll never learn, will you? You should have phoned in sick; they can't stop your pay, then. Sid couldn't get in that day either, but he got paid.'

'How do you know that?'

'I've got my contacts.'

'Why did they pay him, anyway?  He said he was sick, did he?'

'Engineers are never sick. They're either on flexi time or they're working from home. During the blizzard he phoned Fred and told him he had his paperwork with him to work at home.'

It was then Gerwyn sat up, surprised. 'Phoned the Met' Office did he? Or can he tell the future? He's crafty. I suppose he took the papers home knowing there was going to be a blizzard.'

'He'd make a better prophet than an engineer, that's for sure.'

'He knows my future; whether I'm getting grade eight or not. And he knew of the redundancies of the production boys.'

Just then, Fred Crabbe's office door opened and Jonathan came out. He walked past the two electricians without saying a word.

'Take a seat. Take a seat,' invited Fred, sitting behind his desk, as the two walked in.

Steve and Gerwyn sat opposite him. Gerwyn rubbed his hands together under the table and cleared his throat nervously.

He looked around, avoiding the glances of Fred, whose eyes were darting from one man to the other, waiting for one of them to begin. Steve pretended he was interested in some papers he'd produced from his overall pocket, scanning them seriously.

'Fred I--'

Fred jumped back in his seat, ham-acting, his hand on his heart. 'Good god, Steve, I thought you were going to hit me then. It's not going to be an aggressive meeting, is it?'

Gerwyn smiled politely at the engineer's playful ways.

'I hope you're not the nasty type, Gerwyn,' Fred said to the little man, puckering his lips and slanting his eyes.

'Me, Fred? Oh no. I don't look for trouble.'

'Steve can be frightening sometimes. He terrifies me, you know.'

Steve's brown eyes went up into his head and he looked at the ceiling. He waited for Fred to stop his acting. Fred got the message and placed his hands under his chin, then gave a stare of intense attention.

'As I was going to say, Fred, I think these delaying tactics regarding the upgrading of Gerwyn's grade eight are becoming farcical.'

Fred gave a start and sat up. 'He's already been upgraded,' he said, shocked. 'Hasn't he been paid yet?'

'He's been upgraded?' asked Steve, suspiciously.

Gerwyn looked at Steve, a big smile on his face, and he sighed with great relief.

'Listen,' said Fred, with a profusion of sincerity. 'When you told me last week that Gerwyn wanted to be upgraded, I replied with confidence that there would be no problem. As far as I'm concerned there has been no problem.'

'Thank you Fred,' said Gerwyn. 'I'm sorry to have troubled you. I didn't know you'd sanctioned it.'

'Gerwyn, I told Jonathan, the same day you asked me, that you deserve it, and by god you do.'

'Fred,' broke in Steve. 'Gerwyn has not received grade eight status'

'What? I can't understand that.--Don't go away.--I'll find out about this immediately. I'll telephone Jonathan and know the reason.'

The Senior Engineer dialled on the internal telephone. He waited for a few seconds then replaced the receiver. Leaning on his desk and looking thoughtfully into space, he shook his head.

'He's not there. I wonder where he can be. I thought he was going to go straight to his office.'

'Bleep him,' suggested Steve, a twist on his lip. 'I expect he's got his pager with him.'

Fred raised his index finger. 'Good idea, Steve.  Good idea.'

Fred picked up the phone again. 'Hello, switchboard?  Fred Crabbe here, bleep Jonathan Pallet and ask him to ring my office straight away. Pardon? He's gone to District Office? Oh, right, thank you. Ask him to ring me the minute he comes back.' Fred looked up at the two men.  He placed his two forefingers together over his lips and looked at Steve. 'Jonathan has left the factory for the time being. He'll be back. He'll be back. The problem is mine. I'll sort it out.'

'He must have had a rocket up his...'

'Steve...Steve, protested Fred. 'He rung the office and said he was going to District'

Steve blew a frustrated breath through puckered lips. 'Oh come on, Fred. It's been going on long enough. You can telephone the wages office and authorise it.'

'I can't do that. I've given Jonathan the responsibility of grading and promoting. I can't take it out of his hands. You know what he's like. I think he was spoiled as a child. I don't want another problem for overruling him. It wouldn't be right to go over his head. -- What do you think, Gerwyn?'

Gerwyn appeared shocked at Fred consulting him. 'Whatever you say, Fred. I don't know how this place is run. I wouldn't want you to offend Jonathan on my behalf.'

'See, Steve. Gerwyn understands.'

Steve sat in his chair stubbornly for a few seconds, and then stood up. He looked at Fred for a while, pulled out his notebook from his breast pocket, and scribbled something in it.

'Fred, I shall have to take it further. Come on, Gerwyn. Let's get back to work.'

'I'm sorry about that, Steve. Don't you worry, I'll sort it out, I'll see Jonathan.'

Steve and Gerwyn left. Fred was still pleading his innocence as they closed the door.

'We're having the run-around, Gerwyn, boy. They're taking the proverbial piss out of us.'

'But I'll be having my grade eight, now that Fred has promised.'

'You must be joking.--If that's the way they want to play it, I'm game.

'What do you mean, Steve?'

'Relax, Gerwyn. I won't involve you anymore. Just leave it to me.'

# Nine

Ceris, Gerwyn's attractive fourteen-year-old daughter, was in the front room listening to pop records. Her slim figure lay on the floor, stomach down, knees bent and her shoeless feet kicking the air. She rested her elbows on the flowery, nylon carpet, her pretty face cupped in her hands. She had closed the Flemish-glass sliding doors that separated the living room from the front room, in a vain attempt to stop the beat music from penetrating to her mother. She and her mother, having earlier finished preparing the Sunday lunch, had made themselves a mid-morning cup of tea, then took up their different pastimes in separate rooms.

'Turn it down a bit, love. It's very loud,' her mother called.

'Oh Mam I won't be able to hear it if I turn it down any more,' she answered, but then reluctantly got up and turned it down as little as possible. Just as the record was coming to the end, she heard her father come in.

'How did the job go?' she heard her mother ask.

'Not too bad. She only wanted one wall socket. I made a fiver out of it. Hardly worth getting up for on a Sunday morning.'

'Anything is better that a clip around the ear. That's what my mother used to say.--I expect you could do with a cup of tea?'

'I wouldn't mind.--Ceris, turn that noise down.'

'This is the last song,' she called back.

'Where are the other two?' Gerwyn asked, referring to his youngest daughter and his sixteen-year-old son.

'Bethan is still over at her friend's, and David is still horizontal,' answered Hilary from the kitchen.

Gerwyn frowned, then hung his head. 'I'm worried about that boy, Hilary. He's lazy and has no ambition.  He's got his exams coming up this year, but I never see him pick up a solitary book. I wish I had my time over again.'

'I'll give him a call now,' said his wife, and she went to the foot of the stairs in the hall and yelled. 'David! David!'

'Whaaaa,' came the tired voice from the bedroom.

'Do you want a cup of tea?'

'Yes, alright. I'll be down in a minute.'

'He sounds as though he's doing us a favour,' grumbled Gerwyn. 'Maybe he'd like me to take it up on a tray.'

'It's only the way he talks,' said Hilary, as she passed him and went back to the kitchen. 'He doesn't mean anything.'

The music from the front room ended. Ceris slid the glass doors open and came in carrying a full mug of tea. 'Hiya, Dad.-- Mam my tea's gone cold, I'll have another.'

'Hello, love,' Gerwyn responded, giving his daughter a disapproving look. 'Don't you wear anything else than those jeans and that yellow sweater?'

'They're comfy, mun, Dad.'

'Comfy? They look as though they're strangling you.'

The door to the hallway opened and the lanky figure of David shuffled in. He'd wrapped himself in the bed duvet, only his face and bare feet could be seen. His thin face was pale and drawn, his brown eyes half open.

'It's like a butcher's freezer in here,' he mumbled. 'Isn't there a fire on?'

'What do you know about a butcher's freezer?' Gerwyn asked, sharply. 'Put some clothes on. What's this time you're getting up, anyway?'

'I don't know. I haven't got my watch on,' he said, as he made his way to the gas fire and turned it on full. He lay on the settee and stretched out, pulling the duvet around him and, groaning.

Gerwyn slumped into the upholstered armchair that matched the settee and frowned at his son. 'David, have you done any

80

studying for your exams lately?'

'I just put down my history book, Dad.'

'Don't treat me like an idiot, David. You make me mad at times.'

'I did, honest. I don't know why I tell you the truth, you never believe me.'

'But I never see you studying. You've always just finished or you're going to do it afterwards.'

'Come and get your teas,' Hilary called from the kitchen.'

'Bring mine in, Ceris,' David said, seeing his sister moving towards the kitchen.

'Get it yourself, lazy. I'm bringing mine and Dad's.'

'Don't do me any favours, will you? Mam, bring mine in and a chocolate biscuit.'

His mother brought him his tea and chocolate biscuit and then stood behind the settee.

Gerwyn's face began to redden. Hilary noticed her husband's anger. In the past she had calmed things by pointing out the good points David had, which always helped to prevent a verbal conflict. She couldn't understand her husband. He was gentle and passive with most, but David was like a red rag to a bull to him. Her son was always dressed tidily and had a normal haircut. Not like those punks that Gerwyn detested. But Gerwyn was expecting big things from his son and there was no sign it was happening.

The previous few years had seen David coming home and getting stuck into his school work without having to be told. But his recent lack of interest infuriated her husband. It was as though he believed his son was on the downward road. One aspect of David which pleased Gerwyn was that he was the tallest member of the family. He had told Hilary how glad he was that their son was taller: five feet eight inches; eight inches taller than her husband, and five inches taller than herself and Ceris. But Gerwyn had said that that was no reason for him to be complacent. His lack of interest in the future exasperated Gerwyn. She could see he tried to reason with him most times, but he always ended up being frustrated at David's indifferent attitude, leaving Gerwyn depressed.

'David!' he suddenly yelled, startling everybody.

David coughed, choking on the biscuit he was eating. He collapsed back on the settee spilling some of his tea, but managing to clear his throat. Ceris laughed, but her mother shook her head.

'What? What's the matter?' David yelled.

'Stop monopolising the settee and let your mother sit down, boy.'

'Alright. Alright.  I didn't know Mam wanted to sit down.'

'I was wondering whether to hang some clothes on the line, or sit and do some knitting.' She picked up her knitting and sat at the side of David.

'What are you going to do after your exams, David?' snapped Gerwyn.

'I'm leaving school, definitely,' he asserted sharply.

'But what are you going to do after you leave school?'

'Go on the dole, innit? There's nothing else to do.' He glanced at his father. 'Now don't go on about jobs Dad, because there aren't any to be found. It's easier to find a Dodo than a job.'

Hilary looked up from her knitting: 'Talking about jobs, Gerwyn, I've got a chance of a job in town.

Gerwyn's face lit up. 'Honest. A genuine chance of a job?'

'It's ninety nine per cent certain.  Mair Thomas is a supervisor in the supermarket and she promised me she would try and get me in if a vacancy arose. Well, there has and Mair is putting my name forward.'

'What's the money like, Hilary?'

'It's only part time. About forty five pound a week.'

'A bit of good news at last,' sighed Gerwyn.

'Where is it, Mam?' asked David.

'Beels Superstore in High Street.'

'Does that mean I can have a couple of quid extra pocket money?'

'No, it bloody-well doesn't,' yelled Gerwyn. 'You get out and earn some.'

'Tell me where I can get a job, Dad, and I'll take it.'

'You won't find one lounging on the settee, that's certain.'

'You want me to go looking for a job right now, is it? Sunday morning and he wants me to go looking for a job. That's brilliant.'

'Not now, stupid. You've got plenty of time go looking for a job in the week days.'

'You want me to study. You want me to go looking for a job. You want me to help around the house. Anything else you want me to do in between jobs?'

'When I'm eighteen,' interrupted Ceris, I'm going to London if I can't find a job.'

Her father gave a huge sigh of despair. 'Don't say that, Ceris. Don't go saying things like that, it upsets me.'

'You're definitely not going there,' said her mother.'

'When I'm eighteen I can do as I please,' she said softly.

'I wish David had your enthusiasm,' said Gerwyn.

David sat up and pointed at his father. 'Oh! He wants me to go to London, now. You do, don't you?'

'Of course not. But you could write a few letters and get your name down in readiness for when you leave school. Anything to prevent you from believing you're not going to get anywhere in life. You'll automatically grow useless and lazy, David.'

'Thanks a lot, Dad. I haven't left school yet and already I'm useless and lazy.--My mate left school last year and he's already written 150 letters. Each time he's spent part of his dole money on stamped addressed envelopes. Do you know how many replies he's had.--Twenty. And those all said NO VACANCIES!--If they want me I'm available.'

David stood up, adjusted his duvet and shuffled his way to

the hall.

'Where are you going now?' asked his mother.

'To my room, I'm going to go over my chemistry file; give me a call if a job turns up, won't you?' He had been up in his room five minutes when the rhythm of his music came vibrating through the ceiling.

Gerwyn got up and put his arms around his daughter's shoulders. 'You're not serious about London, are you love?'

'Well, if there's nothing around here....'

Gerwyn drew his arm away and went into the kitchen. There, he fumbled around in the medicine cupboard until he found his Valium. He took one and returned to the lounge where he sat by his daughter and put his arm around her again.

'Listen Ceris, love, the first nice day we have in the spring, we'll drive to Torpantau, shall we? Just you and me.'

'And what about me?' asked Hilary.

'You already appreciate the difference between the big city and the countryside,' replied her husband, with a light tone. 'Besides, you'll be too busy working.'

'Dad, I've been to Torpantau tons of times with you and Mam. I know It's beautiful.'

'You used to love going there when you were a little girl.'

'I know. I still love it.'

'Right then, the first nice day in spring, just you and me.'

Ceris gave a reluctant nod.

# Ten

Jonathan looked up at the faded gold number on the fanlight glass above the brown, grubby, panelled door in the side street of Cwm Morlais. He was relieved to see it was the number he'd been looking for. It was a tall building, three floors at least, he thought. On the wall inside the door was a polished brass plate reflecting the miserable drizzling weather. A film of condensation covered the name, M. Mabie & W.E.Myte Partners. The door was open and led immediately to a bare, steep stairway that ascended into the shadows. He made his way up the stairs, two steps at a time, and came to another brown door on the gloomy landing of the first floor. He stopped and remembered why he had come to this practice of solicitors.

The previous day he'd scanned the telephone directory in search of a suitable solicitor. He'd failed to get an answer to his first preference, the secretary of his second choice said she couldn't possibly get him an appointment until next week, so in a moment of frustration he committed himself to his third option.

Smartly dressed in a dark blue suit, collar and tie, he straightened his shoulders and knocked on the panelled door. A loud female voice called from inside. 'Come on in, whoever you are.' Jonathan thought the order was a little unprofessional, but opened the door and walked in. He wondered had he done the right thing. The small congested room had two desks facing each other, and the elderly woman who squatted between them under a solitary fluorescent light, ignored him. She was busy tending a young child in a pushchair who was pulling grotesque faces and was on the verge of crying. Jonathan looked around.

The office was a cave of a room with shelving on all walls reaching to the ceiling and packed untidily with bulky files and law manuals. A smell of old books pervaded the room. A smell which had deterred him from borrowing books from the local library. He suddenly saw himself sitting up in bed reading a well-worn, grubby brown-edged thriller. It had left his fingers smelling and had made him get out of bed to wash his hands. From then on he bought all his books.

The two plastic waiting chairs and a couple of waste paper bins left little space for anything else in the room. The grey head of the middle-aged woman lifted above the desk and her sharp hazel eyes glanced at Jonathan, and then her attention returned to the child.

'Sit down, love. I won't be long,' she called to Jonathan—'There, there, don't cry. Look at the lovely dolly you've got.'

'I've come to see Mr Myte,' said Jonathan, inspecting the plastic chair, then sitting and feeling a draft coming from the door.

'Yes. He won't be long. He's got a young lady with him at the moment.--He's talking to mammy, isn't he my darling? Mammy won't be long, will she? No of course she won't. Who's a little treasure, then? You are. Yes you are.'

She stood and began to push the buggy back and fore the few inches the area allowed; towards the end of the desk and back again. The child looked at Jonathan as he came into view, then disappeared again, whimpering.'

'It's alright, my darling, he's not going to hurt you.'

Jonathan shuffled on his seat. 'Maybe I should come back when you're not so busy,' he said, sounding annoyed and looking for an excuse to change his mind.

'No no. What time is your appointment?' she asked without looking at him.

'Eleven o'clock.'

She looked at the clock on the wall. 'Another five minutes, then.'

Jonathan looked at his watch.  10.55. He was five minutes early. He sniffed. It wasn't the waiting he minded, it was the impression he was getting of the place. 'I suppose I am a little early.'

'Never mind, better too early than too late. He won't be long.'

He stared coldly at the woman. It was obvious she was the secretary. The grey blouse she wore was covered by a thickly knitted woollen cardigan which added to her stout figure. Her full hips were covered by a heavy green skirt. The dingy office was like something out of a Charles Dickens novel, he concluded.

He heard light footsteps coming down the stairs from the upper floor. The door opened and the mother of the child came in, thanked the secretary for looking after it, and then made her way with the pushchair out of the office, forcing Jonathan to stand out of the way. He detected a pleasant perfume coming from her. He sat again, listening to the bumping of the buggy as it went down the stairs.

Footsteps were heard coming down the steps of the second floor again. This time an attractive young lady, possibly in her late teens, came in and pushed past Jonathan and sat behind one of the desks. Jonathan gave her a cursory inspection. She had short cut blonde hair and wore a white blouse and long black skirt.

'This gentleman is waiting to see Mr Myte,' the older secretary said to her. 'Is he free now?'

'Yes, you can go up,' she replied, looking at Jonathan and giving him half a smile.  'I'll give him a buzz and let him know you're coming. What is your name?'

'Jonathan Pallet.'

'Right, Mr Pallet, you can go up now. Just follow the stairs and you'll come to a door on the right. That will be the one you'll want.'

Jonathan nodded to her and made his way up. It became darker and musty the further he climbed, but a forty watt bulb on the upper landing gave just enough light. He came to the door and knocked gently.

'Do come in, please,' called a tenor voice.

He was relieved to enter a spacious office with a large, brilliantly polished, oak desk in the centre of the room resting on a thick red and black patterned carpet, which left a border of polished floorboards around the room. He detected the scent of the previous client. Behind the desk was a young man dressed in a smart slate-grey suit. He smiled at Jonathan and gestured he take a seat at his desk. Jonathan sat on a maroon leather-covered chair which had a high upholstered back.

'I won't be two moments,' the young man said. 'Just making a few notes on behalf of the lady who just left..'

'That's all right,' replied Jonathan.

He looked around the room. It had an old fashioned look about it; left over from another age, he thought. The walls were covered in a green embossed, patterned paper, which appeared to be velvet in texture. It was bordered by a frieze six inches from the ceiling and painted in an even darker shade of green. The modern young man looked quite out of place. As he inspected the room, the solicitor looked up at him and smiled.

'Not my choice of decor, I'm afraid,' he said.

'Sorry, I didn't mean to....'

'That's all right. Just don't judge us by the antiques. They're part of our agreement with the owner of the building.--Right, to business. What can I do for you, Mr Pallet?'

'I'd like your advice on a building being constructed next door to me. A so-called developer has bought the house and is planning on building a double storey extension at the rear.'

'And you have an objection to its erection?'

'Yes. I most certainly have.'

'Have you made a formal written objection to the town planning office?'

'I have. And I did get the plans refused.'

The fresh-faced young man raised his eyebrows. 'Then

there's no problem. He can't build if planning permission has been refused.'

'It's not as simple as that. I received a letter off the council stating that planning permission had been refused. But later, when the building was underway, I received another letter stating that the first letter had a typing error and planning permission had been approved.'

The solicitor sat back in his chair and twiddled a pencil in his fingers. 'Mmm. If planning permission has been approved, as it seems it has, you may not be able to do anything about it, other than take it to court. If there is a clause in your house deeds stating that light and view must be protected, you have grounds to sue the developer.'

Jonathan sat up. 'That sounds promising. But he is a very determined builder. He'll listen to nothing. Just goes on building.'

'Well, to prevent him from progressing with the work I can get a court injunction to stop him until such time the matter is resolved. In the meantime I can write to him directly and instruct him not to build any further until the court has made a decision.'

Jonathan thought for a moment. There was nothing decisive in what the solicitor had said, and it was sounding expensive.

'Is it possible that Mr Bull, the developer, is in the wrong and he has no right to construct the building? I would like something a little more definite. I mean if I take it to court and the court finds--because he has planning permission--he has the right to build it...where does that leave me?'

'If the case goes against you, that is, if it eventually goes to court, then, of course, you will have to pay the costs. But firstly, we can try one or two bluffs. A bluff can go a long way.'

Jonathan raised his eyebrows. 'A bluff? But what if a bluff doesn't work?'

The solicitor eyed Jonathan as though making his mind up of a client who wasn't going to be very profitable. 'I could claim legal aid on your behalf, of course. But I'm afraid you'd have to be very poorly off financially to receive it.'

'Legal aid? How much is the case likely to cost? I mean, I have a good regular job and so does my wife. I can't see me qualifying for legal aid.'

'You're looking at the worst scenario. If we win the case the developer will have to pay the costs.'

'But if I lose I'll be stuck with an expensive bill?'

'I'm afraid so.'

'Approximately how much would that be?'

'Legal expenses are quite high these days, could be as much as three or four thousand pounds. On the other hand, the judge may rule that both should share the expenses.'

Jonathan made a throaty sound and his face expressed indignity. 'I don't want a prolonged legal battle. I was hoping that I...that you could give me more positive advice. Something more clear-cut.'

This type of case may have to go to court before anything definite is arrived at.'

'Is there anything else I can do?'

'Does this developer require any access to your land to complete his extension?'

'He's all over my property. He'll need to render the walls facing my kitchen. He can't do that without erecting scaffolding in my yard.'

'Has his construction encroached on your property? A yard, a foot?'

'I don't think so. The trouble with terraced houses is that it's difficult to know where the boundaries are.'

'Well, he can't come on to your property without first having permission. I'll need the deeds of your property to clarify things.'

'Can you write him a letter forbidding him to come on to my property?'

'Yes, I can do that. If he does, however, you cannot use any force to eject him off your land. That would be illegal. If he comes on your property you must inform the police and ask their assistance to remove him.'

Jonathan thought about it for a minute. He suddenly felt he was getting into a situation which could make his life unbearable. He imagined Charlie Bull walking all over his garden, trampling his flowers, damaging his property, scaffolding in his broken yard. He could see himself telephoning the police; a police car outside his house; neighbours coming to see what the trouble was. Then there were the expensive legal bills. But he wasn't going to let the ignorant bastard walk all over him.

'Are you all right, Mr Pallet?'

'Right?' he said. 'Yes, yes. You send him a letter forbidding him access to my property, and I'll bring my house deeds in as soon as possible.' Jonathan stood. 'I won't take up any more of your time, Mr Myte.'

'Very good, Mr Pallet, I'll have a letter typed immediately.'

Jonathan hurried down the stairs and into the drizzle with mixed feelings. I'm going to beat Mr Bloody-Bull legally. He's not going to make a fool of me. And yet, how far shall I go? How much should I spend on this solicitor? Is there any other way I can stop him? I could make life hard for the bastard. Yes, I'll knock the confidence out of cocky cretin. He's not going to have things as easily as he thinks.

He walked to the car park with a satisfied smile on his face, as though he had found the solution. He was a happier man than when he had arrived at the solicitor's office.

# Eleven

Converting the factory's machine shop to an automatic area had been delayed.  It had been planned for the new section to be commissioned in February, but having half of the machine shop on the other side of the wall next to the new robotic section had been proved a mistake.  The vibration generated by the old machine did not suit the sensitive micro-circuits of the computerised newcomers.  As a result the old machines had to be removed completely into another factory. The rethinking had an adverse chain reaction, for the research sterile area required a great deal of oxygen which needed to be supplied from a huge cylindrical tank just outside the workplace. It wasn't until the big oxygen tank was installed that the authorities realised the adjacent incinerator, also newly installed to burn toxic waste, did not meet with the appropriate safety regulations: it was too close to the oxygen tank.  And so, it wasn't until the end of April that everything was reasonably in order and in place. When it was ready, everybody decided to forget all the errors and the considerable extra financial burden it had put on the available funds, and enjoy the glory of the ultra-modern brilliance of it all.

To celebrate the commissioning of the installation, the district Engineer, Mr Morgan, among other notable area officials, came to inspect and tour the expensive conversion. The guide for the prestigious occasion was to be Mr Fred Crabbe, who insisted that Jonathan Pallet accompany him. Fred didn't want awkward questions asked by the District Engineer which he may not be able to answer, so Jonathan was to be the technical expert at hand. At least that was the reason Fred told Jonathan. However, Fred suffered from halitosis, and talking to officials was a dreadful prospect which took some furtive planning and stealthy movements on his part. When cornered, he would suddenly make sharp, darting movements under the gesticulating arms of the person talking to him, then make the excuse he thought he'd dropped something.

The robots had been tried out and thoroughly tested for two days before the important officials made their inspection. With their chests out, and their faces full of pride and achievement, they strolled around the huge automatic production factory with an air of haughtiness, on the momentous occasion that was to be their crowning glory.

It was a complete transformation. No oily machines or grimy interior. The walls were white and the floors shining with a red sealant. Multiple fluorescent tubes high in the roof illuminated a snaking overhead conveyor belt feeding sheets of metal and machine components to the robots below. Once delivered, another conveyor received the parts and took them through a gauntlet of agitated robotic arms that hummed, smacked and flashed; welding, turning, twisting, moulding and finally producing the end product with only a dozen men operating. Thin swathes of electric-blue smoke plumes ascended up to the extract fans, and the smell of burnt metal spread through, but the place at floor level was clean and free from the usual oil leaks, granules, and swarf as in the old factory.

On the other side of the workshop wandering about, holding clipboard and pen, looking very concerned, was Steve in his shop steward capacity. He stopped occasionally and looked up at the sophisticated machinery, wrote something on his note pad, then walked on carrying out various observations. Fred Crabbe suddenly noticed him, and his fiery eyes darted at Jonathan. Jonathan didn't understand at first, but Fred continued to make eyes at him and then at the shop steward. Jonathan followed the optical missile and realised the target. He shrugged his shoulders in silent communication, which appeared to go unnoticed by the remainder of the oblivious inspection party. It was obvious to both engineers that Steve was definitely making his way towards the touring group. Closer and closer he came until he was in audible distance.

'Good morning, Mr Morgan,' he said, loudly and cheerfully, having had meetings with the District Engineer in the past.

Mr Morgan's first reaction showed indignity, but he composed himself and gave a faint smile to the shop steward: 'Well, well, Steve. I haven't seen you for quite some time.'

'Oh I'm always around.'

'What do you think of our new project?'

'It's certainly keeping up with the times, I can't argue with that.'

'Well, we have to keep your lads in employment. It wouldn't do to fall behind with our competitors, you know.'

'That's true,' said Steve, lifting his clipboard to his face and looking around the animated machine shop.

'You're looking quite official this morning, Steve?' questioned Mr Morgan, suspicious tones in his observation.

'Oh this,' said Steve, shaking his clipboard: 'Health & Safety, just observing all the moving parts that are unguarded. Could raise a problem when maintenance is carried out.'

To Fred Crabbe's embarrassment, and Jonathan's annoyance, the group of men followed Steve's outstretched arm that pointed above the production line where the high conveyor belt was carrying the steel sheets around the universal joints. High currant electrodes would suddenly drop, hum for second, give off and electrical flash and return again as the conveyor belt rolled on continuously, feeding and taking away, then storing the products.

'Surely they are all out of harm's way, Steve,' said Mr Morgan.

'There are times when we may have to work above them; shut them down occasionally. Can't have the men up there on scaffolding carrying out maintenance while those arms are swinging about and flashing high currents.'

'I hope such times will only occur when production isn't involved,' warned the Area Production Manager. 'Far too much money has been invested to shut down this particular line. It's the backbone of the factory's production output.'

'There's a lot of lighting, air conditioning and many humidity units above this lot as well as the extract motors and fans. They don't break down at convenient times. It could be quite hazardous working up there. A simple job like changing a fluorescent tube could cost a life.'

'Yes, well, I dare say we can sort something out in the name of safety,' said Mr Morgan. 'Perhaps we can get out heads together. Yes, we'll arrange a meeting very shortly.'

'I'll be seeing you this week sometime,' said Steve. 'That's if everything has been arranged,' he added, looking Mr Morgan in the eye.

'Will you? About what?'

'Oh. I'm sorry my request hasn't got through yet. You've been very busy, I realise that.'

'What request?'

'Nothing important, there's a bit of a snag in upgrading one of our electricians. It's going through the grievance procedure,' Steve added, casually. 'But I don't want to trouble you now. I just thought you knew about it.'

The District Engineer appeared puzzled. 'Upgrading? There's no need to come to me for that.'

Fred cringed, Jonathan looked at the floor.

Steve continued: 'But it's the next stage in the grievance procedure.'

Mr Morgan looked at Fred Crabbe, clearly annoyed at the situation. 'Can't you deal with this minor problem?' he snapped.

Fred appeared indignantly surprised. 'Of course I can. No problem. No problem at all. There's no need for District to get involved, some misunderstanding somewhere, no doubt. I'll sort it.'

'Well I don't want to hold you up Mr Morgan,' said Steve. 'Sorry if I spoke out of turn.'

'Not at all Steve; By the way, I'd like something more definite on the Health & Safety aspect of this new building.'

'Mr Crabbe and me will work something out, Mr Morgan. Unless you'd like me to consult the Factories Inspectorate for some ideas and advice.'

'I hardly think that necessary. I'm sure we can work something out between us. Leave it with me for the present.'

'Very good, Mr Morgan, whatever you say is alright with me. I look forward to working something out.'

Steve left, with Fred and Jonathan waiting for the fall-out. Mr Morgan stared at Fred for several seconds and then pulled them away from the main group. 'What's this all about? Upgrading an electrician and you're bringing the problem to me. I've got better things to do.'

'I don't know anything about it,' said Fred, astonished. 'The first I've heard of it.' He turned to Jonathan for an explanation. Jonathan felt betrayed and could have given Fred a punch in the face, but he kept his composure.

'I...I do seem to remember mentioning something quite some time ago,' stammered the junior engineer. 'But with all...all the work I had on with...with the conversion, I suppose things got a little behind. The conversion was more important than upgrading an electrician.'

'Apparently not to the electrician,' said Mr Morgan. 'It only takes a second to sign an authorisation if the man is eligible. I assume he is eligible?'

Fred looked at Jonathan again.

'Uh, I'm afraid he hasn't got his final City and Guilds.'

'Good god, man, that's no problem. Can he do the job?' he said, staring at Fred.

'All my troops can do the job. I wouldn't have them

otherwise. Yes indeed, I have a good body of craftsmen.'

'Fred, I don't want such trivialities coming to my office. I want the matter settled at factory level. Make the man up. If you must be fussy about City & Guilds, send him to the technical college, one day and one evening, as usual.  In the meantime pay the man if he's doing the job.--And keep that shop steward away from me!'

'I will attend to it this afternoon, personally,' he said, giving Jonathan a wild look, indicating it was his entire fault.


Steve was triumphant when he and Gerwyn left Fred Crabbe's office that afternoon. Gerwyn however, had mixed feelings about the agreement and was subdued, hurrying along trying to keep up with Steve's long strides. His furrowed brow showed a great contrast to the elation on his shop steward's face. He looked up at Steve, mystified.

'Come on, Gerwyn, boy. We'll celebrate with a cup of tea up the canteen.'

'What? Uh...oh yes, a good idea, Steve.'

'He can't get out of it this time, it's all signed and sealed.'

'Yea, it's all in writing, isn't it?'

'Well, cheer up, then. You are now officially a grade eight electrician.'

'Do you think I'm too old to go back to school, Steve?'

'Of course not, it will be a dawdle for you. Your experience will carry you through.'

Gerwyn was ambivalent towards the agreement. It was all signed and sealed. He had to go back to school whether he liked it or not. He could see himself swotting upstairs in his bedroom, his son asking him has he done his homework.

They sat in the empty canteen after cadging a cup of tea off the affable catering staff. Steve sat there like a Cheshire cat, Gerwyn all doom and gloom.

'Gerwyn, what the hell's the matter now?'

'Don't get me wrong, Steve. I'm grateful to you, I really am. I appreciate everything you've done for me.'

'But? There's a big BUT there, Gerwyn.'

Gerwyn looked at Steve as though a heavy penal sentence had been placed on him. 'To be perfectly honest, Steve, I didn't think I'd have to go back to school. Not at my age. It's going to be hard studying at my age.'

'You are not going back to school; you are going to the local technical college. You'll have a day off every week with pay. One evening per week for a few hours, and you've got three years to achieve it. Most of the boys would jump at the chance.'

'But what if I fail? My son will have a field day.'

'Forget about your son. Just enjoy it.'

Gerwyn went into a trance for a while, and then said. 'I've got a nephew who's doing his C & G in technical drawing. He's in his first year. Do you know what he does? He throws rulers and slings paper pellets in the classroom.'

Steve huffed. 'You won't have to do the first year if you don't want to. When Byron did it they assessed him and he skipped the first year because he knew it all. It will be the same for you. What's more, make sure you get the firm to pay for your examination fees and enrolment fees.'

'They'll pay me for going to college?'

'Well of course. It's they who want you to go. It won't cost you a penny.'

'I've got a feeling Shylock isn't going to like this at all.'

'Forget about Shylock. He's a small cog in a big wheel. Don't let him get on top of you. Tell him to piss off now and again. He'll respect you more.'

Gerwyn looked amazed. 'He'd sack me!'

'You tell him when there's nobody around. He hasn't got a witness that way. I use a lot stronger language than that to him when I've got him on his own.--Come on, we'd better show willing.'

That night, lying awake in his bed, his wife snoring

contentedly at his side, Gerwyn was thinking of classrooms, formulas, equations, electrical regulations, exams, Jonathan Pallet and his son David.

# Twelve

Early May, the sun warming the countryside, the fragrance of spring coming through the air vents. Magpies claiming the middle of the narrow road took flight at the sound of the car. Deep green leaves on the bushy hedges glistening in their freshness trembled in the wake of the vehicle. Chirpy birds were in abundance, some flying overhead, others content to perch in trees. Perky brooks and slithering streams sparkled brilliantly, jinking down the hillsides and filling the fir-lined lake. The mountains grew bigger as Gerwyn drove on.

He'd dropped David off in town to meet his mates. Hilary was working. Bethan had insisted on staying behind with her auntie, where she could have more of her own way and Ceris, reluctantly, had agreed to accompany her father to his favourite country spot.

Driving to the crest of a hill, they turned a sharp bend and raced down the precipitous road into the hollow of Torpantau. Passing the solitary but substantial Forestry Commission lodge, it's chimney smoked a vertical grey streak reaching to the blue sky. They bounced over the hump-back bridge and parked in a large empty space at the foot of the mountains where once stood a small farm.

Gerwyn got out of the car, stretched his arms and looked around at the huge mountains where sheep dotted the slopes. Then he turned to the brook that ran parallel with the road, and further, where the forest of firs grew abundantly tall. Ceris looked out from the car window at the little man in his baggy jeans and lose T-shirt. It was a loveable glance from a soft-hearted daughter who couldn't hurt his feelings. 'Are you nice and comfy in those jeans, dad?'

'What's wrong with them?'

'Nothing, I was just wondering.'

'Come on, Ceris.  Let's cross the brook and walk through the trees.'

'Not again Dad. You said we weren't going to be long.'

'Oh come on. I haven't travelled ten miles to have a quick breath of fresh air and go back again. We've got to have a stroll.'

Ceris got out and looked around. In complete contrast to her father's casual appearance, the fifteen-year-old wore her blue jeans and pink sweatshirt tightly showing off her slim figure. 'It's the same old place, Dad. I don't know what you see here.'

'It wasn't always like this. I used to come up here when I was a youngster. My mate lived here for a while. I told you about Jimmy, didn't I?'

Ceris nodded lazily. 'Only about a hundred times.'

Gerwyn didn't hear her. 'There used to be a farm right where we are standing. Jimmy and his family lived here. We'd go all over the place exploring. Freedom, that's what it was, real freedom. We'd swim in the brooks, climb the mountains.'

Ceris had nodded all the time, patiently, having heard it all before. 'Dad?'

Gerwyn locked his car and he and Ceris crossed the rustic footbridge that forded the brook.  They walked through the trees until they came to a glade where the river Fechan, which winds its way through the country and feeds the reservoirs, passes through the open space in brilliant sunlight. Crossing the river by means of another wooden bridge with gnarled wooden handrails, they sat on the rich grass at the side of the slow-moving river. The silence was broken only by a distant cuckoo and the occasional splash of water washing the rocks up-river.

Gerwyn breathed deeply, taking in the redolence of the pines.

'This is the environment people should live in,' he said, thinking aloud, rather than talking to Ceris. 'What a contrast this is to factory work.'

Ceris remained silent, picking fistfuls of grass and throwing them into the water.

'If I came up on the pools, I'd by a piece of property out here.'

'There isn't any property around here, though, is there?'

'No. Jimmy told me the Forestry Commission bought them all up and grew trees on the land.  He had sharpness in his voice when he told me that. But there are farms further on. If we had driven up through the pass and down the Glyn into the next valley you'd see more country houses and farms. Built into the hillsides, they are nestling there, out of reach; untouchable, independent from the world of worry and stress. Self-governed..'

'You'll never win the pools, anyway, Dad. So it's no good dreaming.'

'You never know. Somebody wins every week'

Ceris turned to him and tapped him on his knee. 'Dad, you don't do the pools.'

'I've been doing them off and on for years.'

'That's no good. What are you now, off or on?'

Gerwyn sighed. 'I haven't done them for some time.'

'Huh! Maybe your luck was in when you weren't doing them.'

'I'll do them gain.--This is better than London, though, Ceris. You've got to admit that.'

'It's boring, Dad. come on, let's go.' Ceris stood up.

'Let's stay a little longer,' said her father, grabbing her hand.

Ceris sat back down and leant her elbows on her bent knees and cupped her face in her hands.

'You know, London can be a dangerous place to live in,' continued Gerwyn. 'Muggers hanging around waiting for you, unscrupulous men exploiting the vulnerable--especially girls.'

'You can go to Cardiff and find all those things happening there, Dad. My boyfriend said--'

'Your boyfriend!' gasped Gerwyn.

'He said a friend of his got beat up the other day in Merthyr.

He had three broken ribs and twenty stitches in his face.'

'You're too young to have a boyfriend, Ceris.'

'I'm fifteen now, Dad, I know girls who've had boyfriends since they were twelve.'

'Twelve? Bloody hell! Who is this boyfriend of yours anyway?'

Ceris got up and wandered a few yards away, her father's eyes following her. She looked around to see a mixture of sadness and disbelief on his face. Strolling back towards him she smiled a reassuring smile.

'Oh, he's just somebody I bother with.'

'Bother with? What's that supposed to mean?'

'Just somebody I go around with.'

Gerwyn got up and faced her. 'Well what...what do you do?'

'We go for walks, discos and things. Sometimes we go to the park, other times we go to town together or across the playing fields.'

He sat back down and patted the grass, motioning to Ceris to sit. She sat at his side and began to pick at the grass again.

'Ceris,' he said quietly. 'I hope you're not doing things you shouldn't.'

Ceris looked at him and rolled her eyes mischievously. Whatever do you mean, Dad?'

'You're maturing now, you know.'

'I've got to mature sometime.'

'Has your mother had a talk with you?'

'She talks to me every day. It would be funny if your mother didn't talk to you, wouldn't it?'

'I mean, has she...had a close talk to you.'

'She whispers in my ear sometimes, that's quite close.'

Gerwyn's frustration boiled over. 'For goodness sake, Ceris, has she told you about the facts of life?'

'Of course she has. I'm fifteen not six.'

A thought suddenly occurred to Gerwyn, and he looked at her with some relief. 'Oh well, you won't want to go to London if you have a boyfriend, will you?'

'He's thinking of going to London as well.'

'What!' he exploded, standing up and looking down at her.

'Dad, I'm sure you're going deaf.'

'You're not going to London with a boy.'

'Does that mean I can go on my own?' she asked, looking up at him.

'No! You've got all this around you. Nature at its best,' he said, raising his arms in the air, turning 380 degrees, frustration getting the better of him.

Ceris thought she might have gone too far. 'I haven't said I'm definitely going, have I? It's just a thought if I can't get a job when I'm eighteen. I've got to cut out a career sometime and somewhere.'

He stood behind her, the solitude of the place no longer serene to him. 'I can't understand you, Ceris. You want to go off to another country and you haven't seen your own lovely land yet. This country belongs to you. It's your heritage. I've never had much respect for people who forsake their country because life gets a little hard for them. If all the brains stayed in our country they could work to make it a better place for our kids. Instead they give all their talent and energy to some other place and leave their own country to deteriorate.

Ceris stood up, guilty for upsetting him. 'Come on, let's go home.

But Gerwyn didn't hear her: 'And when they're in foreign lands they sing of their homeland and tell people what a wonderful place it is, and what wonderful people live there, and how they long to go back. Rubbish!—They should have stayed here in the first place. This is a beautiful country and worth suffering for.' He calmed down and looked at her, his face white from anger. Come on. Let's go.'

They walked in silence for a time, Gerwyn thinking, Ceris wondering how she can cheer him up. As they made their way over the brook towards the car, Gerwyn stopped in the middle of the footbridge.

'Look around you, love. Just look.'

'I know it's beautiful, Dad. But there aren't any jobs.'

He moved on again, Ceris trailing behind. He opened the car door and sat in there a while, Ceris at his side, waiting.

'You don't want to be too willing, Ceris. Some people will go anywhere for work and come unstuck in the process.'

'You're always telling David to find a job. You tell him to find anything, as long as it's work.'

'He goes to the extreme. It takes him a week to get out of bed.--Your mother found a job locally.'

'Filling shelves and sweeping floors?'

'She serves the customers, sometimes.'

'She a dog's body, Dad; If anyone's being exploited, she is.'

Gerwyn started the car up and drove off. What sort of job are you looking or, anyway?'

'I wanted to be a physiotherapist.'

He was surprised. 'What made you think of that job?'

'When Mam was in hospital a physiotherapist came into the ward. She looked very smart dressed in navy slacks and a short white coat. I thought what a lovely job that would be.'

'Well, there you are, then. Aim for that job. You don't have to go to London to find a hospital.'

'I asked the career's officer in school what qualification is required for that job. Do you know what I need?'

'No. But it shouldn't be a lot.'

'Two A levels and four O levels. That puts me out.'

He ground the gears noisily as he changed to go uphill. 'Damn.--Why should it? Why should that leave you out?'

'I'm in the wrong stream in school, Dad, mun. I'm only in the B stream. The best I can hope for is a clerical job and they're asking four O levels for that job. They're not so fussy in London. Being a good typist will get you a clerical job there.'

'How do you know all this, anyway?'

'It's common knowledge in school. People talk about it all the time.'

'Kids dream about it you mean,' he moaned. 'London is expensive to live in.'

'Yes, but if I shared a flat, I'd halve the costs of everything.'

'Who could you find to share a flat with, Ceris, love? You wouldn't know anybody up there.--that boy!'

'Maybe.'

'Good god, Ceris, what are you saying?'

'Don't get in a mood again, Dad. I'll be eighteen, then.'

'I'm not going to have my little girl sharing a flat with some scruff of a boy.'

'Don't be daft, Dad. If I said I was going to get married at eighteen, you'd think differently, then, wouldn't you?--Watch that bend!'

His brakes screeched as he wound round the sharp bend, his concentration suffering. 'Ceris, you're only a child.'

'I'll be old, then, won't I?'

'Old? Old?' Gerwyn placed his hand on his temple, his left hand holding the wheel. 'You're scrambling my brains. You really are.'

'Well, older, then. I don't want to talk about it anymore. Especially when you're driving...But I've got to say this, if I had A levels and was going to university it would be the same as going away to London. You'd have to trust me. I can look after myself.'

'Yea, that's what they all say.' Gerwyn concentrated on his driving and no more was said. But his mind was in the dark streets of London, his fears picturing his darling daughter being influenced by all sorts of unsavoury people.

# Thirteen

Gerwyn had been thinking a lot about Christianity lately. He'd got to the stage in his life where he believed he needed a better quality of existence; something to make his life worthwhile. He needed somebody to help him find his inner self; spirituality where he would discover peace and contentment. The trouble with his assessment of religion was that his logic couldn't find any continuity in it all. So, believing that Ronnie was an expert on the subject, he frequently picked his brains to find the true way. They were both in the workshop, Gerwyn mending a solder bath on the bench, and Ronnie sorting his tools to go to the machine shop on a job.

'There's a lot of different religions today, though Ron. I mean, not only different religions, but different opinions as well. Why can't Christians believe in the same thing?' he was asking, as he inspected the solder bath in the workshop.

'All the answers are in the Bible, Gerwyn,' said Ronnie, with some condescension. 'You have asked me these questions before.'

'But it's never been clear to me. I mean, a Christian is a Christian. Why can't you all belong to one big family? It shouldn't be like a selection of insurance companies where you shop around for the best deal.'

Ronnie had stuck his head into his large steel tool lock-up, his voice echoing ghost-like from the steel cabinet. 'Our sect is open to anyone who sincerely wishes to join us. But we don't waste time preaching to people who may be the devil's disciples: 'Beware of false prophets, ' Christ said.'

Gerwyn turned around, talking to Ronnie's buttocks, 'I'm not a devil's disciple, Ronnie.'

'I'm not saying you are,' he said, emerging from his locker. 'But there are people who try and twist your words and tempt you away from the true road. Christ paid my debt, and ensured that I would gain everlasting life through Him. Therefore, anything earthly is of little significance. I do my job because I get paid for it. I owe my employer a certain amount of obligation, but I don't owe him my soul. If I get the sack tomorrow, I would just move on to another. I am not dedicated to my employer.'

Gerwyn listened to the calmness of Ronnie's voice and wished that he could be as confident and calm as him. Ronnie was refined and had an air of independence. He was single and settled and was a self-sufficient island in the middle of a choppy sea full of disillusioned people.

'I wish I could believe with as much confidence as you, Ron. I mean, what is going to happen to the ordinary guy who just goes about life but not believing?'

Ronnie's head had disappeared again, his voice reverberating: 'People who do not believe in Jesus are just lost souls. They are in oblivion, to be exploited by the butchers of the world; to be slaughtered in war for the devil's amusement.'

Gerwyn turned the solder bath upside down and inspected it, trying to understand what Ronnie was saying and at the same time squirting penetrating oil on the rusty screw, the pungent smell stinging his nose. 'How can I believe in God who has deliberately misled His people, Ronnie?'

Ronnie retracted his head, shocked. 'What on earth do you mean?'

'If I don't believe in Christ and I'm not prepared to follow his ways, am I condemned to hell?'

'As a Christian you would have to believe that Jesus died to save you. That He came into the world and took away the sins of mankind. Yes you would have to follow Christ to be saved.'

'What if I believe that Christ was just a great philosopher

who loved mankind?'

'You can't be saved if you don't believe He can save you.'

'So all those billions like me, as well as the Jews and Moslems, and the rest, who believe in God but not in Christ, all those are condemned to hell?'

Ronnie tut-tutted impatiently. 'Christ said 'believe in me and you shall be saved. I am the way, the truth and the life,' He said. 'Only through me will you see the Kingdom of God.' Those are the words of Jesus, and it is He that I follow.'

'I can't believe like that, see Ron. I mean, God created us all. And now He's picking and choosing by making daft rules.'

Ronnie sat on a stool, his hands on his knees. 'If you can't accept Jesus, how can you understand the wonders of God? Christ did say, 'In my Father's house there are many mansions.' May be He was thinking of you when he said it, Gerwyn.'

'I hope so. I need to have something to believe in.'

'I pray for people like you, Gerwyn, I really do. And I shall continue to do so.'

'Thank you, Ronnie.  I suppose if I don't make it there will be plenty of people like me where I'll end up.--Is Shylock a Christian, Ron?'

'I don't believe he is.'

'Pray hard for me Ron.'

Just then Jonathan came in, his suspicious eyes observing the two men chatting. He was carrying a thick file of papers under his arm and was looking very serious. On seeing him, Gerwyn took more interest in repairing the solder bath, and Ronnie made an exit with his toolbox and some fluorescent tubes, saying good morning to Jonathan as he hurriedly past him. Jonathan came and stood at Gerwyn's side, making him nervous.

'Good morning Jonathan,' he said, giving him a quick glance, as he dismantled the solder bath.

'Morning,' said Jonathan, abruptly, and he threw a one-inch thick A4 file of papers on the bench.

Gerwyn stared at the file, for it was touching his hand. 'What's that for, Jonathan?'

'It's the workshop manual and additional information on the new robotic system. When you've got five minutes, read through it thoroughly.'

Gerwyn picked up the papers and the glossy booklet that was with them, there were approximately two hundred sheets.

'Aren't we going on a tuition course?'

'That costs money.'

'Well...to be honest, I don't think I'll be able to understand that lot.'

'Of course you will, you're grade eight,' said Jonathan, a smirk spreading.

'Oh, be fair, Jonathan. I need to go on a lengthy instruction course to understand all that,' he protested, pointing at the file.

'You're being paid grade eight money to understand it.--Stick this in your pocket and look after it,' he added, forcing a pager in the breast pocket of Gerwyn's overalls. 'When it bleeps, you must telephone the switchboard immediately. They will tell you if I require you, or somebody else needs your services.'

Gerwyn stopped working and frowned at his boss. 'I have carried a bleeper before! I know what to do. One minute you're telling me I should understand all that bumf, the next you think I don't know how to answer a pager.'

'How long are you going to be on that solder bath?'

'I don't know. The elements have blown and the bolts securing the housing have rusted completely. I've snapped two already. I'll have to drill them out.'

'There are always problems with you. Don't be long. There's a job in the work-tray for some servicing to be done in the sterile department. I promised to have it done today, so make sure it is done today.'

Gerwyn sighed aloud and dropped his hands to his sides, then lifting them, he held them out and looked at them. Showing them to Jonathan, he gave him a pleading look and shook his head at his boss.

'I've only got one pair of hands, Jonathan.'

'So has everybody else, but they seem to manage alright.'

'Has everybody got this bundle of literature to read?'

'Everybody will have it in turn.'

'I'm the first to have it?'

'You're privileged, aren't you?'

'We should go on a course.'

'You will eventually.'

'Will it be a proper course?'

Jonathan gave him an indignant stare. 'What do you mean, a proper course?'

'I thought that pneumatics course was going to be a few weeks in a training centre, but what did I have? An hour in the office with Sid running through a workshop manual.'

'There you are, then. You don't need a course when you've got all the information you need in those papers, there.'

Gerwyn was paling every minute. He looked pathetically at his boss and said quietly. I hope that file is not in German like the one you gave me for that automatic, that time.'

'Stop whinging and get on with it,' snapped Jonathan, as he turned and walked away, his tall figure stooping a little, his arms dangling at his side, his wrists turned to the front.

The job of renewing the elements in the solder bath was comparatively easy, but the extra work of cutting the bolts and drilling and tapping the new holes had prolonged the job. It took him another half hour to complete it. When done, he clamped the heavy apparatus under his arm, picked up his toolbox in his other hand, then hurriedly made his way to the department from where it came. When he was crossing from the electrical workshop to the machine shop, his bleeper sounded with a high-pitched intermittent whine.'

He stood there wondering where the nearest telephone was. He was half way between the workshop and the switchboard.

'I'd better go back to the workshop,' he muttered. 'I bet it's Shylock having a bloody game with me.'

He walked as fast as he could, the heavy solder bath slipping down on his hip bone an inch at a time, his heavy toolbox pulling on his other arm. By the time he reached the workshop the tender flesh around his hip was feeling raw. He dropped the bath on a wooden stool and telephoned the switchboard.

'Hello, electrician here. You bleeping?'

'Oh yes,' came a sweet female voice. 'There's a machine broken down in the tool-room. I informed the electrical engineer, but he told me to pass the job on to you.'

'He would. I've got three jobs on the go now, so it will have to wait.'

'The tool-room supervisor said it was urgent and he wanted to speak to the engineer, which he did. The engineer rang me back and told me not to bother him, I should have got in touch with you.'

Gerwyn grunted. 'Alright, leave it with me.'

He got a hand truck from the corner of the workshop and placed the solder bath in it, putting his toolbox on top. Going to the instrument cupboard he got out a large test meter, a continuity tester called a megger, a tachometer and put them all in the truck.

'Right,' he mumbled to himself. 'I'll take the solder bath back first, then I'll go to the tool-room. If I have time I'll go to the sterile department and make a start on that job. Then tomorrow...tomorrow I'm going on the sick for a few days because I'm not feeling well.'

# Fourteen

Alan!' expounded Lynwen, as she opened the door, dressed in a pale green night-gown, nursing her Pekinese. She beamed at the tall, black-haired man who stood there staring through his dark-rimmed spectacles. It was the thirty-year-old bank manager who worked at the same bank as Lynwen. Dressed in a dark grey suit and highly polished shoes, white collar and striped tie, inferred strongly what his job was.

'Sorry to disturb you on your day off, Lyn, but I had an irate customer on the phone who you know more about than I do.'

'Don't be sorry, Alan. Come in and tell me all about it.'

'A Mr Joseph of Berry Road,' began Alan, as Lynwen escorted him into the lounge. 'He's had a home mortgage for £60,000 over a period of fifteen years and apparently you told him that there...'

'Sit down Al,' she invited, pointing to the settee.

He sat on the settee and was warmed when Lynwen sat next to him.

'Uh...this Mr Joseph said that you'd estimated his repayments at £608.75 per month. Well, he had a letter from our bank this morning with a figure of £659.75 per month. This, in his words, is causing him a great deal of distress.'

'Oh, he's got it all wrong. The £659.75 is before the tax allowance scheme is deducted. He'll only be paying £608.75 a month.'

'I thought that's what the misunderstanding might be, but I wanted to confirm it with you first. I'll ring him back and give him peace of mind. Sorry if I knocked you up,' he said, eyeing the silky dressing gown that was wrapped loosely around Lynwen's figure.

'Glad you called,' she smiled.

His eyes automatically dropped to the low neckline, but he sharply turned away when he realised she was aware of his gaze. 'I did telephone,' he said.

'I took it off the hook when Jonathan went to work.'

'Jonathan? Is that your husband?'

'Of course, Alan,' she smiled. 'You didn't think I was living in sin, did you?'

He gave a nervous shake of the head. 'Oh no, I hadn't heard you mention his name at work, that's all.'

'Cup of coffee?'

'No thanks.' He looked at his watch. 'I'd better be getting back.'

She looked deep into his brown eyes. 'Have a cup. I was just about to make one.'

Lynwen got up and went into the adjoining kitchen, leaving Alan feeling overly warm in the comfort of the central heating. He loosened his tie a little and stood up. The Pekinese had been watching him from the sheepskin rug in front of the gas fire, and growled suspiciously. Looking through the window on to the back yard he could see the masonry mess that had been abandoned at the far end of the garden next door. To the left of the window was the concrete block building, barrack-like, towering up and darkening the room. To the right, he could see Lynwen in the kitchen window, which was directly opposite the grey mass of next door's extension, six feet away.

'That's a huge wall next door, Lynwen,' he called.

'The subject of next door's extension is a very sore point in this house,' she called back. 'Jonathan will have a brain haemorrhage one of these days if he doesn't control himself. He wrote to our MP last week'

'Surely if he had objected to the Planning Department he could have prevented such a monstrosity?'

'He did all that. You wouldn't believe the tricks the cowboy next door played to deceive and thwart Jonathan's efforts. He even submitted two sets of building plans to the council, having Jonathan believe he was building a single storey extension. When the building was up to the roof it was too late. He was working to his second plan of a double storey. I don't know how he fixed it, but he had both plans passed by the Planning Department, and had a letter sent to Jonathan stating that the double storey had been denied. When the penny dropped, and Jonathan went down to the council for the umpteenth time, they told him that the honourable Mr Bull could choose to build from either plan.

'The devious swine.'

'Jonathan was thinking of getting a sledge hammer and knocking it down during the night when Bully wasn't there.'

'You advised him against that course of action I trust?'

'You can't advise Jonathan anything,' said Lynwen coldly, as she entered the room carrying two cups of coffee. She gave one to Alan then sat close to him again.

'What...uh...does his solicitor say about all this?' he asked, looking Lynwen up and down.

'His solicitor doesn't say anything. He writes to Jonathan occasionally asking him for instructions, Jonathan writes back begging him for some constructive legal advice. And so it goes on. He had a letter off his solicitor last week reminding him the case is dragging on.'

Alan looked puzzled. 'The solicitor asked Jonathan for instructions? What did he do?'

'He swore, ripped the letter up, stormed into the garden and threw some of our dog's droppings through the unglazed window of Bully's extension.--You're looking hot, Al. Take your jacket off and relax.'

'No thanks. I'm fine. I'll be going shortly.'

'Take it off for a couple of minutes, love.'

'I'm alright, honestly.'

'Take it off, your face is quite red with the heating on.' Lynwen placed her cup on the coffee table and helped Alan remove his coat. He juggled his cup from one hand to the other, not noticing Lynwen deftly loosening her own gown by pulling at the knot of the belt, revealing an ample amount of cleavage. Alan weakened and stared quite positively at the bronzed flesh, which had obviously gone topless during long sunny spells. He suddenly lost his reserve.

'You're well proportioned, Lyn,' he said, in a loud whisper.

'Thank you, Alan,' she whispered back, and she sat, pushing up against him, the top of her gown opening further, the bottom showing her shapely thighs.

'Is your husband...uh...out for the day, Lyn?' he asked, moving his face closer to hers.

'He won't be back for another two hours,' she replied, opening her lips slightly.

He put his left hand on her shoulder and moved his lips closer until they touched, pressing firmly. His right hand slipped down inside her gown and spread out. Then his heart slammed against his chest as he heard the front door being closed forcibly.

'Hell! What's he doing home?' said Lynwen, in an angered whisper, as she jumped up from the settee and hurriedly bound the belt of her dressing gown.

Alan shot up off the settee in panic and grabbed his jacket, fiercely trying to find the arm holes. He had time to put the coat on, but no time to button it up or straighten his tie, before Jonathan appeared.

There was a mixture of shock and satisfaction as he began to understand the situation. His eyes darted from Lynwen to the stranger in an agitated, excited manner.

'I've got you at last, you bitch!' he snarled.

'Jonathan, don't jump to conclusions. This is Alan, one of our bank managers. He had some urgent banking business to consult me about.'

'I know what he was banking on.'

'It's true,' spluttered Alan. 'A customer of ours--'

'Balls to your customer! Don't treat me like an idiot.'

'Please don't get the wrong idea, Mr Pallet. I did telephone first.'

'To see if the coast was clear?'

'No Jonathan. I left the phone off the hook so that my sleep-on wouldn't be disturbed.'

'Get out you bastard!' he yelled at the bank manager.

'What...'

'Get out before I scatter your banking brains over the carpet,' he screamed, picking up a small table from the nest of tables and holding it shoulder high.

The Pekinese shot into the kitchen and quickly curled itself tightly in its basket, its frightened eyes furtively peeping over it protective paw.

'You'd better go Alan,' said Lynwen, trying to keep calm and dignified. 'I'm afraid my husband can be quite paranoid with jealousy at times.'

Alan gave Jonathan a wide berth as he manoeuvred around him embarrassingly, then made a speedy exit.

'You've slipped up this time, you bitch! Got to clever for your own good, didn't you?'

'It's not what you think, Jonathan.'

'Your face has given you away, my darling. So did the face of that snake that just slithered out. It's no good brazening it out this time. Just get yourself a solicitor. You're going to need one very soon.'

'You're not serious, surely? Don't be so damned dramatic.'

'Dramatic! You're going around screwing all the studs available and you want me to keep calm. I ought to screw your neck!'

'Now you're being vulgar.'

'Listen my fine beauty, you've become a disgusting little

whore. As far as I'm concerned you're out of my life forever. It's been quite a good day, really. Now that I've got rid of you, I can sell this house and rid myself of that bloody idiot next door. Now pack your bags and get back home to mummy.

# Fifteen

Gerwyn was sitting crossed-legged on the concrete floor of the despatch department, testing the motor of the conveyor belt, when his bleep sounded. His tools and testing gear were spread around the adjacent floor area after partially stripping the long apparatus which carried the endless foot-wide rubber. Emergency stop buttons hung on their cables along the length of the conveyor and opened control boxes revealed a mass of connectors, contactors and tangled wires. With beads of perspiration on his brow and oily hands examining the motor's terminal block, he glared at his bleep lying at his side and mumbled words of foul language.

Knowing he couldn't leave his testing gear and tools laying around in case some opportunist might take a fancy to them, he gathered them up. For safety reasons he couldn't leave the machine in its present state, so he went to the distribution board and extracted the appropriate fuses. He then made his way to the nearest internal phone and rang the switchboard. The switchboard put him through to Jonathan.

'Gerwyn, come to my office at once,' Jonathan ordered.

'Can it wait, Jonathan? I've got the despatch conveyor stripped down and the foreman is playing hell.'

'Despatch conveyor? That job didn't come through my office.'

'The despatch foreman bleeped me this morning before you came in.'

'What time was that?'

'About ten o'clock.'

'I want you up here,' he demanded, and then the phone went dead.

Gerwyn strolled up the tiresome journey to the main factory carrying his tools and testing equipment. He could have left them in some safe place, but the last time he did that he needed them on the job Jonathan had given him and had to make the return trip to pick them up. Jonathan would never tell him why he needed him until he reached his office, so he had to be prepared for all emergencies. At times he would give him a job which was near the place he was working, but wouldn't tell him until he was facing him in his office. Reaching Jonathan's office, he noticed Steve leaving the electrical shop, which was only a short distance away from the engineers' office. He could see the chrome strip of Steve's bleeper in his breast pocket and a newspaper hanging out of his back pocket.

'Alright, Gerwyn?' he called.

'I can't be alright if I'm working in this place. I've got the despatch conveyor down and he's calling me up here.'

'Conveyor playing up again, is it? Can't stop, see you in a minute.'

Gerwyn pushed his way into the office where Jonathan sat with his legs resting on his desk, reading the newspaper. The engineer looked the frustrated little man up and down.

'There's a bulb blown in the toilet up at the typing pool. Go and put one in then come back here.'

Gerwyn stood there for a while, speechless.

'Well? What are you waiting for, a route map?'

'You didn't drag me all the way up here just to put a bulb in?'

'Yes!' said Jonathan, staring at him.'

'But I'm on a serious breakdown.'

'So? You don't expect me to go and renew the bulb, do you?'

'No, but you could have asked someone else nearer the job.'

'Why? Is above your station to put a bulb in?'

'Of course not, but it would have saved me walking up here and the job would have been done quicker.'

'Oh. You're an efficiency expert. I didn't know that.'

'The electrical shop is only ten yards away, Jonathan. I'm not the only spark who's working today, you know.'

'Are you refusing to do it?'

'No. I'm not, but I don't think you're being fair.'

'Listen, I'm telling you to do it, I'm giving you a direct order.' Then he bellowed, 'And to save you coming back again, this is the other job I want you to do!' He bent down and picked up a block of solid steel a foot long and three inches square, and some springs and several pieces of broken metal.

'What's this for?' groaned Gerwyn, frowning.

'The Maindy automatic. See those pieces? They were once a spring-loaded, interlocking striker-arm for the main feed limit switch. As you can see it has been smashed by a malfunction in the guts of the machine. Production can't wait for a new one to be sent from Germany, so you'll have to make one. You need to cut a two-inch diameter roller out of this metal block, fit a three by half-inch arm on to it so that it will pivot at least two hundred degrees, and assemble it on a steel plate with a limit switch fixed to both ends, so that the arm can be compressed by the on-coming component as it passes over and activate the switches. Get on with it after you've renewed the bulb.

Gerwyn picked up the block of steel and glared at Jonathan menacingly. He didn't say a word, just glared. Then his anger broke and he slammed the heavy piece of metal on the desk. Jonathan jumped in his chair and brought his legs down off the desk. Gerwyn stood there, shaking, looking at the shocked expression on his boss's face.

'That's not my job, and you know it,' he said, the words choking in his throat. 'The same thing happened months ago.'

'Of course it's your job. You're a grade eight electrician.'

'You know very well the job can't be done without the skills of a toolmaker and a fitter. The job requires a milling machine, a lathe...the whole thing itself...from pivot to roller....'

'Are you refusing to do it?'

Gerwyn's anger subsided to an inward whimper. He knew Jonathan was throwing down the gauntlet. He mustered all the courage he could find, picked up the block of steel and threw it across the office.

'It's not my job! I'm refusing to do it,' he said, in a stifled shout, his face white with anger.

'I'm taking one day's pay off you and giving you a verbal warning, and I shall give you the rest of the day to think about it. If you refuse again I will give you a final warning. If you persist after that I will have no alternative but recommend to management your employment be terminated.'

'Jonathan, I'm not that stupid My pay is my pay and you have no authority to touch it.'

'You are getting money under false pretences.'

'I'm paid no more than any other grade eight man whether he be an electrician, toolmaker, fitter or any other trade. You're victimising me.'

'But you are grade eight. Top grade, top man.'

'I'm a genius, I'm a magician, why don't you issue me with a magic wand?'

'It's not funny, Gerwyn. You are being paid highly-skilled wages. You are expected to turn your hand to jobs outside your craft.'

Gerwyn was gaining confidence. He could feel his boss getting edgy. He put his hands on his hips, his colour returning. 'With training Jonathan! With training. It was only a couple of weeks ago I was a grade seven spark. In that short time without any training or instruction you've expected me to turn into a multi-craft expert.'

'I don't want to hear any more. I'm very busy,' said Jonathan, sorting paper on his desk.

'Busy? Feet up on the desk reading the bloody paper?'

'Don't be impertinent. The job is there, if you can do it. If you can't you'll have to put up with the consequences. And it's no

124

good running to your shop steward, I've already had a word with him.'

Gerwyn left the office with mixed feelings. He felt elated he stood up to Jonathan, but the reference to Steve worried him. He cleared his mind and decided he must do the job in hand. He renewed the bulb in the toilet of the administration block, and then his bleeper went again. He made his way to the typing pool, the closest internal phone. Automatically he went up to the nearest desk where a typist was busy audio-typing, bent down to her and looked her in the face. She jumped back, startled: 'Good god! Where did you come from?' she said clutching her chest, her headphones pulling away from her ears as she fell back in her chair.

'Sorry, I didn't realise you had headphones on. Do you mind if I use your phone?'

'Be my guest. I could do with a break, anyway.'

The switchboard told Gerwyn he was to ring extension 223. He was surprised to hear the voice of Steve at the other end. 'Gerwyn, are you coming to this meeting today or tomorrow?'

'Meeting? What meeting, Steve?'

'The monthly union meeting dopey. The notice has been up on the electrical shop board for the past three days.'

'Oh. I'd forgot about that. I've just had an argument with Shylock. He wants me to do a job straight away--'

'Never mind bloody Shylock. This meeting has been authorised by Fred Crabbe. I thought you were on your way when I saw you earlier.'

'No. Jonathan ordered me up from the despatch department. He's told me to do a job, Steve, which I think is not my job to do at all.'

'Well don't tell me now, bring it up in the meeting. Come on over to the canteen, you're holding the meeting up.'

'But what about the work I have to do?'

'Listen, we've all got jobs do. The on-call man is available for any emergencies.--That's me. Shylock knows where we are if one should crop up. Now come before the allotted time runs out.'

'Right oh, Steve. I'm on my way.'

When Gerwyn arrived at the empty canteen he found the electricians sitting at a table furthest away from the serving counter. Steve was addressing them as Gerwyn quietly approached, pulled up a chair and sat.

'Right, the first item on the agenda is about Shylock cutting times on jobs that have already been given official times by Quality Control and agreed by union and management--'

'That bastard has got to be stopped,' blurted Byron, a stocky, black-bearded man. 'He's getting away with murder.'

'Okay. He's got to be stopped, but we need some constructive ideas how to do it.'

'Drop a lump hammer on the bastard's head,' suggested Byron.'

Steve looked at him and shook his head. 'Constructive ideas, Byron? Remember, we've got a trio of conspirators to deal with.'

Gwyn looked up at Steve. 'Work to rule, or have a day's token strike. That'll sort them.'

'That's not going to get us anywhere, Gwyn. We are committed to go through the grievance procedure,' reminded Steve.

'But we never get anywhere with that procedure. It only goes as far as Fred Crabbe and he makes a hundred promises which we are daft enough to believe. Then he forgets all about them.'

'Let's discuss the cutting of bonus times,' said Steve. Shylock said it must have been an office error. The office denied this and said they could only work on the number of hours that came from the engineers.'

Byron shifted in his chair, irritably. 'They're a bunch of bloody liars!' he said. 'I wouldn't trust them in a confession box. And what happened? What happened?'

Steve huffed. 'I was back and fore between the office and engineers for a week; fobbed off every time with figures and red

126

tape. But the bonus did improve for a time. Now it's back to rock bottom again. We've got to prove that Shylock is fiddling the times.'

Ronnie couldn't believe an engineer could stoop to such practices: 'If he is cutting the times, Steve, (A) for what purpose would he do it, and (B) what could he possibly gain from it?'

'(A) Ronnie, he's trying to put a feather in his cap in an attempt to prove he's running a super- efficient department, impressing the Area Engineer. (B) He's intent on undermining the Time & Study boys. He thinks he's all-powerful.'

'You're complicating things, Steve,' said Byron. 'The truth is, he just likes to make up his own rules and regulations, then change them when they don't suit him.'

Gwyn had an expression of concern on his lined face. 'If we're going to let him cut times again and again, we're going to be running around like blue arse flies and getting no bonus for it.'

'Let him cut the jobs to impossible times but don't do the job in all its entirety,' said the shop steward. 'Let him cut them to the extreme so that even the simplest member of management can see through it. Just make sure the job is safe. Let's face it, you're almost doing it now. The jobs we do on maintenance now are impossible to complete if you stick rigidly to the bonus manual—how much time did he give for the universal grinder, Gerwyn?'

Gerwyn was surprised Steve spoke to him; his mind was still on job he was supposed to be doing. 'Uh...well...the universal...I think he gave me two hours, but last week he cut it down to one hour forty minutes.'

'Bloody hell!' blurted Byron. 'The last time I had that job there was three hours on the card.'

'Exactly. And I bet you both signed your cards, job completed? Those signatures hold you responsible for guaranteeing you have carried out all the work as listed in the bonus manual. So, let's do exactly what they want until they make a fool out of their own bonus system.'

'Give them enough rope to hang themselves, you mean, Steve?'

'Right, Gerwyn. You're catching on. Does everybody agree?--One thing I want to warn you lot about is this: The last meeting we held, the engineers knew all about it before I had chance to discuss it with them. If I find out who's leaking information I'll have him up before the Branch Committee.'

There was silence for a few seconds while everybody tried to appear innocent.

'What about this new technology, Steve? asked Byron. 'These robots are no good to us.--And by the way, let me remind you I was the only one who didn't have overtime out of the robotic installation.'

'Overtime should be cut out altogether in my opinion,' said Gwyn. After all, there are plenty of our members on the dole.'

'Don't be so bloody naive,' blurted Byron. 'They're earning more than us collecting dole and doing a few jobs on the side.'

'Let's not start getting personal,' warned Steve. 'Byron if you want an overtime roster, then propose it and we'll vote on it. But remember the last time we did this Shylock stopped all overtime, and even squeezed in a contractor here and there. The only reason you don't get as much overtime as others is because Shylock hates your guts.'

'He doesn't like me, either,' said Gerwyn. 'He gave me a load of literature to read up on robots. He's either trying to make me hand in my notice or sack me for some reason or other.'

'He doesn't decide who is to come or go, Gerwyn,' said Gwyn. 'He's just a little fish in a big pond.--A pain in the arse.'

'I really don't see why you are worried,' said Ronnie. 'If redundancy should occur in this factory it will be me who'll go first; I was the last to start here.'

Byron sneered. 'They may decide on popularity, Ron. That would mean I would be top of the bloody list.'

Steve was losing patience. 'We're going off the point, now.

Redundancy hasn't been mentioned.'

Just then, Gerwyn bleep sounded.

'Who's bleeping you? asked Steve. 'I'm the duty electrician.'

'I expect it's Shylock, Steve,' said Gerwyn apologetically. 'He's bleeping me all the time.'

'Is he? Well, I'll answer it, and we'll see how I can help him.'

'Oh thank you, Steve.'

The shop steward rose from his chair and went to the wall-mounted telephone just a few paces away. Picking it up he dialled the switchboard who informed him to ring 888. He did, and it was Jonathan who answered.

'Gerwyn, what are you doing now?'

'This is Steve. What do you want, Jonathan?'

'I bleeped Gerwyn.'

'Gerwyn is with me in a union meeting along with the rest of the boys. Besides, all emergency bleep jobs are supposed to come to the duty electrician. That's why we are called, duty electricians. The rest of the work staff should be busy on allocated daily jobs. The day man is second on call.'

'That's a mouthful, Steve.'

'Just thought I'd remind you.'

'And whose rules are they?'

'It's an agreement between management and union. You should know that, Jonathan, you were there at the signing.'

'Who said you could hold a meeting?'

'Fred Crabbe, two weeks ago. And if you cast your mind back, you were present at that meeting too.'

'I thought you had that meeting.'

'Jonathan, it's marked on your calendar. Now if you've bleeped just to interrupt the meeting, I'll ask Fred Crabbe for extra time.'

'I had forgotten all about your meeting.--I want Gerwyn over here.'

'He's part of the meeting. Unless it's urgent, I think you're being unreasonable in asking him to leave.'

'It is urgent! So get him over here immediately.'

'What is it that is so urgent?'

'Never mind what it is. I'm saying that it's urgent. So it's urgent. Now send him over.'

Jonathan slammed the telephone down leaving Steve tight-lipped and fuming.

'What is it, Steve. Is he asking for me?'

'Yea, he's asking for you. Tell me, Gerwyn, why should he want you and none of us?'

'I don't know, Steve. He's on my back all the time.'

'Is he victimising you?'

'I didn't say that, Steve.'

'Earlier on you said you wanted to see me about something?'

'He wants me to make a spring-loaded, retractable arm to operate the limit switches on the new automatic.'

'The bastard!' said Byron. Me and Freddie the fitter took that out. We told him at the time it needs to go to the tool-room for replacing. It needs machine tooling, milling and tempering. It's got to be precise to a thousand of an inch, the silly git.'

Steve looked at Gerwyn. 'What did you tell him, Gerwyn?'

'I told him it wasn't my job, but he threatened to sack me, in a roundabout way. He's already given me a verbal warning and he says if I keep refusing he will recommend me for dismissal.'

Byron couldn't believe it. 'I've had a gutsful of that idiot,' he said. 'It's about time we did something about him.'

'Let's keep our cool now, Byron,' said Steve. 'Listen, Gerwyn, he can't give you a verbal warning without your shop steward as a witness. As I wasn't present, it means he's shooting you a load of bullshit.--Are there any items arising from this meeting?' he asked the rest of the men.

'No, no,' said Gwyn. 'You go and sort Gerwyn's problems out.'

'Aye. Don't bother with that bastard, Shylock or Fred Crabbe. Go straight to Mr Morgan at area office.'

'We'll go through procedure, Byron. We'll end this meeting

now.'

The men went back to their jobs while Gerwyn and Steve hurriedly made their way to Jonathan's office. The pace made Gerwyn hot as his short legs struggled to keep up and his furrowed sweating brow portraying the trauma within.

Ken James

# Sixteen

Steve knocked hard on Jonathan's door and charged in before an invitation could be offered. Gerwyn followed timidly behind with so much hesitation the spring-loaded door closed on him before he could get through. The providential sign induced him to remain outside in the corridor. The knocking and sudden thrust of the door made Sidney jump in his chair and look around with a startled expression on his spectacled face. Jonathan looked up sharply from his paperwork.

'Steve, would you mind not barging through the door like that.'

'Sorry, Jonathan,' said Steve, over-politely.

'If you've come here to be disrespectful I suggest you turn around and go back out.'

'I've come in my official capacity to represent Gerwyn, here,' said Steve pointing to the missing electrician.--'Where the hell is he?'

Steve opened the door and saw Gerwyn standing with his hands clasped together behind his back and one knee slightly bent.

'What are you doing out there?'

'Do you want me to come in now, Steve?'

'Of course I want you to come in. I'm going to look a dick in there on my own, aren't I?'

'Oh, right, Steve.'

'I wanted to see Gerwyn privately,' snapped Jonathan. 'So I would appreciate it if you would leave my office and get on with your work.'

'I bet you would. If I leave I'm taking Gerwyn with me, and I'll make a telephone call to my full time official reporting a case of victimisation at this workplace.'

'Victimisation? Who is being victimised and by whom?'

'Come on, Jonathan. Let's be man enough to face up to the situation. You're continually on Gerwyn's Back.'

'In what way do I treat Gerwyn any different from the rest of the men?'

'You've been on his back for months, and you know it. You exploit his disposition. You expect him to do impossible tasks. You are generally making life hell for him. I've turned a blind eye to it because I wanted him to make the first move, but when he explained in the meeting what was happening, the men gave me a mandate to look into his case officially.'

Jonathan sat up straight in his chair and shot an angry glance at Gerwyn. Sidney did the same as though in support of his colleague. Jonathan said, 'Gerwyn can speak for himself, surely?'

'He tells me he has tried but his words fall on cloth ears.'

Jonathan eyed Gerwyn again. 'Cloth-eared am I, Gerwyn?'

'I...I didn't exactly use that expression, Jonathan. But you must admit you don't listen to a word I say.'

'Don't I?' asked Jonathan. 'Well, well. I thought I hear every word you say.'

Gerwyn shuffled nervously. 'Well...yes...you listen, but you don't take any notice of what I say.'

'Don't I?' he repeated with the same sarcasm in his voice.

'Uh...no. And you sort of...insinuate things...And threaten.'

'Threaten! Good god, Sid, I threaten him. He claims I threaten him.'

Sidney clicked his tongue in a tut-tutting fashion and shook his head like a teacher despairing over a dunce. 'Gerwyn,' said Sidney, 'let me give you a little advice, choose your words carefully when you make such a serious charge against your engineer.'

'This is nothing to do with Sid,' warned Steve. 'In fact I'd be grateful if you would be kind enough to leave us in private until this meeting is over.'

'Oh,' said Sidney, indignantly. 'Oh Oh. It's like that, is it? Let me remind you that this is my office as well as Jonathan's.'

'You stay where you are, Sid. If Steve is using Gerwyn as a witness, I'll need you for the same purpose.'

'Oh I'm not going anywhere.'

'Right, Gerwyn,' asserted Jonathan. 'You've used the word threaten. Let's hear more. Come on, let's hear more.'

'You threatened me with the sack earlier on, Jonathan.'

'I most certainly did not.'

'You said if I didn't make a striker for the interlocking mechanism, you would recommend me to area office for dismissal.'

'You must have misunderstood me, Gerwyn. I said nothing of the sort.'

Steve broke in. 'You know very well that making that particular piece of control gear is nothing to do with an electrician,' he snorted. 'So why are you trying it on? Byron has already told you it requires machine-tool operation.'

'Because Byron can't do the job, it doesn't mean that Gerwyn is incapable. I shall ask whoever I think is best for the job.'

'Ask? Maybe. Threaten? Definitely not.'

'I did not threaten anyone.'

'You gave me a verbal warning Jonathan,' prompted Gerwyn. 'Said you'd dock me a day's pay.'

'Hells bells, where do you get these stories from? You must be hearing things, man.'

'You said you'd give me time to think about it, and if I didn't change my mind you'd recommend my dismissal.'

Jonathan looked at his colleague. 'Did I say any such thing, Sidney?'

Gerwyn gasped with astonishment. 'Sidney wasn't there!' he yelled.

Sidney was shaking his head. 'Oh I was here, and I heard no such comments.'

Gerwyn was agitated now. Looking at Steve, then at the engineers; twisting his hands tightly, stressed.'

'I'm sorry, Sidney, but you must be thinking of another person at another time. You weren't here with me and Jonathan earlier on.'

Sidney lowered his glasses and twisted his thin lips into grin, and then looked Gerwyn straight in the eye. 'I distinctly remember you refusing to do the job, Gerwyn. I was sitting right here in my chair, trying to do my paperwork. We have enough problems in this office without you causing a lot of extra unnecessary work.'

Gerwyn, ageing with every lie, his face ashen and lined, stared at Steve. He clasped his hands in front of him, sad and defeated, tilting his head as though to hide. But he managed to mumble. 'Steve...it wasn't like that...honestly. They're lying...It wasn't like that, Steve.'

'It's alright, Gerwyn. Don't let them get to you.--Okay, Jonathan. If that's the way you want to play it, that's okay with me.'

'Play it? What are you insinuating now?'

'You know what I mean. I'll take it from here.--Anyway, getting back to the reason of such importance for which you bleeped Gerwyn in the middle of a union meeting, and a subject so personal you couldn't discuss it in front of me, maybe you'd like me to leave the room so that you can have a talk with Gerwyn.'

Jonathan imagined Steve outside the door eaves-dropping on every word he might say to Gerwyn.

'No. It's not all that personal. But if you insist on being present every time I want to see Gerwyn, then so be it.--Gerwyn, you're working night shift tonight. I thought I'd get in touch with you as soon as possible so that you could go home early and get some rest.'

Gerwyn looked up, shocked. 'Nights? Me, Jonathan?'

'Yes you Gerwyn. It's all part of grade eight agreement. Grade eight men can be called upon at any time when a shift is left empty by unforeseen circumstances. Peter has phoned in sick. You are the obvious candidate,' he said, raising his eyebrows.

'But I thought I'd be called if a shift man finished working here, or somebody went on long term sickness, said Gerwyn, looking at his shop steward.'

'That's what Fred Crabbe inferred,' said Steve, thoughtfully. But he didn't put that in writing. You don't have to work tonight, anyway, so don't worry about it.'

'I'm telling him he's got to work tonight,' Jonathan yelled.

'Twenty four hours, Jonathan, smiled Steve. If you're bent on working to rule, then we can work to rule as well.'

'What? What are you talking about?'

'It's all in writing. If you want a man to work shifts, you must give him at least twenty four hours' notice. It's all in writing, Jonathan.'

Jonathan's cheeks reddened. 'How the hell can I organise cover for tonight?'

'You always offer the off-duty man to cover. So what's the problem?'

'I phoned him. He wasn't at home.'

'Of course he's not at home. And you bloody-well know why. You know that he's up the canteen attending a union meeting.-- It's Byron!'

Jonathan's eyes sparkled with hatred just then, but he kept cool. 'Seeing as you know his whereabouts, maybe you can inform him that I'd like him to work an overtime shift tonight.'

'I'll do that for you. He might faint with shock, but I'll tell him. Besides, if I didn't I might be accused of being as petty as you.-- Come on, Gerwyn. Let's go'

'Gerwyn,' called Jonathan in a silly friendly voice. 'Remember you're working nights tomorrow night, won't you? The shift begins at ten o'clock, incidentally.'

'Oh I'm glad you told me that, Jonathan,' said Gerwyn, all reserve gone. 'I would never have known the shift begins at ten. Well, well, fancy that. I hope me working on nights makes you very happy.'

The two electricians left the office, Steve infuriated, Gerwyn saddened.

'It's a good job we've got shop stewards, Steve. People like Jonathan and Sid would drive us all to suicide.'

'He might drive me to busting his nose, but I wouldn't give him the satisfaction of anything else. I can just see my fist landing one on him.'

'Don't do that, Steve. He'll sack you.'

'I'm aware of the consequences, Butty, but sometimes my temper goes against my better judgement.'

Gerwyn, in the mists of confusion, was thinking of the past couple of hours, shaking his head, trying to understand what made Jonathan the way his is.

'Do you think he had a bad upbringing, Steve?'

'Who, Shylock? Completely the opposite, I'd say Spoiled brat, that's what he is. He still thinks he's in university playing games with his fellow students. He can't handle men, that's his trouble.'

Gerwyn shook his head. 'I think he can. That's the problem: He handles me only too well.'

Steve looked down at his mate, 'Gerwyn, you've got to make a stand against him, otherwise your life will be hell.'

'I try, Steve. I do try.'

# Seventeen

Mr Bull, his denim shirt opened at the front, his shirt sleeves rolled up past his impressive biceps, was slowly walking backwards up the rear lane of his property. He was gesticulating to a lorry driver who was reversing his vehicle, loaded with concrete blocks, up the lane and as close to Mr Bull's rear garden as possible.

It was a fine day. The sun warmed the mountain of debris in his back garden he called his building site. Occasionally the breeze swept up a grey-slate haze of dust from the masonry rubbish. But he was well pleased with the progress he'd made on his extension. The roof tiles hadn't been put in place, but the timber framework of the extension's apex was complete. Being behind on the payment to the roofing contractor meant that the contractor had insured himself by leaving a big hole in roof of the house after partially tiling, and fixing no tiles at all on the new extension. Bull was eager to build the inside partition walls of both house and extension and his excitement showed he couldn't wait for the concrete blocks to be unloaded.

'Back a little more,' he shouted to the lorry driver. 'Whoa, that'll do. You can swing them into the garden from there.'

The lorry driver got out of his cab and looked for a substantial piece of ground where he could rest the compact bundles of multiple blocks.

'What garden?' he asked as he looked at the mess, which not only filled the rear space but over-spilled into the lane.

'Oh just dump them on top of that lot and don't be so fussy.'

'They'll topple over, mun.'

'Never mind, they'll come to rest somewhere.'

The driver climbed on to the back of the lorry and began to operate its crane. He gently dropped the suspended blocks on top of the nearest mound of rubble. As soon as he released the block from the clutches of the hoist, it toppled over and crashed into the adjoining dry stone wall of Jonathan Pallet's property. The wall caved in, tumbling over on to Jonathan's border of flowers and shrubs. Stones from the wall brought down a fuchsia, burying the flowers and spreading stones of all sizes on to his garden path.

'I'm not taking responsibility for that,' said the worried lorry driver.

'Don't worry, I'll patch it up with a few blocks.'

'Where the hell did all that mess come from, anyway?'

'I've got to earn a bit of dough to keep this lot going, haven't I? I fix up fronts of houses. All the old rendering and mortar I strip off I dump here. I'll get a couple of skips one day and get rid of the lot.'

'Don't the neighbours complain?'

'They grizzle about the noise sometimes, about water coming into their roof, about broken gates and falling timber. I usually get a ear-bashing from somebody or other. I'd never get the job done if I listened to them all.'

'You're not flavour of the month, then?'

'The guy next door takes things too seriously, mun. He moans about loss of light, loss of view, loss of valuation on his house. He's a pain in the arse.'

Just then one of Bull's unemployed helpers called from the extension. 'Charlie, come here, quick. We've got a nasty problem here.'

'Problem, what the hell's the matter now?'

Charlie clambered over the rubble using large stones as steps and jumping from one ridge to the other, lashing out at grey wooden laths sticking up, like someone cutting through the jungle. He kicked at crumpled metal buckets, slates, cardboard

140

boxes and eventually pushed away some rusting scaffolding tubes before jumping down on the new concrete path that surrounded the new extension.

His helper, a short scruffy little man with a red face and terrible acne, was shaking his head and looking fearfully at the building. As Bull approached him, the man pointed to the side wall of the extension where the large opening for the kitchen window was to be installed. His finger directed Charlie's eyes to a crack in the wall which was two inches wide and ran diagonally from the top right hand corner of the window up to where the new extension was joined to the main wall of the house.

Charlie stared not believing what he saw. 'Bloody hell. How did that happen? The wall is ruined. The whole bloody wall is ruined.'

'Subsidence?' suggest his worker.

'Don't be bloody stupid. My footings went down six feet. Besides, there's nothing wrong with the slabs,' he added looking at the base of the concrete floor.

It was then he noticed the concrete blocks at the bottom of the window opening. The blocks were powdery and appeared to be compressed, as though some heavy weight had crushed them. His eyes rose to the lintel of the window which had been lifted off its supporting blocks and was cracked in half. He shook his fair curly head, and his hard stone-like features looked puzzled and worried.

'I don't understand it. I don't bloody-well understand it at all. This will put the job back weeks if not months.'

By this time the inquisitive lorry driver had scrambled over the mounds of rubbish and arrived at the scene. He sized up the situation and an enigmatic twist came to his lips as though he had solved the mystery.

'You've got a determined enemy, Charlie boy,' he said. 'There's only one name for it, sabotage. Wilful sabotage.'

'How do you know? Tell me! Tell me!'

'I've seen it before. You place a powerful hydraulic jack in the window, pack it with steel plates at top and bottom, and simply jack it up. A good hydraulic jack will lift tons of material easily when the brick-work hasn't had time to set.'

Charles Bull thought for some considerable time on the subject of past upsets. He couldn't deny he hadn't pleased everybody in the vicinity of his home or those he had done work for in the past. But nobody had ever gone this far. To destroy his hard work in such a mean and cowardly way was unforgivable. There was that old roofer he owed money to. And the wall he built for Mrs Macdonald. She was happy with the wall but not too please when he hand-mixed his cement on her prized patio, and failed to bring it to its original beauty afterwards. She was furious and deducted some money off the bill, so she'd had her revenge. And there was Marie, his ex-wife who had sworn to get even with him, but that was a couple of years ago. No, this had been coolly thought out by somebody who had easy access to the property, to a hydraulic jack, to easily jump in from next door in the middle of the night and work away unnoticed. Yes this had been engineered.

'I'll kill him!' he suddenly burst. 'It's that bastard next door. I swear I'll kill him!'

He jumped up onto Jonathan's small yard, where half the concrete had been torn up accidentally by the excavator, and thudded his fist on the kitchen door. He placed his hand over his eyes and peered through the kitchen window, then went to the lounge window and looked through. Not a sign of life anywhere. He tried the door handle but it was locked. He turned around in rage, his elbows at ninety degrees, his fists clenched. Then he calmed down and jumped back onto his own property. The two men had been silent, just looked at him, fear showing in their eyes. The lorry driver decided it was best if he left, so he made his way to the lorry. Charlie looked at his labourer.

'Come to think of it, it's been very quiet around here lately.'

Then he thought some more. 'I know where the lanky bastard works. If he doesn't show up here, I'll pay him a visit at his factory. He's not going to get away with this—Jim, start knocking the top half of the damaged wall off, we'll start on that now.'

# Eighteen

He woke at six in the morning; too early to get up, his first nightshift to come. He'd forced himself to lie in, but didn't feel any better for it. In fact, it made him feel worse. The joints of his limbs seemed to ache deliberately as he lay there watching the diffused sun force its way through the lemon curtains and light up the room. Hilary had lain at his side, peacefully, breathing lightly and contentedly. He'd felt himself doze off, then woke again, then fell back to sleep. Off and on he'd dozed till eleven o'clock. Hilary had gone, slipped out during one of his naps. He urged his sluggish muscles out of bed went downstairs for breakfast but a cup of tea is all he'd managed to stomach. Hilary was in work and the kids were in school, so he was all alone and didn't like it. His muzzy head remained with him all day and when the children came home from school and played their music it had not helped. He kept his patience and silence all day until Hilary placed his favourite supper of bubble and squeak with egg and bread and butter, but nightshift stomach gave it no appeal.

And so, with heavy heart and lingering headache he found himself clocking in a few minutes before ten o'clock for the hated nightshift. He made his way to the electrical workshop where he became even more depressed, for on top of his locker were several works orders left for him by Jonathan. The first works order read:

(1) Locate and rectify fault on domestic scrubber/polisher. (In cupboard up

in admin block.)
(2) General office has reported photo copier
has developed a squeak.  Strip down and
grease. (key with security guard)
(3) Remove and clean thoroughly electrodes on
boilers No's 1 – 4 in main boiler house
(4) Make a list of appliances in room 1442
of Research Department including serial
numbers and makers names.

The second works order read,
(1) renew spent lamps and tubes in the
 following departments:
I Room 101 Processing Department.
ii  Personnel Records.
iii North stairs, Admin Bock.
iv Above conveyor belt Despatch Department.
v  Trace and rectify fault on blow heater,
Quality Control.

The third works order read,
(1)  Carry out E1 yearly maintenance on all
lighting in Clean Area Department,
ensuring that all diffusers are
thoroughly washed inside and outside.

'Bastard!' is all Gerwyn could mumble as he opened his tool
locker and began mentally planning the best way to get around
all the work as quickly as possible. He decided to get stuck in
and see how things would progress. He took as many tools and
accessories as he could to save time going back and fore the
workshop.

The nightshift fitter, toolmaker and lubrication officer,
(Better known a Ollie the Oilier) were in the fitting/electrical

workshop sitting around a makeshift table, which was, in fact, an oil drum covered with a piece of plywood. It was five o'clock in the morning and they were passing the time away playing cards, three card brag. They were fantasising big stakes with the help of matchsticks. A used matchstick was only £50.00 but a live match was worth twice as much.

The bulk of the nightshift work was complete and unless an emergency arose within the next two hours leading up to finishing time at seven o'clock, there would be nothing to do except play cards or dose the last part of the shift away. The night had been comparatively quiet with only a few breakdowns in the main machine shop. The maintenance group was always grateful for a quiet night, especially since the main machine shop had been moved up to the north end of the factory complex. Access to it meant a lengthy walk in the open air, and though the stroll was appreciated in summer, it was not appreciated during bad weather conditions.

However, Chris, the burly six-foot fitter, who sported a full grown fuzzy beard and could be compared to a muscular lumberjack, was unlike most of the other men. He liked to be busy so that the night would pass quickly. Furthermore, he only played cards when the night dragged on endlessly, as it was doing so then. When he did play cards he soon got bored and would amuse himself by annoying the other players, such as not taking the game too seriously and raising the stakes to a ridiculously high bragging peak. This would infuriate his workmates. As Chris was not only muscular, six feet tall and always ready for a friendly wresting match, he didn't have too many people complaining about his mischievous ways. Raising the stakes to a £1000.00 pounds when he only had a hand of eight high or a Jack high, soon left him without any matchsticks to play with. On occasions he would break pieces of plywood off the top of the table and claim they were worth at least £500.00 pound each. Though he'd had dark looks from his opponents, they kept their peace. Being out of matchsticks, he pulled a cigarette from his overall breast pocket, stole a live match from Oliver's winnings, lit his cigarette with it and threw the dead match back into Oliver's pile.

'You've cost me £50.00 now, Chris,' complained Oliver, in a muffled moan. 'That's not fair.'

'I couldn't light it with a dead match, could I?' said Chris, logically.

'Try and be serious, Chris,' said Billy the toolmaker,' a short, middle-aged man with balding head. 'The game's gone all to cock. You're spoiling it, Chris,' he said, with a high-pitched tone.

'It's a stupid bloody game, anyway,' replied Chris, gruffly in his gravel voice.

'Play it properly and you'll find there's a lot of skill to it.'

'Skill? Don't talk daft. It's all bloody luck and you know it.'

'There's a lot of bluff and cunning in the game,' insisted Billy.

'If you were playing it properly you'd be playing for money, matchstick head.'

'We're certainly missing Peter tonight,' said Oliver, making obvious inference to Chris's disinterest. 'We normally enjoy a good game of brag.'

'You asked me to play to make up the number,' retorted Chris. 'If you didn't want my skill and expertise, my charm and my wit, you shouldn't invite me.'

'We only asked you because Gerwyn is knackered. He would have taken the game seriously, that's for sure.'

'Where is he, anyway?'

'He's got his head down,' answered Billy.

'What?' said Chris. 'He can't last out one single nightshift without crashing out?  He'll never make a shift-man.'

'Shylock's not playing fair with him, is he?  If one of the regular sparks was working tonight Shylock wouldn't have left half the work out.'

Chris shook his head with disgust. 'Gerwyn's daft enough to do it, that's his problem.'

'What can he do, Chris? If he's told to do it, he's got to do it.'

'He should do what we all do; Byron finds complications with the job in hand and books all night on it. Peter goes to the production foreman and asks for a few emergency requisitions to cover him. Steve books all night on a problem job and miraculously finds the fault just before finishing time. They all get a pat on the back for working conscientiously all night.'

'Come on, Chris,' said Oliver. 'It's your turn to brag or drop out. Don't forget you owe me fifty quid for that match you struck.'

Chris broke off a piece of the table top, threw it over to Oliver, and took away four live matches and one dead match. Then he smiled genially at the astonished Oliver.

'There. We're quits now,' he said.

'Come on, Chris, you can't do that. Be fair.'

'I've had a gutsful of this game. Ask that lazy git of a machine setter to play instead. I expect he's got his head down in the cloakroom.'

'He's a cheeky git,' said Billy. 'He's not there tonight though,' he mumbled'

'He gives you a job-note when you're short of time,' said Chris. 'You don't mind him coming over then.'

'I told him to stick his requisitions. Last time he gave me one I had to make him a garden rake the following night.'

'Are you playing or not?' persisted Oliver.

'No. I'll make a cup of tea.'

'Make me one the same time,' said Billy.

'I may as well have one,' said Oliver.

'You're a crafty pair of swine.'

As Chris got up the internal phone rang. Picking up the receiver he listened for a minute, then assured the caller he'd sort it out straight away.

'Trouble?' asked Billy.

'No, not really, there's a couple of sheep come down from the field and parked themselves in the canteen compound again. They're knocking the swill bins over. I'll go up and throw the buggers back over the fence.'

'What about the tea, Chris?'

'A great idea, Billy, put the kettle on, I'll have one when I get back.'

'We might as well give up this game,' sighed Oliver, as he rose stiffly from his stool. 'I'll make the tea. Chris won't be back for a while. That's made his night that has. He'll be like a bloody rugby player up there; running around under the floodlights tackling those sheep.'

When the beefy fitter returned through the narrow passageway into the fitting/electrical shop, passing the cloakroom on his way, he was chuckling to himself almost uncontrollably. Then as he approached his two mates he burst into a raucous laughter.

Oliver looked at him with cynical, grey eyes and snorted quietly, 'I suppose there's a full moon out tonight?'

The fitter controlled himself and wiped his eyes. 'Well, if there is we're going to see a machine-setter over the bloody thing any minute now.'

'What do you mean?' asked Billy.

Chris was laughing again. 'I've...I've just thrown...thrown a sheep into the cloakroom...where that cheeky bastard is sleeping,' he said, hardly able to finish the sentence before roaring with laughter again.

Oliver and Billy looked at each other, shocked. 'You stupid bugger,' said Oliver. He's not in there tonight. Gerwyn got there before him. Jim has gone up the main cloakroom.'

They ran to the closed door of the small cloakroom knowing that Gerwyn would be lying there in complete darkness. They were too late, for already screams of terror were vibrating through the door.

In the darkness of the confined space, Gerwyn was kicking,

150

punching and calling for help from God, not knowing what demented monster was pounding on his chest, bleating high decibels that could burst the eardrums. Then the door flew open and a huge block of blinding light flooded in. The terrified ewe bolted through the door knocking Billy off his feet, then out through the open exit and disappeared into the darkness.

By this time Gerwyn was on his feet, still swinging punches, crying out at the walls, the air, the light and anything else he imagined. He kicked at the electrical tubular heaters at the base of the walls, tore overalls off their hooks and furiously swung around in circles. His flaying hands got bruised and grazed on the roughness of the sand-brick walls, his voice snarling like a trapped animal.

'Gerwyn! Gerwyn! Calm down,' shouted Oliver. 'Are you okay, boy?'

Gerwyn was not okay. He was uncontrollable. Oliver made a tentative move towards him but Gerwyn's gyrating body and flying fists soon made him retreat. Oliver was aware that he was bigger and younger than Gerwyn, and under normal circumstances he'd have no fear of him, but the man was clearly out of his mind and unpredictable. Then hefty Chris, instigator of the tragedy, full of remorse and obviously worried, switched the cloakroom light on. He quickly went to Gerwyn and had a fist in his chest for his trouble. It didn't deter him. He clamped his powerful arms around the little man, lifted him off his feet and hugged him closely. He carried him into the workshop fully realising the stupid thing he'd done and the shock he had caused the electrician, for his mate's body was shuddering, his legs twitching in spasms.

By the time they had got him to a chair and sat him down, he'd become quiet and still. The only parts of his body that gave any movement were his eyes which darted right and left in his motionless head. His face had lost all colour and was lined extensively. Chris caught him by the shoulders and rocked him gently.

'Gerwyn, Gerwyn, are you all right, mate?'

Gerwyn's glazed eyes calmed, and he stared at the fitter, the lines in his face beginning to fade, his stiff body relaxing.

'What...what was that? What the hell was it, Chris?'

'I'm sorry, Gerwyn, boy. I'm really sorry, I thought the setter was sleeping in there.'

'Who?...Oh Jim. No...He said I could go in there tonight. I'd...I'd been a bit busy, see, so he let me sleep there. Gerwyn held his hands to his head as though trying to hold it on to his body. He looked up and saw the worried faces of Oliver and Billy staring at him.  'I don't understand, though...what was that...It was so real...Hell, what a nightmare.'

'It wasn't a nightmare, Gerwyn,' said Oliver. It was this bloody big bear of a fitter,' he said pointing to Chris. 'He put a stray ewe in there.'

'He put you in there?'

'No, no, Gerwyn,' owned up Chris. 'I put a sheep in there for a laugh.'

'It was a sheep, was it? I was dreaming I was lost in the woods up at Torpantau and a big monster jumped out at me.'

Chris hugged him again. 'I tell you what, mate, you put up a bloody good fight. You can be on my side any day.'

'Come on,' said Oliver.  The kettle's boiled. First cup is Gerwyn's.'

'I'd love a cup, please,' said the electrician.

'It's a good measure of whisky, you need,' said Billy. He winked at Gerwyn. 'I've got a little drop in my locker.'

# Nineteen

I don't know what makes that grey matter of yours slurp around in your head, Gerwyn. You've been working here for three years and I still don't understand you,' said the bearded Byron, up the stepladder. He was putting up a fluorescent fitting in one of the administration offices, and at the same time trying to be patient with Gerwyn. Gerwyn had related his latest reasoning when they had walked across to the Admin Block.

'What do you mean, Byron?' moaned Gerwyn, looking up, his two hands on the sides of the ladder, his one foot on the first rung.

'Ronnie's a Bible puncher, isn't he? He's no more than that. It's no good asking him those crazy questions of yours.'

'But he talks a lot of sense, Byron. There must be more to our existence than the short time we spend on this planet.'

'I think you're from another planet.--So you think there's a little man running around inside your head, do you?--Hold the bloody ladder, this fitting's heavy,' he yelled as the ladder rocked. 'Keep a tight hold.'

'Sorry Byron. Something fell in my eye.--I don't think there's a little man running around inside my head. It's just that I said to Ronnie, if a man had a soul you'd see it leave his body when he died.'

'That's it. You stick to logic,' said Byron, holding the fitting with one hand and scratching his irritating beard with the other. 'If you keep talking to Ronnie you'll end up on the street corners preaching to exhaust fumes.--Pass the bush spanner. These twin

153

fittings are heavy.'

'If we had scaffolding I could have held it for you.'

'Shylock reckons there's no time on this job for erecting scaffolding. I'd like to see him try and do the job on top of a step ladder.'

'Maybe we should go and see Steve and ask his advice.'

'Waste of time. If I can manage I'd rather not discuss it with Steve. He's getting management-minded.--Anyway, where did this little man in your head come from?'

'Well, when I said about not seeing the soul leave the body, Ronnie said it wasn't important. To have faith and believe, that's what's important, he said. But if I needed something tangible, as he put it, then the soul could be any size. He said, when you see a rocket ship being launched, the only picture you see is a gigantic piece of technology lift into the sky. But if you took the whole ship to be a human body, and the small capsule at the top to be the human head, then inside the capsule you have all the electronic controls and computers which can be assumed to be the human brain. But the soul of the ship is actually the astronaut who is in control and guiding the ship through life.

'I think you should find the nearest wall socket and put your finger in it. You need shock treatment.'

'I'm only making conversation, Byron. I'm not going mad. Anyway, I had enough of a shock when I was on nights.'

Byron laughed. 'I heard about that. Chris is an idiot, isn't he?'

'He's too much of it.--Do you want a change up there?'

'Thanks mate. I've done all the heavy work and now you ask. You can connect the three wires.'

Byron came down and Gerwyn climbed up to make the final connections. Byron held the steps looking up at Gerwyn standing on the top step on tip toes just managing to reach the fitting.

'I reckon Darwin had the right idea,' said Byron. 'I believe in evolution rather than God and religion. But there's one problem; we have evolved over millions of years and have finally arrived at the stage where we produce people like Shylock. Was it worth

154

it?'

'Ronnie says that religion is in you when you're born. It's not something that's been put into you by the preaching of other people. Like a robot being programmed to know that somebody had made it.'

'I know where it will all end up, bloody test tubes. They'll be producing babies in the laboratory. Sex will be ruled out.'

'Good god, Byron, you know how to bring a depression on a man. Well, I won't be around then, anyway. Pass the tube, I can put the diffuser on then. Brighten the place up a little.'

'Man will be God, then,' continued Byron. Give them crazy scientists enough time and they'll change the whole structure of the world and we won't be able to do a bloody thing about it.'

'Shut up! I don't want to hear anymore.'

'Do everything you want to now, Gerwyn boy. There's nothing after this life.'

'I see you're at the bottom of the ladder again, Byron,' broke in Jonathan, who had managed to slip into the long office without either man noticing.

'I can see you've got your bloody daps on again,' retorted Byron. 'The way you materialise you must be a regular member of rent-a-ghost.'

'How do you always manage to be leaning on the bottom of a ladder every time I see you?'

'Every time you see me? That can't be too often, you're never in bloody work. It's your turn to be in today is it? Our Sid having a lie-in, is he?'

Jonathan sniffed at the remark. 'I've got to come in at all times of the day and night if I'm called. That's why I work flexible hours. I can't clock off and forget about it all. But that doesn't alter the fact that Gerwyn's doing all the work.'

'You missed it, mate. If you had come in early you would have seen me doing most of the job. Twenty minutes sweating my guts out on top of that stepladder, when the job should have been made easier and safer with scaffolding.'

'What do you want on a Saturday morning, one man out and scaffolding, or two men and a stepladder? Make up your mind, I can't afford both.'

'I don't suppose you can stretch to two men and scaffolding?'

Gerwyn looked down feeling guilty. 'To be honest, Jonathan, Byron's done more than me. If I was taller, I would've offered to do more. You can get portable scaffolding these days.'

'Portable scaffolding, you've still got to put it together. The weekend would be gone with you two figuring it out.'

'See what I mean, Gerwyn.  It's not worth the hassle arguing with him.'

Gerwyn put an apathetic expression on his face and looked down on Jonathan, questioningly.  'I'm glad you came now, Jonathan. I was four hours short in my pay on Friday. Why was that?'

'Why didn't you tell me on Friday?'

'I came to your office a couple of times but you weren't there.'

Byron gave a grunt. 'That's no excuse, mun, Gerwyn. You should have asked BBC radio to make an announcement. He's never there these days.'

Gerwyn ignored Byron. 'Sid said you were in town, Jonathan.'

'He did, did he? Well, well. If you've got a pay query you'll have to fill in a pay query form, won't you?'

'I telephoned wages. They told me they paid me the number of hours that you put on my time sheet.'

'It can't be my fault. I don't make mistakes. Incidentally, did you service the fork-lift truck last Saturday morning?'

'Yes,' answered Gerwyn, coming down off the steps. 'Why, Jonathan?'

'What water did you use to top up the batteries?'

'What do you mean, what water did I use?'

'It's a simple question. Where did you get the water from?'

Gerwyn decided to climb back up the steps and look down on his boss, pretending he had a final screw to tighten. 'The usual place, Jonathan, where we always get it from.'

'Where is the usual place, Gerwyn?' sneered Jonathan.

'Water...er...water tap, isn't it?'

'Water tap!' exploded Jonathan. 'Do you realise you should only use distilled water?'

'We've never used distilled water as far as I can remember.'

Byron pretended to butt his head on the stepladder. He looked at Jonathan, his eyes full of fire and contempt. 'Have you had a queer turn, or something?' he said to his boss. You're alright, are you? Has that grey matter solidified?'

Jonathan was stone-faced now. Hurt at the disrespect Byron showed. 'There is nothing wrong with me. However, at this precise moment I am talking to the butcher not the block.'

'Well the block is answering you. We all service the fork-lift trucks in turn, and we all use tap water. We have done so for the past six years.'

'You should have been using distilled water.'

'Where are we going to get it from? Shall I try the canteen fridge? You haven't supplied us with distilled water for six years.'

'There is distilled water available,' said Jonathan, a smirk on his face. 'Gallons of it.'

'Where the bloody hell is it, then?'

'It's in the chemical store where it should be. If you'd looked you'd find it.'

'In the chemical store? After six years he buys distilled water, puts it in the chemical store and expects us to know it's there.'

Gerwyn, hanging on up the steps, and whose head had moved like an umpire at a tennis match, thought he'd better show support. 'We're grade eight, Jonathan, not clairvoyants.'

'Don't get upset, Byron,' said Jonathan, triumphantly. 'You'll burst a blood vessel. Now get on with the next fitting or you'll never finish the job.'

'We would have had another one up if you hadn't come along

and cocked up our momentum.'

'Never mind the wise cracks. Just get on with it,' said Jonathan, and he walked away.

'And he wonders why I don't like him,' said Byron, looking up at his astonished mate, who had whipped out his handkerchief and was wiping his brow.

'Duw, duw,' spluttered Gerwyn, then repeated himself. 'Duw, duw. You told him Byron. You told him alright.'

'I'll tell him a lot more before I'm finished here.'

Gerwyn heard footsteps and looked through the fanlight into the corridor. 'Steve's coming,' he said.

'The bloody cavalry's arrived has it?'

The shop steward bounced in with a carefree air, adding to Byron's prickly mood.

'Why are you looking so hot and bothered, Byron? And you, Gerwyn, been fighting or something?'

'That bastard's upset me again. After all the years we've used tap water for the batteries, he's now conjured up distilled water.'

'Distilled water? There's no distilled water here. We had a chemist to analyse the tap water years ago. It's fine. Hardly any lime in it at all. It would be cheaper to change a battery now and again than spend money on thousands of gallons of distilled water each year. Fred Crabbe knows that.'

'What's Shylock on about, then? He reckons there's distilled water in the chemical store.'

'The chem...the childish git. There's five gallons in the chemical store that have been there for short time. I was in there a fortnight ago and he wanted to know what was in the five-gallon drum. I told him it was distilled water which is used for special instruments in the Clean Area.'

'Five gallons? We'd use that up in one day on the fork-lifts. Where's he going to get more from?'

'He's not. He just wanted you to know that he knows something you didn't. He's a supercilious bastard, isn't he?'

'What's he on about then?'

'He just loves upsetting you pair, doesn't he? And you idiots fall for it every time.'

Byron looked at Gerwyn as though it was all his fault. Gerwyn tilted his head and said, 'Shall we put another fitting up, Byron?' Byron kicked the cardboard carton in which the fitting came in. Steve shook his head.

'Anyway Byron, I came up here to see you. Do me a favour on Monday morning, clock me in. I'm having a late night on Sunday over the valley,' he winked, 'I maybe a bit late getting back. I asked Peter but he gave me a Christian look and told me it was embezzlement.'

'I told you before that it was the last time I'll do it. This is the last time, don't ask me again.'

'You're a pal, see you on Monday.'

Gerwyn stared at Byron. ' I'm glad he didn't ask me, I'd get caught, I know it.'

Ken James

# Twenty

Which is the worse, Mam, having your appendix out or having a baby?' asked Ceris, as she helped her mother wash the dishes.

'Having a baby is worse. An appendix operation, and the pain it causes, only lasts a few weeks. Having a baby takes nine months. Nine months of thinking and worrying if the baby is going to be alright and if the birth will be okay. I've you three kids, and I love you all, but I'm not having anymore.'

'Have you told Dad you don't want anymore?'

'Oh yes. He agrees.'

'Well, that's alright then, isn't?'

'He agrees but he hasn't done anything about it.'

'What can he do, then?'

'Well, there are operations available.'

'Don't you take the pill?'

'I was going to but your father stopped me. He heard it causes serious side effects. But he still won't do what I want him to do.' She pulled the plug, leaving the water out of the sink, and Ceris threw the tea towel on the worktop. 'Let's have a sit down.'

They went into the sitting room where Gerwyn was sitting in his favourite chair watching the Sunday afternoon film on the television. He looked down-in-the-mouth and was staring through the TV rather than looking at it.

'What's the film about, Dad?'

'I don't know. I haven't been taking much interest in it. I think it's one of those soppy romantic things.'

'You don't want it on, then?' asked his wife.

'No. It's a waste of a TV licence.'

'Good. I can put Coronation Street on then. If I don't watch what I've got on video soon, the next episode will be here before you know it. I don't get much time these days.'

'I can't stick that lot,' grizzled Gerwyn. 'I'm going for a drive. Coming, Ceris?'

'I don't fancy another lecture on the evils of London.'

'I'm not going to lecture you, just come along for company.'

'I'm going to watch Coronation Street with Mam.'

'Why am I the only one in this house who hates soap operas?'

'There are not many programmes you do like, love. Mind you, you've got your eyes glued to it when there's a bit of spice on.'

'I'm going for a drive.'

'There are always those few jobs that need doing around the house?'

'I've been doing jobs around the house for the past two weeks. That's when I haven't been doing the washing and ironing and cleaning up after the kids.'

'Only because I've been working full time and the kids are busy at school. You can't expect them to come home from school and do housework when they have homework to do.--Where's Bethan, anyway?'

Gerwyn thumbed towards the closed glass door of the front room. 'She's in there with her imaginary friend.'

Hilary slid the doors open quietly and saw her eight-year-old playing in the corner with her Teddy bear and some fluffy toys. 'You okay, love?'

Bethan turned round, her chubby figure and full face very much like her father, but her dark hair taking after Hilary. 'Teddy isn't doing what he's told today, Mam.  I'm going to send him to his room if he doesn't listen.'

Her mother smiled, 'Isn't he, love? You send him to his room if you want to.'

'I'm going to give him another chance, first.' Then she turned back to her toys and began pointing her agitated finger at Teddy.

Hilary watched her for a while, amused and pleased at the same time. She'd been content with a boy and a girl and both she and Gerwyn had decided on no more. Bethan wasn't intended, but now the quiet, no-trouble, independent little girl was a treasure to her, though too independent for the company-loving Gerwyn.

'Mam's going to make a cup of tea in a minute. Do you want a milk shake?'

Bethan nodded without turning round, engrossed in her fluffy children.

Hilary closed the doors quietly and sat on the settee with Ceris. 'She's in a world of her own in there. She keeps things very tidy, though, I must say.'

The comment made Gerwyn think of his two daughters with some satisfaction, but David was another matter. 'David should sleep in a builder's skip. He'd be more at home there,' he said.

'Don't start having a go at David,' said Hilary. 'Just because you're in a mood.'

Gerwyn stood up. I'm going for a drive in the car. He left the house and jumped in his old black Anglia. There was a low pressure of gloom hanging over him. It was in contrast to the Sunday afternoons he loved when the children were small. They'd be singing in the back of the car. He liked that. Then they'd stop and he'd by them ice-cream. Then there were trips to the seaside, drives to Torpantau, basking in the sun, swimming in the river, climbing the mountains. They'd lost interest in all that. They wanted to be independent. At least the sun is shining, he thought and the car was warm.--Soap operas. False that's what they are, bloody false. Everything is hypocritical these days. Two-faced actors and actresses are blown up into heroes and heroines, making the gullible believe they're some kind of gods. Pop stars are the same. Listen to them on the TV and radio and they sound great. They're miming every bloody thing that's why. Listen to them live and they sound like the grinding workshop on a busy day. He smiled to himself, pleased with his joke. Food! That's the biggest sin; all additives and colourings, preservatives and flavourings. You can't trust anything or anybody. You can't believe in anything anymore. A man should have something to believe in. Can't believe in God because there are hundreds of different denominations, it's confusing. Politicians only want your vote. Solicitors only want your money. Doctors have had a gutsful of their patients, can't get rid of you fast enough. They haven't got any patience with their patients. He smiled again. Mayors only work for charity when they're in office. Oh god.'

Gerwyn suddenly found himself braking gently, and he came out of his mental soliloquy realising he was on a country road behind two girls on horseback. They were riding abreast with a blind bend fifty yards ahead of them. Gerwyn subconsciously slowed down and followed behind them. The girls looked around at Gerwyn but made no effort to pull their horses to the side, so he was compelled to follow them at a very slow pace until it was safe to overtake them.

I suppose I could buy Ceris a horse, he thought. Maybe she wouldn't go to London, then. I bet she'd love to have a pony of her own. She could go for rides at weekends. That's probably the trouble with Ceris; she hasn't got a local interest to give her a challenge. She could enter competitions as well as mix with a better class of people. Like those two kids. They look classy.

Gerwyn looked up at the two girls and realised he'd driven past the bend that had been holding him up. The road ahead was straight and clear. He turned his indicator on and smiled at them as he passed, but was given a couple of icy stares in return.

He followed the road until he came to a section of an old railway that had been cleared and made into a picnic area. There were rustic benches and tables hewn out of logs overlooking a wooded valley. He pulled onto the gravelled parking area, got out of the car, stood akimbo and breathed in the country air. After taking in the rural scene with its hazel trees and beech

164

trees in the foreground and green rolling hills in the distance, he sat at one of the benches and dreamed about improving his life style. He was definitely going to make a great improvement for himself and his family; a life of happiness and contentment.

He was gently brought to awareness by the distant clip-clopping of horses. The two mounted girls approached looking elegant and socially superior. Gerwyn admired the serenity and grace of their composure and could already see Ceris sitting there with pride and skilfulness.

'Yes.' he mumbled. I'll make enquiries tomorrow. Ceris you are about to become an equestrian, my girl. You nagged me for a pony when you were a little girl. I thought it was a daft idea then. But you were right. I haven't given you enough opportunity in the past, but I'll make it up to you. You can prove to me just how classy you can be.

He got back in his car, his heart lighter, the future and brighter and a pleased expression on his round face.

Ken James

# Twenty One

W e've got to! We've got to!' gesticulated Fred Crabbe, his loose, alter-neck, khaki jumper hanging at the sleeves as he raised his arm in despair at his two Junior Engineers. They sat opposite him in his office, after being summoned to an emergency meeting. 'The directive has come from Head Office: All departments in all areas have to find some means of saving money. They've closed a factory in South Glamorgan. They'll be closing down units in this area if we can't find some means of saving money. It's because of the government's involvement with our products and its subsidies, we have to listen to the government's directives.'

'What do they expect us to do?' asked Jonathan. 'We're engineers not general managers. We've got enough paper work as it is.'

'Yes, engineers you may be now,' answered Fred, running his fingers through his untidy hair. 'But you may be engineers surplus to requirements soon.'

Sidney adjusted his thick-rimmed glasses, a nervous tic on his high cheekbones. 'Is it really as serious as that, Fred?'

'Of course it's serious. There's a rumour they have been looking at the number of engineers in the industry and asking is the number justified? Tell me, you two, my left and right arms, are we overburdened with work?'

'I've had a terrible time trying to keep my paperwork up to date,' said Jonathan.

'Paperwork! Paperwork can be done by a schoolchild. Your paperwork does not justify the wages of an engineer. I've always given you complete freedom as long as the men are kept busy. But if you count the amount of time you have off, together with the hours you spend writing out works orders, requisition forms, etcetera, etcetera, you'll find that you do very little engineering work.--Well? Well?' he asked, expecting them to come up with some excuse.

'What are you getting at, Fred?' asked Jonathan.

Fred looked at him, astonished: 'Jonathan, there are three engineers in this office. Now, if you were the manager of this area, you wouldn't be looking at three people, not on paper, not on paper. 'You'd be looking at two electrical engineers and one mechanical engineer. If you were the area manager who had been asked to look at the latest staffing levels with money-saving schemes in mind, what would you be asking yourself at this precise moment? Mm? Mm?'

'I...I don't know...Tell me, Fred.'

'You'd be asking yourself, why have we got two electrical engineers and only one mechanical engineer? The second question would be: If we can manage with only one mechanical engineer, why can't we manage with just one electrical engineer?'

Sidney smiled to himself and relaxed back in his chair, his angular face beginning to cool down. Cut-backs in the past merely meant playing musical chairs to make the books look good. Sidney didn't mind such games, but the seriousness of the present situation had him worried until Fred had made that remark. Sidney was the last engineer to start at the factory which made him think he'd be the first to go.

'Are...are you saying that I have to go, Fred? asked Jonathan, shocked. 'Is...Is it me?'

'No, Jonathan. I don't want to lose you. I've got enough on my plate as it is without doing your work, too. Even though, it may not be a lot. We have to make some cut-backs, however.'

Jonathan sighed. 'We know that, Fred. We've been discussing it long enough. But you're holding something back.'

'Calm down, Jonathan,' Fred growled. 'There's nothing on my mind. I want some suggestions from you two. Now, if you were the manager of this establishment, looking on paperwork in a logical and rational manner, taking into consideration the large financial investment our company committed itself to lately, and you were asking yourself what was the purpose of that investment if we are not saving by the modernisation, where would you look to justify that expenditure?'

'I was under the impression that there would be an immediate return on the investment by wages saved on those who were made redundant, Fred,' reminded Sidney.

'Yes, yes, the production staff have made their sacrifice, Sidney.'

It was Sidney's time to be shocked. 'You want to get rid of me, Fred?'

'No, no. I don't want to get rid of either of you. For god's sake wake up!'

Both Junior Engineers looked at their boss knowing now what he intended doing. Both knew he would not commit himself to an adverse decision about his troops. He could not face his men if they thought he was responsible for sacking any of them, and he didn't want the union pestering him.

Jonathan looked at him, some contempt showing through. 'I suppose we could manage without a spark or two less if it was necessary. Since the robots were installed I've had to justify the department's staffing level by extending routine maintenance. But that can be covered by those remaining. We could at least afford to leave one spark go.

'Jonathan. You can afford to leave a spark go, but on paper it just doesn't work. We haven't lost a lot of maintenance, but we have lost a great deal of breakdown call-outs. On paper we have an agreement with the electrical union that the numbers of electricians will not be decreased other than by natural wastage. No way can we suggest a redundancy in the Maintenance

Department, particularly in the electrical unit. You know as well as I do that Steve could find a mountain of maintenance work that has been neglected over the years because of under manning and doing things our way; for instance, your methods of impossible times on the bonus scheme. Let's not stir up a lot of dirt.'

'Alright, alright.' expounded Jonathan, as ideas began to germinate in his mind. 'Leave it with me. I'll sort things out one way or another.'

'Good. I can forget it now, can I? You will not fail me?'

'How much authority and backing will I get?'

'As long as you remain within the rules, you'll have the backing of the company.'

Sidney shuffled uncomfortably in his chair. He had heard enough and didn't want to hear anymore. 'If you don't want me Fred, I've got a lot to do,' he said, and stood up.

Fred gave him one of his suspicious looks. 'Go on. You can go.'

Sidney left, closing the door quietly behind him. For reasons known only to him, he hissed loudly in the corridor and shook himself. He walked down the corridor with the gait of a cowboy that had just got off his horse.

Jonathan stood up to go but Fred held his hand up. 'Wait! Don't go. I haven't finished with you yet. Listen', he said, lowering his voice. 'This meeting we've had isn't personal, you understand? I'm just giving you the facts, that's all.'

'You mean you're throwing the ball into my court and you don't want it back.'

Fred pursed his lips and blew. 'You're taking it personally. I know things aren't going well for you lately. And if there's anything I can do to help, let me know. I'll be there like a shot, you know that. You know me, Jonathan? I'm always there if you need me. If you want to take some time off that's fine with me. Just see that things are watertight in the department. As long as I'm left alone to work things out my end, it'll be alright. I've got a lot of programming to do on my computer. Have you patched

170

things up? Your personal problems, I mean?'

'Patched it up? Hell, no. I'm selling my house.'

'I'm sorry to hear that, I really am. You deserve better. You've tried hard. I know that. You can't be blamed for not trying. No man could have tried harder than you.'

'Yes, Fred. Okay. Fred.' said Jonathan, dryly.

'I mean it. I feel for you, Jonathan. You've had a rough time and borne it bravely. Have you got a buyer?'

'The proceedings are well on their way. I've got a decent solicitor this time.'

'You gave up on the other one?'

'Nothing else I could do. He was absolutely useless. He was asking me all the time to advise him on what I wanted him to do. Then he had the bloody nerve to send me a bill for £60.00.'

'Did you pay him?'

'I had to. Sixty quid for a couple of letters and an interview.'

'But you've got a top man this time. Good. What about the builder? Have you got him under control? I hope you haven't let him put one over on you.'

'I've got even with that idiot.'

Fred thought he must continue to take interest in Jonathan's affairs. Give the man opportunity to get things of his chest. 'How did you do that?'

'Suffice it to know that I made him pay dearly.'

'Right, right, I don't want to know the details. As long as you've sorted him out. Well done, Jonathan. Well done. Right, off you go. And remember, I'm here if you want me, but only for you. I don't want to see any members of certain trade unions turning up.'

Jonathan stood up again. 'Right, Fred. I got the picture.' Then he left, and Fred turned around and faced his computer.

* * *

Steve had been given the job of checking and "Repairing if required," all the extractor fans in the office block, research department, clean area department, kitchen and canteen, which meant walking the entire slab of concrete on which the huge complex had been built. His tall figure revealed his disgruntled attitude as he bounded along carrying his toolbox, his long brown hair bouncing on his shoulders. Along the way he had several requests from employees asking him to do simple jobs: toilet attendant wanted a light bulb changed, a domestic asked him to look at her inefficient vacuum cleaner, the crane operator said he'd bring his kettle in for Steve to check it over. His bad mood was reflected in the sarcastic replies he made to each favour asked. Then his bleeper sounded, adding to his irritation.

'Who the hell wants me now?' he grumbled to himself.

Switchboard informed him it was Jonathan. He rang him.

'Steve, is that you?'

'Very clever, Jonathan, I don't know how you work these things out.'

'Never mind the sarcasm. I want you in my office immediately.'

'Does that mean now?'

'This is serious. Procedure dictates that you be present at this meeting. So get over here.'

'You work to rule when you want to, don't you? Why procedure, anyway?'

'You'll find out when you get here.'

'The telephone went dead which gave Steve an opportunity to whisper some foul language down the line. As he made his way to the office he had a bad feeling about it. Jonathan sounded too cocky. "Procedure dictates your presence," he quoted to himself. Sounds like disciplinary action. He's having a go at Gerwyn again. As he approached the office door he could hear the raised voice of Byron yelling at someone.

'You lying bastard! I saw you wrap it up. You've lost the bloody thing, haven't you?'

'Don't call me a ba...bastard. Or I'll sack you now,' shouted Jonathan back at him.

'Don't provoke me any further or I'll come around that desk and...so help me, I won't be responsible for my actions.'

After a few moments Steve began to whistle aloud and opened the office door. Both men inside were red-faced. Byron was leaning over Jonathan's desk in a menacing manner, spittle on his beard. He pulled back when he realised his shop steward had come in.

'Okay, let's hear it, what's it all about?' asked Steve, coolly.

'Mr Perfect is giving me a written warning for threatening behaviour,' he said to Steve, then turned back to Jonathan. 'I know a few things about you, mate. Just remember that.'

'And did you threaten him, Byron?'

The flustered Jonathan answered for him. 'I have a wit...wit...witness, Steve. The tool-room foreman heard him. He's not go...going to get away with it.'

Steve sat on the chair at the side of Jonathan's desk and looked at Byron, despairingly.

'Well, he bloody provokes me, mun. He treats me like a school-kid. It wouldn't be so bad if he knew what he was talking about, but he tells me to do things the hardest way, knowing I can do it an easier way.--And I've got the qualifications.'

'Let's stick to the fact, Byron,' said Steve. 'What exactly happened?'

'The same as usual; he prevents me from doing my job. I was there, in the tool-room, carrying out a necessary repair on a milling machine. He came in, like the most important man in the country, abrupt as ever, wanting to know what happened to a roller-bearing off a motor I worked on two bloody weeks ago. I gave it to him the same day as I took it off the motor with all the technical details. But he's gone and lost it and he's accusing me of not giving it to him. He came in the tool-room like a headmaster talking to a naughty boy, in front of everybody.'

'I don't remember him giving it to me,' said Jonathan, who had composed himself now that Steve was there. 'If he'd given it to me I would have it somewhere. But that's not the point. I've become afraid to talk to this man. He blows his top for no reason at all. I only asked what he'd done with the bearing so I could get the serial number and order a new one.'

'You took two weeks before you decided to order a new one?' observed Steve.

'There you are. That's efficiency for you,' butted in Byron.

Jonathan ignored the two: 'He was like a volcano erupting. Before you knew it he was threatening me with a spanner. But he's got caught out this time. I've got a witness.'

'He provokes me, Steve. He drives me bloody crazy.'

'Are you admitting that you threatened him?' asked Steve.

'Of course I didn't threaten him. I admit I called him a lying bastard. But that's the truth.'

'I've got a witness, man! I've got a witness,' reminded Jonathan.

'There he goes, I've got a witness, I've got a witness,' aped Byron in a squeaky voice. 'The awkward bugger called me up from the despatch department the other day just to open the workshop door. Said he forgot his key.'

'Do you want me to take the case up for you Byron, to make it official?'

Byron thought for a few seconds, turning his head one way then the other, scowling at his boss. 'I wouldn't want to put you to the trouble. Not with him and his bloody witness. I suppose I'll have to accept it, won't I?'

Jonathan handed the sheet of paper with the written warning on it. Byron reached out then snatched it from him.

'Right, you can go now,' said Jonathan, triumphantly, and sat back in his chair with a great deal of satisfaction.

'Thanks!' snapped Byron, as he left, slamming the office door behind him.

'Don't go, Steve. I've something rather unpleasant to do now.'

'You're not going to fart, are you?'

'Don't so disrespectful. It is my unpleasant duty to tell you I

174

have to leave one of the men go.'

'Go where? What do you mean? A training course or something?'

'No. Finish him. Give him his notice.'

Steve looked at his supervisor with disbelief. 'Jonathan I think you've flipped your lid. You can't get rid of people just like that. We have a redundancy policy here, natural wastage only.'

'I'm not making anyone redundant, the man will either have to hand in his notice to save himself embarrassment, or I'll have to dismiss him. Whichever way, he has to go.'

Steve leaned back in his chair and folded his arms. 'What the hell are you on about? Who are you on about?'

'Gerwyn Freeman.'

'Gerwyn! You're mad. On what grounds?'

'On the grounds of bad time-keeping.'

'And what about procedure?'

'Procedure has been exhausted.'

'Since when?'

'Since I gave him his final warning eleven weeks ago.'

'That was over three months ago. He's back to on a final warning now.'

'It's not three months. It's eleven weeks.'

'Let me see his record.'

Jonathan handed Steve an A5-size record card which had been lying on his desk in front of him. Then he sat back in his chair while Steve scrutinised the record looking for a mistake or loophole. He couldn't find either. He looked across the desk, contemptuously; his eyes working their way up and down Jonathan's flushed face.

'You're stooping pretty low,' he said in a low, cold voice. 'You haven't got a good name in this factory. There's not a department that has a kind word for you. Do this to Gerwyn and you'll be despised by the whole workforce.'

'I don't want any abuse from you.'

'Have you told him yet?'

'I've sent for him. He should be here soon.'

'You don't really intend going through with this?'

'Since I gave him his final warning he hasn't been acting in a responsible manner. I can't put up with it any longer.'

'What's he done? I haven't heard of him doing anything. He's the most inoffensive man in the department.'

'Inoffensive? He offends me. He was on the sick again last week for three days.'

'That was because his nerves were playing him up. And you don't help in that department.'

'If the job gets him down, it's not my fault. I want men on shift who I can rely on. Men who don't moan about the work I put out for them. I can't afford to have people taking days off just when it suits them.'

'The engineers seem to do all right. They take time off whenever they like. That privilege is strictly for the hierarchy, is it?'

'If you have any complaints about your supervisors I suggest you take them to Fred Crabbe.'

'A lot of good that will do.'

Just then a gentle tapping came on the office door. Gerwyn walked in, insecure and nervous.

'Oh, I'm sorry, Jonathan, I didn't know you were having a meeting with Steve. I'll wait outside.'

'Come in, Gerwyn,' said Steve. 'Your guardian angel of a supervisor has something to tell you. You'd better sit down.'

Gerwyn sat in Sidney's vacant chair and faced Jonathan, rubbing the sweat off his hands on his overalls. He looked at Jonathan, full of attention. Steve waited for the shock-wave to hit Gerwyn.

'Gerwyn,' Jonathan began, then faulted. 'I'm afraid you've exhausted the disciplinary procedure. This sort of behaviour cannot go with impunity. With higher management biting at my heels to control the situation I have to be hard sometimes. I'm

176

afraid I will have to leave you go.'

Gerwyn tilted his head. 'What do you mean, Jonathan?'

'I mean that...uh...you've been on the sick so many times, I have no alternative but to release you from your duties.'

'Are you taking away my grade eight because I went on the sick for three days?'

'No Gerwyn, you are dismissed.'

Gerwyn stared at his boss. 'Sacked? You're sacking me?'

If a mother had thrown a young child out in a raging blizzard, there would not have been a more pitiful sight than the expression which spread across the face of the little man. He looked at his shop steward despairingly, but Steve had fixed his blazing brown eyes on Jonathan.

'I will have to bring my Area Secretary in on this,' he said, coldly. 'My full-time official will have something to say. You can expect all hell to break out, I'm warning you. You don't get an iota of cooperation from me or the men from now on. That will include the whole department, not just the electricians.'

'I'm working to the rule book, Steve; I am working to the agreement which was signed by your union Official. Even area officials recognise the need to stop the abuse of the sick scheme. If you want to bullshit your men, that's okay with me. Don't try and bullshit me, brother, yours fraternally, etcetera, etcetera.'

Steve stood up and leaned over the desk, almost nose to nose with Jonathan. 'You've waited a long time for this, haven't you, Mr Jonathan Shylock-Pallet? If that's the way you want to play it, then that's the way it's going to be. Come on Gerwyn; let's see what we can do.'

Gerwyn sat in his chair, his eyes fixed on Jonathan. He had to beg: 'Will you please give me another chance, Jonathan? Please?'

'I'm sorry, Gerwyn, the rules have to be applied. It's nothing personal. You're the man who's been abusing the system. Now, I'd like to carry on with my work.'

'I think there's venom running through my veins from a

poisonous snake,' said Gerwyn, quietly. Then he stood up slowly.

'The two craftsmen left the office, Steve slamming the door with such force, some of the ceiling tiles lifted off the suspended ceiling. He walked quickly, his mood foul, his steps lengthy. Gerwyn scampered behind him.

'Do you think there's some kind of chance for me Steve? Do you think he just wants me to sweat for a day or two?'

'Gerwyn, I know how management work. If they've decided to cut down in some way or other, they'll find any excuse to get rid of people. And they'll give full support to the supervisors. Just before you came, he'd given Byron a final notice. But Byron keeps a note book on all Shylock's misdemeanours. Shylock's afraid of what's in that book. Top management don't know of Jonathan's absence record, or his shopping sprees in town during working hours. Trouble is, we can't prove it.'

Gerwyn thought for a few seconds about Byron. 'It's not just me he's trying to get rid of then, Steve?' he said, as though there was some redeeming feature for his low morale.

'No, he'd sack the lot of us if he could employ a new workforce; he'd be able to manipulate new men better.'

'Last year the boys went on a work-to-rule because their bonus was late. Will they think my sacking is more important?'

'Last year we had the upper hand. They couldn't afford to lose production. They have the robotic system now; still under guarantee.'

'I don't know what I'm going to tell Hilary. I can't say I've been sacked for a bad sickness record. I'd be the laughing stock of the village. I'll have to tell her I've been made redundant, that's all. There have been cut-backs. That's it.'

Steve shook his head. 'You'll get another job, Gerwyn.'

Gerwyn was hurrying as fast as he could to keep up with Steve's long strides. 'You think so?'

'Yes. And you've got your C&G now.'--Then he stopped. Oh no, you haven't have you?' he said, looking down at his mate.

Gerwyn was glad for the breather. 'Still studying, I've been

178

stuck in my front room swotting while my kids have been enjoying themselves. I won't have to take the examinations now.'

Steve shook his head again, and then resumed walking.

'Do you know,' continued Gerwyn, keeping up with him. 'I've been looking back at my past life. I've made a balls-up of everything. I should have stuck to one job. I always thought the grass was greener elsewhere.'

'It just hasn't worked out this time, that's all,' Gerwyn. You probably find yourself in a cushy job this time next year and all this will be forgotten. Have a few months on the dole. Work the system. There are some good fiddles around. Look on it as a holiday.'

'I'll have to try that, Steve. Thank you.'

'Come on, we'll have a cup of tea and balls to them all.' Then he stopped again and put his hands on Gerwyn's shoulders. 'And while you're working your month's notice, remember you don't have to worry about the job.'

'I might go on the sick I've got nothing to lose now.'

Steve thought about it. 'A cup of tea is definitely called for.'

# Twenty Two

The Freeman family were sitting in their large kitchen enjoying a late tea which Hilary and Ceris had hurriedly prepared. It wasn't often all five members of the family had opportunity to eat the same time. However, such were the circumstances of the day they all managed to be present. Hilary, as always was the last to sit, making sure everybody had everything they wanted. She sat at the head of the oblong table facing Gerwyn, the sisters at one long side and David having the most room across from them.

'You're all very quiet,' remarked Hilary, picking up a tuna sandwich.

'I've got things on my mind,' said Gerwyn, in between bites. 'No job and a mortgage to pay. A few small jobs on the side are all I have. Some security is that. They won't always be around. Besides, I'm afraid the dole people may catch me at it. We still owe on the mortgage, you know.'

Hilary swallowed hard. 'I'm full time at my job now love. My wage isn't so bad.'

'How much do we owe, Dad?' asked Ceris.

'It doesn't concern you, love,' answered Hilary. 'I wish you wouldn't talk about such things at meal times, Gerwyn. Let's live for today and worry about shortages when they come.' She looked up at her son with a hopeful expression. 'David will be having some kind of benefit soon.'

David shook his head, his elbows on the table, a sandwich in one hand, a cup of tea in the other. 'I'll need that, Mam. I'll probably be needing a lot of things before long.'

'As long as you spend sensibly. What you buy for yourself I don't have to spend on you. As for the mortgage, Gerwyn, you said your redundancy money will pay off a lot of it.'

Gerwyn felt uneasy in his chair. He sniffed loudly and nodded. 'I know that, love, but not enough. I hate having that hanging over my head at the best of times, but when I haven't got a job, it's threatening.'

As Gerwyn's eyes went into distant thoughts, the doorbell rang and brought him sharply back out of them again. He was getting up to answer it but Bethan was quicker than him and was through the living room before he could straighten up.

'That kid will do herself an injury one of these days,' said David, using the incident as an excuse to speak. 'By the way, I've got something to tell you,' he said, pushing his plate away.

His mother and father waited as he paused, looking for the right words to begin.

'I've gone and s--'

'It's a policeman!' blurted Bethan, as she burst back into the room. 'A policeman at the door, Dad,' she repeated resting at her father's side. 'I haven't done anything, honest.'

Gerwyn and Hilary looked at each other, questioningly. So did Ceris and David, while Bethan looked at them all in turn. Then she went quite pale and looked at the table.

'You'd better go and see what he wants,' Hilary instructed Gerwyn.

Gerwyn hurried to the front door where the policeman waited, his flat hat in his hand and his police car behind him, engine running.

'Mr Freeman?'

'Yes. What's the trouble, constable?'

'Mr Gerwyn Freeman?'

'That's right,' answered Gerwyn, tilting his head. 'Is there a problem?'

'I don't quite know, M Freeman. My colleague called at your house earlier but failed to get an answer. He asked me to call this evening. He'd appreciate it if you will come down the police station in the morning so that he can ask you a few questions.'

Gerwyn's eyes widened and he clasped his hands in front of him. 'What about constable?'

'I have no idea, but it must be something which concerns you, otherwise he wouldn't be asking for you in particular. But if you come down sometime in the morning, he'll be at the station and I'm sure he will clear the matter up with you.'

Gerwyn held his stomach. He felt dulled and puzzled. He looked at the policeman in disbelief.  'It sounds very ominous, constable.'

'Oh, I'm sorry, I didn't mean it to.'

'I don't want to be worrying all night about it. I'll never get any sleep.'

'I'm sure it's nothing to worry about.'

'So you do know what it's about, then?'

'No, I assure you I don't.'

Gerwyn's eyes got agitated. 'How do you know there's nothing to worry about, then? Please tell me,' he asked plaintively.

'I honestly don't know, Mr Freeman. It's best you go to the station in the morning and PC Davies will tell you all about it.'

The policeman shrugged his shoulders waiting for Gerwyn to terminate the meeting with a, thank you, or close the door. But Gerwyn was not satisfied. 'But can't you tell me anything at all to ease my concern?'

'Nothing at all, I'm afraid, but if you haven't done anything wrong, you've got nothing to worry about, have you? Can you come down in the morning?'

'Yes. I'll be there.'

Good. That's settled, then. Just ask for PC Davies. Cheerio now.'

Gerwyn remained at the door until the policeman got in to his patrol car and watched him drive off. He looked up and down the street. The early evening sun had encouraged a number of people to stay outside doing a few mundane chores; some were giving their windows a wipe, others were just having a chat. All had a furtive glance at the patrol car as it drove down the street, knowing which house it had visited. He raced back in the house, pushing past Hilary who had hung on every word in the hall, and went straight to the medicine cupboard in the bathroom. He unscrewed the top of a Valium bottle and took a pill. He came back into the kitchen and sat at the table looking pale.

'Good god! They want me down the police station in the morning.'

Hilary had come back in and sat at the table, looking at her worried husband. She wasn't worried because the policeman called, or that Gerwyn had to go to the police station, but anxious about him taking things so deeply, unable to cope with problems.

'What for?' Asked Ceris.

Gerwyn shook his head, harshly. 'He wouldn't say.'

'Well he should have,' said David, firmly.

'Well, HE BLOODY-WELL DIDN'T,' yelled his father.

'Alright, alright keep calm.'

Hilary looked at her children. 'He said he was only passing a message on,' she told them.  'It's probably nothing to worry about.'

'What on earth can it be about,' wondered Ceris, out loud.

'That's what I'd like to know,' said Gerwyn, scanning the faces of his children. 'Have you kids been up to something?'

'Don't look at me,' said Ceris, indignantly. 'I've haven't done anything.'

He looked at David. 'David?'

'You're alright, are you? What do you take me for, an idiot?'

'Bethan?'

Bethan looked sheepish. She shuffled in her chair, then looked at her mother, dolefully.

'It wasn't my fault. I didn't want to do it. He said it would

184

make me feel great.'

'What are you talking about, Bethan?' her mother demanded.

All eyes were on Bethan.

'Me and Julie were playing behind the garages this morning and we saw two boys with their heads inside plastic bags. We asked them what they were doing and they said for us to try it.'

Gerwyn dropped his head, then quickly raised it again. 'Glue?' You were sniffing glue, Bethan? What the hell's got into you? Weren't you in school?'

Bethan's eyes were glassy now, and looked as pathetic as her father. 'Yes, I was in school, Dad. Playtime, me and Julie went behind the garages and these two boys were there.'

'Did you sniff the glue, Bethan?' her mother asked, gently.

'Only once and then we ran away.'

'Don't you ever do it again, love. Do you hear? It's not a nice thing to do.'

'I won't, Mam. It was awful.'

'That's not the reason the police came,' said David. 'They probably know nothing about a couple of school kids sniffing glue.'

His father looked at him, hoping he had an answer. 'What do think, then, David?' Then he buried his head in his hands; 'Oh no!'

'What's the matter, Gerwyn? What have you done?' asked Hilary, believing her husband had finally realised the reason.

'I've got a feeling somebody has reported me to the tax people or the dole for these fiddles I've been doing.'

'I can't stand this,' said Hilary. 'Telephone the police station and find out what it's all about.'

Gerwyn put his hand to his mouth, then sighed. 'It can't be that, though. A couple of years ago my mates got caught hobbling. The tax people sent a letter to his house saying they wanted to see him immediately.' Then he went into a depression again. 'What can it be?'

'Go and telephone the police,' demanded Hilary. Ask for the inspector in charge. He probably knows what it's all about. Do it now, Gerwyn.'

Gerwyn got up and reached for the telephone directory. Thumbing through the pages he eventually found the number of the police station. Going into the hall where the telephone sat on a golden ornate wooden shelf, he dialled the number and waited, looking sadder and sadder with every passing second. The police answered.

'Hello, police station. Sergeant Evans speaking.'

'Oh, hello. This is Mr Freeman. One of your constables called to my house a short time ago asking me to come down to the police station in the morning to see PC Davies, but he couldn't tell me what it was all about. Well...eh...my wife and I are a bit concerned, you know. It's quite worrying, not knowing what the matter is all about.'

'PC Davies is not on duty this evening, Mr Freeman. And I'm afraid I don't know what it's all about, either. I think it's best you wait for him.'

'I can't wait till morning. Do you think I can speak to the duty inspector?'

'Well, he's a busy man. But, if that's what you want I'll see what I can do for you.'

Gerwyn waited, glancing up at his wife who was standing at his side, anxiously waiting for the tension to be broken. Then Gerwyn raised his hand to her as he heard the phone being picked up at the other end.

'Hello, Mr Freeman?'

'Yes, that's me.'

'Sergeant Evans has explained to me your concern, but I'm afraid I can't help you. Your case has not been discussed with me, and the officer concerned is not on duty. You'll have to wait until morning.'

'I was hoping to put my wife's mind at rest before morning. We are very worried that it's something serious. I was hoping

186

that you could help us. Please.'

'I'm sorry, Mr Freeman but I can't do anything until the morning. I'm sure if it was anything of a serious nature PC Davies would have informed me.'

Gerwyn sighed. 'I see. So it's not serious. Thank you very much.'

Gerwyn looked at Hilary. 'He said if it was serious the policeman would have informed him. So it can't be serious.'

'Thank goodness for that.'

They both went into the lounge where the children had eyes on the TV and ears tuned into the conversation in the hall.

'It's alright, kids,' he said, light-heartedly. 'It's not serious. The inspector said he doesn't know the case, but it can't be serious or he would have been informed.'

'Can I talk to you and Mam, now Dad?' asked David asserting himself.

David's manner was so abrupt that Hilary and Gerwyn sat down and paid full attention. Even Ceris sat up, but Bethan said she wanted to go to her room, so David waited until she'd left.

'I was trying to tell you before the doorbell went, that I've decided to sign up for the Army.'

'The Army?' repeated his mother, concerned. 'I don't think I like the sound of that, David.'

Gerwyn said nothing, surprised his son was so positive about an army career. But he felt ambivalent, too. Was this to be more worry, or the beginning of a new era in his life as well as David's? Or perhaps just a passing whim. No. Don't think too much about it, he told himself.

'You won't change my mind, Mam. I was in town today and there was an Army recruitment portable cabin there. I went in and asked all about it. I can choose my regiment and learn a trade. That's why I want to save some money. Get some under my belt, sort of thing.'

Hilary thought about it while David watched her for some

conclusion to her thoughts.

'It's come as a bit of a surprise, love,' she said. 'But if that's what you want, I won't stand in your way.'

'What about your examination results?' Gerwyn wanted to know.

'I've got to have them before the Army will advise me on what's best for me. But they'll be out in a few weeks, so I'll know then.'

'I know I've nagged you, son,' said Gerwyn. 'But I'm not pushing you into the Army, am I?'

'Of course not, Dad, there's nothing round here for me. Training courses that get you nowhere, that's all.'

'I don't know whether I like the idea or not, son. But I'll tell you this: The Army is not just a place to get a job or apprenticeship. There are trouble spots in the world that you'll be sent to. There can be danger as well as job security.'

'I know. I've thought it all out.'

'Best of luck, David,' said Ceris.

David smiled at her. 'Thanks Sis.'


When Gerwyn and Hilary lay in the darkness of their bedroom that night, neither could sleep. Gerwyn had been thinking aloud for twenty minutes jumping from one subject to another. He had talked of David with a mixture of pride and concern. While Hilary worried if her son would be all right. Then Gerwyn talked about the loss of his factory job, of mortgage, of the little private jobs that brought in little money. But each time he would return to the summons to the police station. Hilary would answer him in single syllables picturing David in uniform, hoping her husband would tire and fall asleep, but he kept on. Then she suddenly thought of something that might me the reason for the police calling.

'I've got it,' she said. 'I bet I know why the police want to interview you.'

Gerwyn immediately sat up in bed. 'What? Tell me, Hilary.'

'Do you remember, a month ago I think it was, when that white van ran into that blue car?'

'Yes. So?'

'Well, that's it. The drivers were arguing whose fault it was. One of them turned to you and asked would you be a witness.'

'Yes. I tried to get out of it but you said it was the van's fault and you gave my name.'

'Yes. You didn't speak to me for days. Anyway, you saw him come out of the side road without looking.'

Gerwyn thought and decided quickly. 'Yea. That's it. It must be. I told you I didn't want to get involved, didn't I?'

'If somebody bumped your car and it wasn't your fault, you'd want a witness, wouldn't you?'

Gerwyn sighed. 'I suppose so. Thank goodness that's sorted.-- Bethan sniffing glue, Ceris wanting to go to London, David off to the army...good god.'

As there wasn't much prospect of sleep, Hilary decided to get something off her mind. 'Yes, well, those problems will sort themselves out eventually. The important thing is we don't have any more children, Gerwyn,' she said, with an air of accusation. 'As we are alone and wide awake, I think we ought to have a little talk. I'm in a bit of a dilemma myself. We've cleared up your little worry, now it's time to clear up my major problem. We've discussed it before, haven't we? But we've never solved it.'

'Do you know, love, I feel better already. I'm glad you thought of that.'

'Are you deliberately ignoring me?'

'What's that, love?'

'You haven't heard a word I've said.'

'What did you say?'

'I said we don't want another little Bethan coming into the world. It's time we did something about it.'

'I told you before. It must have been a faulty sheath. It wasn't my fault.'

'That's not the point. One of us will have to be sterilised. I don't want any more pattering of tiny feet, dirty nappies or the worry of inoculations.'

'Those inoculations drove me scatty, love. Especially when they mentioned brain damage.'

'Well, then? You don't want all that again, do you?'

'You're going to mention vasectomy again, aren't you? I get a pain in my testicles every time you mention that word.'

'One of us will have to be sterilised. I'd have to give up my job if I got pregnant again. We'd be in real financial difficulties then.'

'Faulty sheaths are one in a million. It couldn't possibly happen to us again.'

'Famous last words. Knowing our luck there's one waiting in the next five hundred and it's got you name on it.'

Gerwyn turned his back on her with some considerable impatience. 'Bloody hell, Hilary, you settle my mind on one thing then wind me up on another.'

'Keep your voice down, Gerwyn. Ceris is just in the next bedroom, remember.'

'But I feel myself getting all knotted below whenever I think of it,' he whispered.

'It's got to be faced, Gerwyn. Either you have a vasectomy or I'll have to be sterilised. Sterilisation for a woman is a terrible operation. It's worse than having your appendix out.  They'll have to cut my stomach open and--'

'Alright! Alright! I can do without the gory details. Let's talk about it tomorrow.'

'Tomorrow I'm going to phone the doctor and make an appointment to have myself done, seeing as you can't face a simple operation that takes five minutes.'

'Don't do that. I can't let you go through that.'

'Well, one of us has to.'

'Oh god, why is my life so complicated? Alright, I'll have it done. I'll probably develop some incurable side effect.'

Hilary leaned over him, put her arm around him and kissed

him gently on the cheek.

'Thank you, my love. Thousands of men have it done. It's a small operation and very safe.'

'Maybe...maybe. It's just that...well, if it was on some other part of my body...but down there...Oh.'

'You'll be alright. You'll be glad you had it done.'

Oh, I'm sure. What is it? A miracle cure for everything? A panacea! I'll be skipping down the road shouting, I've got my job back, my mortgage is paid, my kids are no problem, the police don't want me. I've had the snip, you see.' Then he lay on his back for a while staring at the ceiling, the street light giving the room a faint yellow glow. He turned to his wife. 'Are you going to sleep now, love?'

'Yes, love, I'm shattered. Have you taken your sleeping tablet?'

'I've taken two, but they don't seem to do a lot of good. I took one last night without it having any affect at all. I think my body is getting used to them.'

'You're relying on them too much.'

'I can't help it. I hate lying awake for hours on end. The night drags and my brain pesters me with worry. But when the tablets do take effect, it's a lovely feeling. Those last few seconds before I fall asleep...no worries...uncaring...complete bliss.'

'Try and relax, now. Goodnight, love.'

'Goodnight,' said Gerwyn, sorrowfully. 'Do you know when you go to sleep I feel quite lonely. It's as though you're going on a long train journey and I'm left standing at the station.'

'You're daft as a brush, Gerwyn Freeman. Go to sleep, now.'

'I think it's beginning to rain outside.'

'Just relax and make your mind a blank, Gerwyn.'

'Goodnight, then. Have you got enough continental quilt?'

'Yes Gerwyn. For the last time, goodnight.'

Soon Gerwyn could hear his wife breathing deeply. He lay there for another half an hour before the tablets began to relax his arms and legs and finally his mind. The he drifted into oblivion.

Two o'clock in the morning Hilary was awakened by the writing and moaning of her husband. She switched the light on and found him wet with perspiration, his face shining with sweat, his pyjamas wet and clinging. There was ghastly expression of fear on his face as he whimpered and screwed his limbs in all directions. She shook him gently and called to him, but it took a slap on the face before he came to, staring at his wife in breathless disbelief.

He was shaking and wiping his brow. 'Oh god, Hilary. I've had a terrible nightmare.'

'You can say that again. I've been trying to wake you up.'

'I had my old job back...was summoned to a hospital...Shylock and Sidney were in the operating theatre dressed as surgeons...My name was Grade Eight...Ceris was a nurse...they told me I had to carry out an operation because I was Grade Eight...said I'd get the sack.' He took off his pyjama top and threw it on the bed. 'I had to take a woman's appendix out using my tools...I had to cut open her stomach with my sharpened hacksaw blade...It was too blunt...had to press hard on her stomach...harder and harder...then a big hole opened up and the blood spurted all over me...I looked at the patient...it was YOU.'

Hilary threw quilt back and handed Gerwyn his dressing gown. 'Come on. Down stairs for a cuppa until you calm down.'

# Twenty Three

Gerwyn arrived at the police station after having the front bumper of his car badly dented on his way there. As usual he was quite depressed in the morning. Over breakfast he'd thought about David going to the army and had concluded it was not a good idea. He loved his son and could only see him being posted to some overseas trouble spot. Imagery had gone through his mind of land mines blowing up and snipers hiding in secret places. He'd been thinking of him as he drove along when the mishap occurred. The female driver who he'd collided with blamed him for it and the thought crossed his mind that his wife is a witch. He was convinced that had she not mentioned the accident he'd witnessed some months ago, he'd not have met with the accident that morning. The young lady who had crashed into him, as he overtook a parked car on a blind bend, called him and idiot. She'd drove off, her black eyes daring him to take it further. He hardly believed it happened at all, for he suddenly found himself walking into the police station, not remembering the last two miles he'd driven.

'Yes sir,' enquired the tall, mature policeman, who stood behind the thick, bar-like counter, pressing the palm of his hands on its polished surface. 'Can I help you?'

Gerwyn looked at him nervously. 'I've come to see PC Davies,' he replied, defensively, keeping away from the counter.

'He's busy at the moment. He won't be long.'

'The policeman opened a hatch behind him and looked through. 'Phil, I believe the gentleman you have been waiting for has arrived.' He closed the sliding hatch and turned to Gerwyn.

'He won't be long.'

'Oh right. I...uh...don't know what it's all about, really. A policeman called to my house last night and asked me to come to the station this morning.'

'Ah, I see.' Then the man sat down.

Gerwyn looked around the small reception area. It was cold and bare. The cream walls were hand-smudged, and the grey vinyl floor tiles were grimy. There was a stale smell which reminded him of a grotty little house he once worked in. He tried to cope with the insufferable silence by taking interest in the posters around the wall. The longer he waited the more disturbed he became. He looked at the constable sitting behind his desk and thought he'd be better employed sorting out the drivers who parked on blinds bends, causing accidents to innocent people.

'There are a couple of cars parked dangerously on a blind bend in Seewas Street, constable. They were to blame for me bumping my car on the way here this morning.'

The policeman looked up from his work and gave Gerwyn an officious glance. 'Are you making an official complaint, Mr....?'

Gerwyn was surprised at the question. 'Freeman. Gerwyn Freeman. No, no. I just thought that you might like to know.'

'Like to know? Why should I like to know?'

'Well, it's...uh...against the Highway Code, and it's...it's dangerous.'

'It most certainly is. I agree with you.' Then he resumed working on his paperwork.

'And it's causing accidents.'

'I agree with you again.'

'Well, don't you think that...uh...people...the people who park their cars like that should be told to park them safer? In a place where they don't force other motorists to overtake on a blind bend? You know, make it safer for other road users; pedestrians as well.'

'Are you making an official complaint, Mr Freeman?' he asked

194

again, not bothering to look up from his writing.

'Well...you see...No.'

'Did you make an effort to locate the owners?'

'Well, no. I didn't know who they were.'

The constable looked up again and sighed. He stood and came to the counter, leaning on it with intimidation, staring at Gerwyn. 'Presumably you were in collision with another vehicle?'

Gerwyn backed away from the counter, not giving the policeman such advantage of the dominating position. 'Yes...but it wasn't my fault.'

'Did the owner of the vehicle you came in contact with accept liability?'

'No. She didn't.'

The constable straightened up and scratched his head. 'It must be your fault, then.'

'No. It wasn't my fault or the woman's. I was forced to drive on the right hand side of the road on a blind bend because of the cars parked on the bend outside the homes of those people. It was they who were breaking the Highway Code, so it's their fault.'

'So you think they were parking outside their own homes. Do you realise if this case goes to court it will cause a lot of trouble for those people who were parking there. And even then you may find the judge will put the fault squarely on you for not attempting to ask the owners to move their cars. It's a very expensive process.'

Gerwyn sat down on a wooden chair. 'I just thought I'd report it, that's all. Sorry.'

Just then another policeman appeared from around a partition wall that hid the room around the corner. He was carrying a file of papers and was looking very serious. He had no tunic on but was dressed in the light blue shirt of the Force and had his navy tie knotted tightly.

'Ah Phil. This is Mr Freeman. I believe you wanted to see him yesterday for something.'

The young constable stared at Gerwyn with steely blue eyes for a second, then lifted the flap of counter and came around. He passed Gerwyn and opened one of the grimy doors the other side of the reception area and began to go through. He looked back at Gerwyn, grave and suspicious.

'This way, Mr Freeman,' he demanded.

Gerwyn followed him down a dimly-lit passageway that had a stale smell of cigarette smoke, and into a room where there was a wooden table with a chair either side of it. The wooden table was four-foot square and had scratch marks on it as though someone's finger nails had dug into it. The constable slammed the door behind him, then sat on the chair nearest the door. He gestured to Gerwyn to sit on the chair opposite him. Gerwyn sat in silence facing the man who was spreading papers out on the table. He didn't like the situation, he decided. He didn't like the room nor the policeman. His knees felt weak and a knot began to tighten in his stomach.

'Now Mr Freeman, delicate matter this,' the poker-face policeman said, his voice deep and guttural. 'I hope we can clear it up,' he said, flicking the papers with his index finger.

'Clear up what, constable? I've hardly slept worrying about it.'

'Worrying about what, Mr Freeman?'

'Whatever it is you've called me here for.'

'Surely you know why you are here, Mr Freeman.'

Gerwyn tilted his head. 'I've no idea.'

'Mmm. Do you own a black Ford Escort?'

'Yes I do,' he admitted, his brow furrowing, his eyes searching the policeman's face.

'Is the registration number, AAX1 44CD?'

Gerwyn swallowed hard and his face turned a shade paler. He rubbed his sweaty hands down his trouser legs. 'Yes. Why?'

The policeman sat in silence for a minute, looking Gerwyn

straight in the eye, making him glance around the room and back to the constable again. Gerwyn placed his hand on his abdomen and caressed it gently as the knot tightened causing irritation there. The policeman began playing with his papers again, flicking them over as though he were making sure of the information contained in them. He spread his hand over them in a spider-like fashion. Then, in a drawling, ominous tone of voice, he resumed his questioning.

'Do you take rides in the country on Sunday afternoons, Mr Freeman?'

Gerwyn felt himself blinking his eyes uncontrollably. There was accusation in the man's voice serious accusation.

'I do...um...on occasions.'

'Was one of these occasions three weeks ago?'

'I don't quite remember, it could be.'

'Could be? Don't remember? What about last Sunday and the Sunday before that?'

'Yes...yes...I did go last Sunday.'

The policeman sat back in his chair twisting his ballpoint pen around his fingers and looking at Gerwyn with slit eyes. Gerwyn could stand it no longer, and averted his eyes, looking down at his shaking knees, and licking the inside of his dry mouth.'

'Do you have company on these rustic excursions, or are you one of those loners?'

'Sometimes I go alone, other times I take company.'

'Why do you go alone sometimes, Mr Freeman?'

'Oh god! Because nobody will come with me most of the time.'

'I'll come to the point, Mr Freeman. You have been reported for following young girls around the countryside. What do you say to that accusation?'

Gerwyn felt his hand clasping his stomach. His head tilted again, but his fury was greater than his timidity. 'Liar!' he yelled at the policeman. 'It's all lies. It's not true.' Then he felt his breath being taken away. 'Who said these terrible things?' he gasped.

'You have been following two teenaged girls while they were out riding their horses.'

His mind went back to the time he saw those girls. It might have looked like that, he thought. Oh Lord you know it wasn't like that. He looked at his accuser, 'I wasn't following them,' he pleaded. 'I...I have a daughter of my own...I wouldn't....'

'Having a daughter of you own doesn't make any difference whatsoever. The fact is you drove your car behind them for some considerable distance. Is it also true that you tried to make yourself known to them?'

Gerwyn knew he had to calm himself. He musn't appear guilty. 'I...drove behind them because they were approaching a bend in the road and I didn't want overtake on a blind bend...' Then his morning's accident came into his mind and he couldn't believe what life was doing to him.

Just then the door opened and the other policeman popped his head through. 'Everything alright in here, Phil? He's not still going on about that bend in the road, is he?'

'He has mentioned a bend. Which bend do you mean?' asked the interrogator, thinking Gerwyn had slipped some evidence unconsciously to his colleague.

'He was driving on the wrong side of the road this morning and he had a bump in his car.'

'No. We're not talking about that,' he said, disappointment on his face. 'It's OK I'm managing alright.'

Before the policeman went he took a hard look at Gerwyn then closed the door.

'You have a lot of trouble with bends then, do you, Mr Freeman?'

'If I had overtaken those girls on horseback and a car came round the bend like it did this morning, those little girls may not be alive today to make those stupid allegations,' Gerwyn said very deliberately, but with shaking voice.'

The interview continued. 'Is it true that you eventually passed the girls then lay in wait for them at an enclosed area further down the road?'

'I was not lying in wait!'

'And after they went down the road you drove after them and caught them up?'

'No! No! I was out for an afternoon drive,' yelled Gerwyn, hysterically. 'An afternoon bloody drive, that's all! There's no crime in that, is there?'

'There may be intent, Mr Freeman.

'Oh God, give me strength.'

'The same girls alleged that you were in a similar place again last Sunday, and the Sunday before, following them.'

'I was not following them, you've got to believe me. I...I have a daughter who wants to go to London to live...and...and I'm trying to think of some way of encouraging her to stay here, you see...I thought...well...it might be a good idea if I bought her a horse and taught her to ride. It would be an incentive, you see, to make her stay home. She could enjoy riding around the countryside instead of the streets of London. I thought if I could have an opportunity to have a chat with those girls they might give me a few tips...where to buy a horse...what riding schools there are or...or somebody they may know may be able to help....'

The constable stopped him. 'Why don't you take your daughter with you when you go for these rides on a Sunday?'

'She likes to rest and watch television with her mother. Sometimes she comes with me.'

'There's a lot of brutality about these days: sex attacks, beatings, muggings. Society has gone mad. The situation is very sensitive. What makes you different from those sorts of people?'

Gerwyn felt the tears come to his eyes. He was crumbling into apathy. He suddenly heard himself sobbing pitifully. He tried to stop himself but he couldn't. Believe me...please believe me, I....I had no intention...Oh God believe me.'

'There's a lot of perverts about, Freeman. The father of one of those girls is in no doubt that you are one. The one girl complained to her father and he followed behind them last Sunday, saw you there took your car number.'

Gerwyn dropped his head and clasped his hands tightly. 'I'm no pervert...believe me. I wouldn't hurt a fly.'

'That's what they all say. Now listen, and listen carefully. This could be a very serious situation. I have now made you aware of the situation. There has been no charge made against you so far, so heed this warning. If you are reported again I will have no alternative but to book you for intent. Now compose yourself and go. But remember, you have been officially made aware of the situation.'

Gerwyn wiped his cheeks with his fist. 'I can go?' he asked with immense relief.

The policeman began collecting his paper together. 'Yes you can go. Just don't forget this official warning.'

He walked to his car in a painful daze, and drove home through the streets as though he were flying in a dream. Cars and buses dove past as though they were asteroids in space flashing by. When he got home he didn't stay very long, just five minutes. Just long enough to make his way to the bathroom and drinks cupboard. David, who attempted to make conversation with him, was perplexed at his father's mumbling and lack of response. He was even more puzzled when his father wrote a note, then left as quickly as he had come. He watched Gerwyn leave the house and shook his head dismissively, then returned to the television programme he'd been watching. He decided to make a cup of tea. That's when he glanced at the note his father had left. It wasn't often David showed any signs of concern, but his father's note was cryptic and confusing. He decided to telephone his mother at work. He went into the hall holding the note in his hand, reading it over and over again. He picked up the telephone and dialled the number.'

'Hello, could I speak to Mrs Freeman, please?'

'Mrs Freeman is busy in the store,' replied an abrupt female voice. 'Can I take a message?'

'This is her son speaking. It's important.'

'Very well but you'll have to hang on. She may take some time coming to the phone.'

When she did come to the phone, Hilary sounded breathless. David doubted his wisdom calling her at work, wondering was he making a mountain out of a molehill. He felt as silly as his father, worrying.

'What is it, David? What's the matter? The manager is not too keen on me leaving my work.'

'It's Dad. He's acting strange. Funny like, you know?'

'Strange? Funny? What on earth do you mean?'

'He came home earlier, after being down the police station, and was acting daft. He came in mumbling, ignoring me, went into the bathroom, dived into the cupboard, wrote you a note and shot back out again. I just read the note and it doesn't make any sense. All it says is: 'Hilary, I've gone to Torpantau to pay the mortgage off.''

'Are you sure it says Torpantau?'

'Yes. I can read.'

'And that's all it says?'

'Yes.'

The telephone went quiet. David wondered if his mother was still there. 'Mam, you there?'

'Yes. I'm trying to think. Read that note again, slowly'

David huffed, impatiently. 'I'll emphasise every word for you. This is what it says. HILARY, I'VE GONE TO TORPANTAU TO PAY THE MORTGAGE OFF.

'To pay the mortgage off,' repeated Hilary. 'David I want you to go to the bathroom,' she said, her voice positive and grave. Have a look in the medicine cupboard above the wash-hand basin. Tell me if your father's bottles of tablets are there, one marked Valium the other marked Mogadon. Hurry!'

Hilary waited, her female intuition telling her that her day was going to be a disastrous one. The only way the mortgage could be paid off is by claiming insurance on Gerwyn's death. 'David! David! Are you there? Answer me. She heard the phone being picked up.

'Mam, there aren't any bottles marked Valium or Mogadon.'

'Oh my God he's taken them with him. David, listen. You stay there until Ceris and Bethan come home. Don't mention your father's behaviour.'

'What are you going to do?'

'I'm going to look for your father.'

'How are you going to manage that? You haven't got transport.'

'I'll ask my friend in work. She has a car.'

'Mam...do you think Dad's done something, well, you know.'

'I don't know what to think at the moment. But I must find him. I'll have to go now. I'll have to explain things to my boss. He'll just have to understand, that's all.'

'Where are you going to look, Mam?'

'Torpantau. Bye, love. Look after the girls.'

'Don't worry about those, Mam. I'll look after them.' The dialling tone was sounding before David could finish his sentence.

# Twenty Four

The telephone made Sidney jump in his office chair as he momentarily thought the fire alarm had sounded. He composed himself, rested his elbow on the desk and drawled down the receiver a reluctant hello.

'Sid!'

'Yes, Fred,' he answered in a tired, bored way.

'Have you heard?'

'Heard what, Fred?'

'Obviously not. Brace yourself. They've just found Jonathan on the tarmac at the foot of the office block'

'He often goes around there to see if he can catch the boys skiving.'

'Dead! You fool. Dead!'

Sidney sat up slowly, hardly believing what he heard. He always wanted to appear cool; he was proud of that side of his personality. He refused to be ruffled in any situation. But this was an event he had not experienced before.

'Good god! Dead? Dead?'

'He's on his way to the hospital mortuary now.'

'I can't believe it. Jonathan dead?'

'Yes, Jonathan.'

'What happened?'

'I don't know myself, yet. But what I do know is that the police are involved. They want to interview me. Do you know why Jonathan was up on the roof?'

Sidney thought about the busy morning of visitors and began to relate the story in a serious but slow manner. 'Steve insisted that he go up and do the checking. Since Gerwyn's dismissal the electricians have been awkward. Steve has been the worst of them all. He's found a thousand things wrong with the H&S aspect of the job. This morning he refused to work on the office extract fan units on the roof of the office block. He reckons they were too near the edge of the roof and that there should be protective railings there to safe-guard the men from falling off. He said it is against the H&S Regulations. Section 7 or something.'

'Yes, yes, he's right. There should have been railings put up, but management wouldn't sanction the high cost of installing them. Anyway, brace yourself again: The information I have received through grapevine is that the police are suspecting foul play.'

'That can't be true, surely. Good grief, no. He must have lost his balance.'

'They say he was either pushed or jumped. He was too far away from the base of the wall to have accidentally fallen. He had nothing to jump for, had he Sid?'

'Not unless his wife was playing on his mind.'

'No. He was telling me he was glad to get rid of her. No, no. Definitely not.'

'She was up here earlier on, you know.'

'What?'

'That's what I was about to tell you. She was in a foul mood, too.'

'Did Jonathan see her?'

'Let me tell you it all. I told her to wait because he was up on the roof, but she shot out of here like a bat out of hell. That's not all, some guy by the name of Charlie Bull was looking for him just after that; a mean-looking guy. Within five minutes Gerwyn Freeman came looking for him. He was in a right stupor. Just kept saying, 'Shylock, where is he? He owes me holiday pay.' Repeating himself. I got annoyed with him and told him to go and look for him up on the roof. I had to get rid of him, he was

204

acting queer and I can't really cope with him. He stared at me and said, I need every penny, then he left. '

'You'd better come up to my office. The police will want to have a little chat with you. Besides, I'm not going to face them on my own.'

'I don't particularly want to get involved if it's not essential, Fred.'

'Sidney?' growled Fred.

'Yes Fred.'

'Get up here!'

Sidney sighed. I'm on my way, Fred.'

Sidney slowly stood up and straightened his V-neck ruby jumper, then looked in the small mirror on the wall at his side. Yes, his brown plain tie was knotted nicely against his tan shirt. He sauntered out of the office and grudged every step up to Fred's office, his slight figure moving like a cool cowboy, his legs slightly bowed. Even the thick mist and the penetrating drizzle would not make him hurry, though most of the way was taken indoors through workshops and machine shops, all overhead lights blazing because of the dark miserable day.

'Yes, I realise that', Sidney was saying, trying to keep cool under the constant questioning of Inspector Masterman in Fred Crabbe's office. 'What I was going to say is that I'll help all I can, but I don't honestly know whether I can.' His hand was occasionally stroking his cheeks, and a nervous finger adjusted his glasses often, betraying the calm front he was attempting to put on. 'I don't want to bring about a situation where people may think I'm pointing an accusing finger at them. It was just a coincidence this morning when so many outsiders were looking for Jonathan. I remember saying to myself how popular he is this morning.'

The six-foot inspector, standing over Sidney, held his finger to his shiny red lips in concentration, looking through Sidney with his bulbous brown eyes, rather than at him. He suddenly swung his two hands behind his back and clasped them together, causing his mackintosh to open at the front and reveal his light grey suit. He paced the room, his long oval face full of introspection. Then he scratched his greying hair and came back to Sidney.

'What time was this?' asked the Inspector, his voice sharp.

'As I recollect it was at the time he was...uh...had the accident.'

'Why did you say, he was, and then change your wording?' asked the accompanying sergeant, who was leaning his stout body against the closed door. 'He was what? Killed, pushed, jumped, or do you mean murdered?'

'No. I meant it was around the time he was up on the roof.'

'Who were these people, Mr Soper,' continued the Inspector.'

Sidney looked at Fred sitting behind his desk who was enthralled with the questioning, his eyes darting from one man to the next. He gave Sidney a gesture with his open hand as though he were pushing him along.

'Well,' said Sidney, his cool lost, face pale and worried now. 'In order of appearance, firstly his wife was asking for him. A few minutes later a builder by the name of Mr Bull wanted to see him, and then lastly, one of our ex-employees, Gerwyn Freeman was asking for him.'

'And all three came before Mr Pallet met his death?'

'I can't say that. I don't know when he met his death. All I can be sure of is that they all came to see Jonathan after he went up on the roof.'

'Did any of them give any indication why they wanted to see the dead man?'

'No. In fact I would've thought they would be the last people wanting to see him.'

'Why do you say that?'

'He was divorcing his wife. Jonathan told me she had gone back to Newport where her parents live. So it was quite a surprise to see her turning up at the factory. The builder is being sued by Jonathan for damaging his property--That's right isn't it, Fred?' Fred gave a reluctant nod.

'What about this ex-employee?' chirped in the sergeant.

Sidney turned to him. 'He wanted some holiday money he believed was owing to him. He must have thought that Jonathan was responsible for not paying it. But he had no business being here. He doesn't work here anymore.'

'Was he sacked?' asked the Inspector.

'Yes.'

'The reason?'

'He was a bad time-keeper. Too many occasions on the sick'

The inspector turned to Fred. Fred nodded enthusiastically. 'Is he the type to hold a grudge?' he asked Fred. Fred held his hand out towards Sidney, as though Sidney was the better judge. The Inspector turned back to the Junior Engineer.

'I don't know,' said Sidney, shaking his head.

'What were the specific times of those arrivals, Mr Soper? What time did his wife arrive?'

'In my opinion--mind I was busy this morning,' he said looking at Fred. Fred's eyes went up into his head. 'So busy, in fact,' emphasised Sidney, 'I missed my early morning cup of tea.' Fred puckered his lips at him. 'I was looking forward to lunch, so I remember looking at the clock. It was 11.15. A few minutes later Mr Pallet came in. So it must have been about 11.30 when Jonathan went up on the roof.'

'And then Mr Bull?'

'About ten minutes later Mrs Pallet arrived, then Mr Bull a little later and then Gerwyn came in...Oh, I don't know. Probably five or six minutes after that, I think, I`m not sure exactly.'

'This Gerwyn character, judging by your timing he would have been looking for Mr Pallet about 12 noon.'

'Yes, give or take a few minutes.'

'And nobody enquired about Mr Pallet after that?'

'Not after. The shop steward came in earlier as he frequently does.'

'And what did he want?'

'He came to complain about the safety aspect of working on rooftops without safety rails being present.'

'Was the discussion heated?'

'When Steve and Jonathan are together there are always raised voices.'

Fred nodded enthusiastically.

'And this morning was no different?' asked the Inspector.

'No different. As normal.'

'Can you remember any of the raised-voice dialogue?'

'I didn't stay in the office very long. I don't like getting involved with their problems. But Steve--I can remember his exact words, he said, "I'm not going up on that bloody roof to risk my neck for you, Shylock".'

Fred sat up, shocked. The Inspector quizzed: 'Shylock?'

'Yes, they call him that behind his back. Sometimes it slips out in heated discussion.'

'I see. Carry on.'

'"You've worked up there before, bloody Samson," said Jonathan--Samson refers to Steve's long hair and as well as his weakness for women.—"I think you're just being awkward", said Jonathan. Then Steve said, "If you're so...effing clever, get up there and repair the unit yourself.  That's providing you can use the tools." That 's when I got up and went out of the room.'

'I see. So Steve actually suggested that Pallet go up on the roof?'

'Yes.'

'Why did Pallet accuse the shop steward of being awkward?'

'Because of the sacking of Gerwyn Freeman; they withdrew their cooperation.'

Fred nodded again.

'So there is a lot of bitterness around,' said the Inspector.

'You could say that.'

'Where is the shop steward now?'

'He's here at work. I can have him paged if you want to see him.'

'Yes. I'll be obliged if you do that Mr Soper. I don't think we need to detain you any longer.'

'Right,' said Sidney, slowly rising. He ambled to the door feeling as though he had given a good account of himself. He gave Fred a wry look. Fred raised his eyebrows in surprise.

'One more thing, Mr Soper, was Mr Pallet generally popular throughout the factory?'

Sidney turned around, his hand on the door knob. 'Speaking quite candidly, I'd say the majority of people complained about his sarcasm and his unhelpful attitude.'

The Inspector looked at Fred, but his lips had dropped into a sad expression, his eyes scanning the ceiling. The Inspector turned back to Sidney.

'Right, thank you, Mr Soper, you have been very helpful.-- Sergeant, ask the cleaning lady to come in.'

Fred stood up. 'You won't need me now, Inspector?'

The Inspector shook his head. 'No. Thank you Mr Crabbe, you've been...helpful, 'he said reluctantly.

Before Fred made his exit, he held his arms in the air. 'I don't know what it's all coming to. Use my office for as long as you wish.--Do you want a cup of tea?'

'That would be very nice,' said the Inspector.

'I'll see what I can do.' Then he brushed past the cleaning lady as she came in, followed by the sergeant.

Ken James

# Twenty Five

The following day Inspector Masterman was sitting at his desk at CID headquarters after being dropped off by his sergeant. The two detectives had been driving around in the hot sun all day trying to track down the evasive Mr Bull. Although the weather was in complete contrast to the previous day, both men agreed it wasn't the ideal day to be stuck in a car. Mr Bull, unaware he was being sought, was carrying out minor jobs in different parts of the town to pay for the high cost of building his own house extension. They eventually found him rendering a wall on a small house in a side street. However, after some initial questioning the Inspector advised him to call at the police station for a further interview. As the two detectives progressed and questioned suspects, the routine inquiries were eliminating all the possibilities and the one probability was pointing to the hapless Gerwyn. As a result, the Inspector had sent his sergeant to the Freeman's home to pick up the suspect and bring him to headquarters.

And so, while the sergeant was on his way to the Freeman's house, the Inspector sat at his desk reviewing the case over and over in his mind. He came to the conclusion that Mr Bull had been very co-operative and showed a great deal of shock when told of Jonathan Pallet's death. He was emphatic when assuring the Inspector that he had nothing to do with the death. He'd admitted he'd called to the factory to see Mr Pallet, but that was only to discuss his extension and ask him permission to erect some scaffolding in his back yard. He'd told the Inspector Mr Pallet was difficult to find lately, and wasn't at home very often.

Very politely and with understanding he told the Inspector that he realised his neighbour was a busy man. The security officer at the factory had seen him (Bull) hanging around and told him he would have to make an appointment and suggested he leave the premises. He said he'd try and see Mr Pallet at his home, then he left and went to his work because "time was money." The security officer at the factory verified Mr Bull's story which satisfied the Inspector.

A similar story was told by Jonathan's wife. She, too, had been advised by the security officer that morning. But the security officer knew Mrs Pallet from previous visits, he advised her to go and wait in Jonathan's office as he usually was there at two o'clock in the afternoon. She'd told the Inspector she wanted to make one last desperate attempt to save their marriage. That Jonathan had changed all the locks on the doors at their home which made it impossible to arrange a meeting there. By confronting him at work, she'd said, he would be forced to talk to her. When she'd not found him in his office she'd thought she would look for him. However, walking around the factory in her bright clothes attracted wolf-whistles from the workmen, so she'd brought the embarrassing visit to an end and left the factory.

The one piece of evidence which was weighing heavily against Gerwyn was that the cleaning lady had seen him in the corridor which led to the rooftop stairway. Not only had she seen him but claimed he'd been acting in a peculiar manner, mumbling to himself and ignoring her. 'He always used to stop and have a chat,' she'd said. When she'd asked him if she could help, he'd left without reply. Though she hadn't actually seen him climb the stairway to the rooftop, he'd been the only one there at the vital time, with the exception of several administration staff who needed to use the corridor to gain access to the upper rooms. She'd also added, that because she'd been between Gerwyn and the stairway, he'd certainly not climbed the stairway to the roof on that occasion. The Inspector kept an open mind about that statement, for he thought Gerwyn could have waited an opportunity for the place to be clear of personnel.

He was in his office for some time pondering over the case when the glass-panelled door of his office opened. His sergeant walked in, paunchy, his tie undone, his shirt open at the collar and his coat hanging over his arm. Though his ruddy complexion revealed he was hot and his forehead glistened with perspiration, there was a satisfied expression on his chubby face. He sat opposite the Inspector and smiled across the desk.

'I think we can close the case now, sir. We won't be seeing Gerwyn Freeman in this office or any other office. He's down at the mortuary lying in a freezer drawer above his ex-boss. And he's been there since yesterday afternoon.'

The Inspector stroked his chin as he looked with some surprise at his sergeant. The sergeant was not unknown to jump to conclusions.

'Facts, sergeant, then, perhaps, I will be allowed to make up my own mind. How did Mr Freeman die?'

'You can add him to a long list of overdoses. He was found near a river bank up at a country place called Torpantau, about eight miles from here. An empty bottle of Valium, an empty bottle of Mogadon and an empty bottle of whisky were at his side.'

'How did you come by this information?'

'As instructed, I called at his home. Walked into the wailing and mourning of his family. The children and his wife were unable to say two words without choking up and breaking into deep sobs. The wife did manage to spit out some remark to me which I didn't understand. She said, and I quote, "It's all the fault of the bloody police." There was a neighbour there who couldn't get me out of the house fast enough. Accused me of being a callous swine. How was I to know? I managed to get some information out of one of the more rational comforters, who told me that Mr Freeman was up at the morgue. I went up there immediately and the pathologist confirmed death by overdose drugs and alcohol.'

The Inspector had listened with great concentration. 'Did he leave a suicide note?'

The sergeant raised his eyebrows and agitated his eyes, the satisfied expression gone from his face. 'I'm not quite sure, sir,, he said. 'I didn't like to intrude by asking too many questions.'

'You forgot to ask.'

The sergeant was deflated. 'I believe it did slip my mind, sir.'

The Inspector shook his head. 'Why are they blaming us, anyway? What have we got to do with his suicide?'

'Freeman had an interview with the boys in blue on the morning of Pallet's death. Mrs Freeman told her neighbour they upset him and must have thrown him into a depression.'

'I think I'd better make a diplomatic visit to the family. Before I do, you get onto uniform section and find out what it's all about.'

'Pardon me for saying so, sir, but it seems pretty straight forward.'

'Does it? Do you think the murder was premeditated, or a spur-of-moment job?'

'Premeditated, I'd say. The cleaning lady saw him in the corridor. He had cause to feel bitter towards Pallet for sacking him. He had three kids and a wife to support. My theory is that he couldn't face up to his world falling apart and wanted to end it all. But first, he wanted to get even with Pallet. He brought the tablets and whisky along with him so that he could go straight to the country and end it all. He knew he was going to do it and also knew he couldn't face the consequences.'

'I see. Who found the body?'

'Mrs Freeman and a friend. Her friend phoned the ambulance, who phoned us. A PC Humphries had all the details. I've had a word with him.'

'I presume the body was searched at the time?'

'Yes. There was nothing found on the body except Mr Freeman's car keys. Apparently he was a very particular man. He had locked his car and put a Krooklock on the steering wheel. Then sat at the side of the river and took his fill of all he had with him.'

'Was the car searched?'

'Yes, sir, nothing unusual found.'

'So we can be sure that Mr Freeman had no murderous weapons in his car or on his person. Not even an offensive weapon. Should we presume, sergeant, that Mr Freeman had a premonition about his ex-boss? Perhaps telepathic message from Pallet letting him know where and when he would be available to be killed? That he was going to be standing on the edge of the roof on the administration block at a particular time on a particular day? Could that be classed as premeditated, sergeant?'

The confidence slowly drifted away from the sergeant as he thought about the case again. Nodding his head, he looked at his superior and scowled slightly. 'What is your theory, sir?'

'At the very least it could possibly be a spur-of -the-moment killing. But I think the shop steward knows more about the case than he is telling us. That he is holding something back which could give us vital clues.'

'He did have an alibi, sir.'

'Yes, a very convenient one. He did, of course, justify Gerwyn Freeman's presence at the factory that morning. The company owed Mr Freeman some holiday pay and superannuation. So in that way, he was protecting the man. If Gerwyn Freeman's last gesture in life was to make things as financially sound as possible for his wife and children, he would make sure that all monies due to him would be made available. He would also look after the car and make sure nobody had it except his family However he was misguided if he thought that the insurance would pay out on a suicide..--It would be improper to call on the

Freeman family until the funeral is over. It's not essential we interview them straight away. We'll give them a few days to come to terms with their bereavement. I must find out if there was a suicide note. In the meantime, bring the shop steward into the station. I'd like to have a few more words with him.'

'Very good, sir.'

# Twenty Six

Steve was impatiently pressing the doorbell on the aluminium-framed glass door of number 9 Hinton Street. He could hear the melodic chimes deep in the house and wondered if there was anyone inside who was going to respond. He pushed his face on the obscure glass panel and strained his eyes to see beyond the threshold. The bright decor inside allowed him a hazy vision of a narrow passage leading to a carpeted stairway. To him the house appeared deserted. He turned his back on the door and thought about the situation, looked at his car and wondered should he drive away and try later

He felt he had to talk to Byron. The police had been asking too many questions and he found himself lacking in his usual confidence. He was about give up hope of finding Byron at home when he heard someone inside grumbling and thudding down the wooden stairs. Byron opened the door with one hand and tucked his shirt in his trousers with the other. His normally neat cut beard had many stray whiskers sprouting, his face pale and tired. He looked at Steve with sleepy surprise, then twitched his head backwards as an invitation to enter. Steve stepped inside; Byron pushed past him and led him to the lounge.

'Wait,' whispered Steve. 'Is the other half in?'

'No. She's out doing a bit of shopping and the kids are in school. Why?'

'I just want a private talk with you, that's all.'

'You'd better come in and sit down,' said Byron. 'I'll make a cup of coffee, want one?'

'I could do with something to drink.'

'You want something stronger?' he asked with sharp surprise.

'No I'll make do with a coffee.'

'What shift are you, then?'

'You know what shift I`m on. Days yesterday and nights tonight, and I know that you`re on your two rest days and back on days tomorrow`

`Oh yea, I forgot you were days.`

'You forgot? Did you forget you rang me at work yesterday morning?`

`Yesterday? Did I? Oh yea about the roof job Shylock`s given me for tomorrow. I told him I`m not doing it without roof railings, ` said Byron as he disappeared to the kitchen

`Yes and you phoned to remind me to begin the grievance procedure with Shylock. Said you wanted it sorted out by the time you came in tomorrow. Well, I did, and he went up to inspect the place and ended up bloody-well dead!` Steve yelled.

Steve heard the crash of a cup breaking on the kitchen floor. Byron came back in to him, a shocked expression on his tired face.

`Dead! Shylock`s dead?` How...what happened.`

`I thought you may be able to tell me. You know how Jonathan`s been really keen on grievances lately, especially when you`re involved. Only you and me knew that he`d be looking for an opportunity to find some means of getting one over on you. Only you and me would know he`d be up on that roof looking for excuses to give you a warning or some kind of admonishment for refusing to do the job`

`You think I had something to do with it? You must be out of your bloody mind. You don`t think that I`d waste a rest day to come in to the bloody factory, do you?`

Steve flopped on to a soft easy chair, part of the three piece suite. Byron slowly sat on the sofa and bowed his head to the tan carpet. They both sat in silence for a few moments.

It was Steve who spoke first, in a quiet, whispering tone. `I`ve got some more bad news; guess who they think was responsible for the death.`

`Not me? Not me!`

`No. Oh no, not you—Gerwyn.`

Byron lifted his head sharply, his mouth agape. `Gerwyn!` They`re all bloody mad.`

`I`ve got some more bad news for you; Gerwyn`s in the mortuary; he`s dead too.`

`I don`t believe I`m hearing this. What` going on Steve?`

`Gerwyn killed himself. A witness saw him up the factory the morning Jonathan died. Gerwyn`s the scapegoat.`

Byron fell gently back in his seat. 'On Gerwyn! They must be desperate. Thick pigs!'

'He was in Admin corridor around the time Shylock was pushed off the roof.'

'Pushed? How do they know he was pushed?'

'They carried out some kind of experiment and measurements. They concluded he either jumped or was pushed.'

'He must have jumped.'

'Don`t be daft. Can you imagine Shylock jumping? No. They discounted that. He was too mentally stable. Besides he`d miss out on building up a case one you. '

'He was a nutter as far as I'm concerned. A right head-case.'

'They're looking for a murderer anyway.'

'They must be mad.--Hang on, the kettle's boiling.'

'They're pressurising me,' said Steve, as Byron went into the kitchen. 'They've had me in twice already, making me feel as though they suspect me as well as Gerwyn.'

Byron came in with two steaming cups, and gave Steve a cup. Byron looked out of the rear window, his cup in his hand.

'Listen,` said Steve, `I don't mind bulling Fred Crabbe now and again, nor do I mind making life hard for the Junior

Engineers. I know how far I can go with those two. But I find myself breaking out in a cold sweat when that Inspector starts questioning me. His eyes penetrate me as though he's reading my mind. And when that sergeant is breathing down my neck I start stammering like Shylock. I haven't mentioned the fact that you instigated the Health & Safety problem on the roof a couple of days ago. It probably wouldn't matter if I did. But I do remember a heavy bit of dialogue from you at the time. Let me quote your exact words: 'Make sure the bastard goes up on the roof in the morning and sorts the safety out.' That was the day before your rest days. And to make sure he went up you rang me the morning of his death to make sure he went up.'

'I credited you with more intelligence,' said Byron, unusually calm. 'I was on my rest day.'

'In that case you won't mind me telling the Inspector of the roof dispute.'

'Why tell him? It's a dispute between management and union.'

'Because he knows I'm holding something back. And until I tell him what I'm holding back he's going to keep on hounding me.' Steve picked up his cup and took a gulp of the cooling coffee. Besides, I can't believe Gerwyn done it, nor should he take the rap. I don't like being used, Byron.'

Byron sat back down and looked at Steve. Softness had come into his eyes, yet determination, too. 'That's great, mate. Thanks a lot. You think I done it, don't you? You want to pin it on me. Listen, Gerwyn is dead. I liked the guy. He was a bit of a fool, but likeable. He can't come to anymore harm now. Maybe he did do it. Why not let them think that way. Don't drag me into it. I've got a wife and kids as well, you know. And you want to incriminate me.-Mate!'

'I won't tell them anything if you don't want me to. But what if they should suddenly turn on me and nail me for it? What if they find some evidence which will prove Gerwyn innocent? I've also got a wife and kids.'

'Alright, calm down. How did Gerwyn top himself, anyway? I mean...did he...blow his brains out, or what?'

'He took an overdose of tablets and whisky. Valium, I think.'

'Valium, uh.'

'What's that got to do with it, anyway? It doesn't alter things, does it?'

'I just wondered, that's all.'

'Don't get me wrong, Byron, but I'm only looking at things in the same way the police. They'll get to the truth.'

'What do you mean the truth? What are you getting at now?'

'If they knew how much you hated Shylock and the way you used to threaten him; If they knew you were aware that Shylock would be up on the roof at a particular time...If they knew that Shylock was trying to get you the sack...'

'Yea, yea. I get the picture. I appreciate what you are saying. It's all stacked against me. Just keep your mouth shut and it will all blow over, okay?'

'I hope you're right. I don't want to be questioned by that Inspector again.'

'It will all blow over, believe me. Let's...let's concentrate on Gerwyn. Poor git. When are they burying him?'

'In a few days, I suppose.'

'Have you organised a collection for him?'

'Not yet. I'm going to.'

Byron went to a cupboard and brought out a small tin box. He took a five pound note from it and gave it to Steve. 'Make that a start. I'll be back in work tomorrow. I'll give you a hand to make the collection. Let's make sure he'll have a good send off.'

Steve took the note, finished his coffee and stood up. 'I'll see you tomorrow when we change shifts, then,' he said, making his way to the door.

Byron followed him to the front door and saw him off. As Steve got in his car Byron called to him. Hey, it will be alright, don't worry.'

'Let's hope so,' said Steve. Then he slammed his car door and drove off at an unnecessary quick speed.

Byron watched him go down the long road, thoughtful, staring, wondering. He waved his hand, though Steve wasn't paying any attention. Then the car turned the corner and Byron went into the house.

# Twenty Seven

Inspector Masterman was being driven in the official unmarked car to Flints Components Factory. It was the third day after Jonathan Pallet's death and he had no definite evidence to give him a serious lead. The prominent features of the Inspector had a vague mask of concentration on them. His sergeant would occasionally take his eyes off the road and glance over to him, expecting his superior to share his thoughts. Silence prevailed, however, as the overcast weather of the mid-morning added an extra gloom to the Inspector's thoughts.

'Any new ideas, sir?'

'Strange case, sergeant, the more I interview people the more I get the impression that Jonathan Pallet won't be missed. Nobody has shown any genuine grief or sympathy towards the man's unfortunate death. Even his wife seemed to be over reacting, as though she wants us to believe she is devastated. But in the words of the bard, the lady protesteth too much. Some of the craftsmen under his authority appeared to be pleased of his passing. All sympathy expressed was for Freeman.' The car stopped at a red light. 'Do you still think he's the guilty party?'

The sergeant wrenched at the hand brake with contempt. 'His suicide indicated very strongly of his depression over the mortgage. Evidence points to the probability that he wanted to clear his family of all debts before he killed himself. The interview he had with uniform the day of his suicide also suggests he had a perverted leaning which nobody had suspected.'

'I have previously stated there was no intention present. He couldn't possibly have anticipated his engineer being on the roof at that particular time.'

The sergeant looked across at the Inspector. 'Well, opportunity knocked and he took advantage of it.'

The Inspector folded his arms and expressed annoyance. The theory was far too simple.

'It was completely against his character. He was a mild-mannered man, sergeant. A short, inoffensive man who, apparently, wouldn't harm a fly.--The lights, sergeant.'

The sergeant drove off fiercely, disgruntled at being prompted. 'You can't tell what goes on in little peoples' minds. Little people are always trying to prove themselves in one way or the other.'

'His interview with the local police only proved he was in the vicinity at the time. He did nothing. Besides, his reasons he gave for being there were quiet plausible. His character references from his work mates and employers suggest nothing to indicate he was a sex pest. No evidence in his past of violence. I can't say I'm convinced he did it.'

The sergeant's tone was caustic now. 'Evidence suggests that Pallet made life hell for him. He may have been stalking Pallet for some time. When he saw him he snapped; a moment of madness overtook him and he went crazy.'

The car drove into the factory and the Inspector unclipped his belt as the sergeant steered into a parking space. They got out, showed their credentials to the security man at the lodge, told him where they were going and entered the building making their way to the west stair tower. After climbing the several flights of concrete steps, panting heavier the higher they climbed, they entered a small room where ascended a metal spiral stairway. Their shoes clanked on the metal plate steps as they slowly made their way up through the dim lighting to the rooftop door. Emerging from the musty stairwell they set foot on the flat gravelled roof of the administration block. With hands on their hips and breathing heavy, they stood in a penetrating

224

drizzle.

'I hope this is the last time we have to come up here, sir,' grumbled the sergeant, puffing.

'You're out of condition,' gasped his colleague. 'Come on, let's make our way to where Pallet met his death.'

They crunched their way along the roof, dodging numerous vents and air-conditioning cowling that jutted up all over the place. The loose stone chippings began to grate under their feet putting pressure on the soles of their shoes. Occasionally they jumped back as startled pigeons flared up before them. Stopping at a large circular aluminium cowl, which housed a big extract motor, they both pondered the situation. They were at the very edge where Jonathan Pallet had toppled off and fell to his death. The Inspector raised his head and looked around.

'We haven't got the panoramic view we had the last time we were up here,' he observed, alluding to the weather. We know that it was quite foggy on the day Pallet died; Mr Soper and others have said so. But even in these misty conditions, a man could make observations from nearby rooftops with a pair of binoculars.'

'Someone could, indeed.'

'The maintenance staff has access to the rooftops at all times of day and night. I dare say, that having all the access points and such freedom, maintenance staff coming and going so frequently would hardly be noticed, unless they made a commotion.'

'What are you getting at, sir?'

'It doesn't take a genius to come to the conclusion that if someone wished to gain access to this place, for some devious reason, he would hardly take the middle stairway as Freeman did. If he did he would have known there was a high risk of being seen.'

'I wish we had taken the middle stairs. They have a lift as far as the top floor.'

'But then you would have to walk the whole of the top floor

to reach the spiral stairway. How many people would you pass on your way? Too many. No, I believe someone knew Jonathan Pallet would be up here. Someone who used a stairway other than the obvious one. Someone who lay in wait behind one of those big cowlings. We know of two who knew Pallet would be up here: The shop steward and the mechanical engineer. There was also Mr Bull and Mrs Pallet.'

'Plus Gerwyn Freeman.'

'Forget Freeman for a while. Now, the shop steward had a fool-proof alibi. He was working in the kitchen repairing an electric oven, confirmed by the kitchen staff. The mechanical engineer was in his office all morning receiving and making phone calls from his senior Mr Crabbe, so that gives him little time to do anything. Bull hardly knew the layout of the factory to find Pallet, besides his alibi is quiet sound. Mrs Pallet? She wouldn't have a clue how to get up here. No, I've come to the conclusion there is another person we have overlooked. Who else have we interviewed and crossed off?'

'Ronnie Peters. But he's straight. It's been confirmed he was working in the clean area. In fact all electricians working that day had sound alibis.'

The Inspector turned to his sergeant and congratulated him. 'Well done, sergeant. That's it. All electricians working that day. Who wasn't working? Byron Thomas.'

'He was at home all day, sir. On sick leave.'

'Quite. But who has verified his alibi? His wife was out, his children in school. He lives just ten minutes drive from here. Furthermore, I have this strange feeling every time I talk to the shop steward that he is hiding something. When I asked him if he thought Mr Freeman was capable of committing a murder, his first reaction was to defend the man. However, at a later interview I brought the name of Byron Thomas into the frame. At that point he began to show a little anxiety, and then encouraged the theory I had put forward about Freeman doing the deed. But look at the gravel at your feet, sergeant. We agreed that it was so disordered when we first inspected it, that a struggle must have occurred. A man of Gerwyn Freeman's stature would hardly be able to take on the height and weight of Jonathan Pallet. No. He would not be able to overpower Pallet.-- What's that? Just there in the gravel.'

The Inspector pointed to a small light-coloured particle in the stone chippings, lying in the shadow of a cowling. The sergeant bent down and picked it up carefully in his handkerchief. Both men uttered simultaneously, 'A tablet.'

The sergeant fell to his knees and made a thorough examination of the immediate area. It took him five minutes to find another two tablets. Both men searched the gravel for another half hour, but found nothing more.

'I lay you odds of 20 -1 that these are Valium tablets,' smirked the sergeant.

The inspector looked disappointed. 'I have no doubt,' he said, glumly.

'I think that's pretty conclusive, sir,' said the sergeant, triumphantly.

'Very strange we didn't come across those tablets before. We made a thorough search.'

'The wet weather has given them a shine..'

'I'm not so sure I can go along with that.'

'It's pretty clear to me, sir. Freeman came up here and, seeing Pallet at the edge of the roof, went up behind him and gave him a hefty push. Don't need a lot of strength to do that. In his panic he dropped his bottle of tablets and scraped at the gravel to retrieve them. When he saw the domestic in the middle stairway earlier he decided it was prudent to take another stairs.'

The Inspector was thoughtful, looking at the gravel, full of concentration. 'Valium are usually in strong plastic bottle with a child-proof screw top. Those bottles don't break open as easily.'

'Ah, but he was in a great hurry when he got home, earlier that day. His son informed me of that when I eventually had a few words with him. He probably took a tablet to calm his nerves.  Besides, the cap of the bottle was cracked, if you remember.'

'Well, the evidence is damning for the man. Too much to be ignored, I suppose.'

'Exactly, sir. Conclusive, I would say.'

'Come on. Let's get back to the station.'


There was a gloomy expression on Masterman's face as he tidied his desk on the afternoon of Gerwyn's morning funeral. The evidence he had against the deceased was enough to convince his superiors that there was no need for further investigation, and the case was closed. His sergeant, in contrast, was elated at the early conclusion of the case and demonstrated a great deal of personal pleasure.

'Penny for your thoughts, sir,' requested the sergeant, smugly. The question brought the Inspector out of his revelry.

'I've been thinking of PC Davies and the report he made out on Freeman's excursions into the country. It's short and official as it should be, but there's nothing in it to suggest Freeman should become overbalanced by it. It simply stated that he advised Freeman to take another route for a respectable time.'

'I know PC Davies, sir. I've worked with him. What he put in his report and what he might have told Freeman could be two different things.'

'Why do you say that?'

'He's been on the Force for a long time and missed out on promotion. He can be intimidating. Like a dog with a bone he won't let go until he has to. His intimidating ways could easily have an emotional effect on a weak man. Even more with a man who was already unbalanced.'

The Inspector looked at the sergeant with a dry smile. 'Yes, I know what you mean, sergeant.  Anyway, I'll have to leave my visit to Mrs Freeman until she has time to get over his death. I can't tell her that her husband is going to be charged posthumously with the murder of Jonathan Pallet so early after his suicide. It was difficult enough interviewing her about his suicide note.  And the children weren't exactly friendly, were they?'

'He was a strange man, sir that I'm sure of.'

Suddenly there was a disturbance in the adjoining room and a female voice commanding, `You can`t go in there!`

A loud knock rattled the glass on the Inspector's door. It was abruptly opened by the person responsible for the intrusion. The Inspector and the sergeant were shocked to see Mrs Freeman walk in followed by David and Ceris. Their black mourning clothes were contrasted by their ashen faces.

'Mrs Freeman,' expounded the Inspector, as he stood up. 'I hardly expected to see you come to the office.'

The corpulent sergeant pressed his back against the wall to allow the three to pass. They stood at the desk facing the Inspector, looking hard, their eyes red from weeping.

'My deepest sympathies to you Mrs Freeman. I'm truly sorry for your loss. I was going to make an appointment after an appropriate time elapsed.'

'I've saved you the journey, then, haven't I?' she said quietly, but deliberately. 'I wanted to leave this visit for a later date, but I couldn`t stop my son coming up, so it has to be now.  You can see at first-hand what you have done to my family. Have a good look on the faces of my children. I want you to see what your system does to ordinary families who just go about their business, trying to live an honest, worthwhile life. You've managed to ruin it all. You've destroyed us.'

The Inspector's face dropped to his boots. 'I'm sorry you see it that way, Mrs Freeman.--Sergeant! Get three chairs and some refreshments.' The sergeant left. 'Mrs Freeman, I don't quite know what you understand of the situation,' said Masterman, softly. 'But I will explain anything to you which you may have misunderstood. I assure you, the police had nothing to do with your husband's death.'

`Liar! yelled David

His mother held her arm up to him. `Let me deal with it, David.` Still keeping calm, but positive and forceful Hilary needed to say what was on her mind. 'My Gerwyn was coping quite well until he was called to the police station. You must have done something to have driven him to his death. Not content with driving him to his death, you now make him a scapegoat for Jonathan Pallet's murder.'

`Who told you that Mrs Freeman?`

`It`s common knowledge up at the factory.`

The door opened and the sergeant struggled in with three chairs and then left.

'Would you like to sit down, all of you?'

'We'll stand,' said Hilary.

'Mrs Freeman, we have evidence--'

'Don't be stupid,' said David, coldly, unable to stay quiet any longer. 'Evidence? That's a laugh.  How many times have we heard that this past decade? You lot can dig up evidence any time it suits you.'

Masterman looked from one pale face to the other, feeling ruffled. He placed his hands, palms down, on his desk. 'Now listen, all of you,' he said, firmly. 'This is not the time or place--'

'I want to know what you did to my husband to drive him to such drastic measures,' insisted Hilary. 'What did you do to him in that half hour he was in police hands?'

The Inspectors eyes became agitated. 'Half hour? he said, surprised.

'Yes, half an hour. I have telephoned the station to try and find out what had happened. After threatening to write to the Chief of Police I was told by the duty policeman that my husband had been interviewed. I asked how long had he been at the station and I was told half an hour. I want to see this PC Davies.'

The door opened and the sergeant came in with a tray of cups of steaming tea. He placed one on the desk for the

230

Inspector, and then offered the family. They all shook their heads, scornfully, so he took a cup himself and placed the tray on a cupboard in the corner.

The Inspector sympathised with Hilary but was unable to grant her the meeting. 'I'm sorry, Mrs Freeman, but that won't be possible. However, I have his report on my desk. If you wish to see it, you can. I must warn you that you won't be happy with its contents.'

'Read it to me. I want my children to learn the ways and the lies of police.'

The sergeant was offended at Hillary's insinuation. 'Shall I escort the family out, sir?' he said, and he touched Hilary's elbow.

'Get your hands of me,` she snapped.'

'And I'll tear you apart if you hurt my mother,' said David.

'Please, please,' demanded the Inspector. 'Let us all keep calm. Sergeant, wait outside, please. I'll call you if I need you.'

The sergeant gave David a hard stare, but left.

The Inspector picked up the report that PC Davies had made out and read the brief statement.

'That accusation is disgusting, said Hilary. My Gerwyn was not like that at all. And I suppose that 30-second reading represent a half hour's interview?' she said, not believing it at all.

'It is an insignificant summary of a routine interview, Mrs Freeman. We had a complaint from a parent which we had to follow up. The young girls probably misread the situation.'

'I often went to the countryside with my father,' said Ceris. My father loved it up there. I know the girls who ride those horses. I went with my father the last time. He wanted me to have a horse.'

'You went with him?' asked the Inspector.

'Yes. I told him I didn't want to be part of that scene. They're a stuck up bunch who aren't very popular at school.'

'I didn't hear any mention my daughter accompanying her

Dad in that report, observed Hilary.

The Inspector seemed puzzled. 'No, there wasn't, was there.'

'They'll be even more unpopular when I get back to school,' continued Ceris. 'I'll tell the whole school what they did. My father was a gentle, loving Dad who was trying his best to discourage me from going to London. He couldn't harm a fly. My god, you police are stupid.'

'That's uncalled for, miss. We have our duty to do.'

'I want to know how this PC Davies did his duty to my husband. He must have done more than just advise him. He had him in there for half an hour. What did he do to him? What did he say? And I don't want that rubbish that's in the report. I want the truth.'

'I'm sorry, Mrs Freeman, but the case is closed. There's nothing I can do.'

'My husband is dead and defenceless and there's nothing you can do? You've already done it.  You've taken advantage of him and made him a scapegoat.

'That's what the system is all about now, Mam,' said David. 'Pick on the weak; the frail, the gullible. The whole country is at it. How many unsuspecting ingenuous people have been made the scapegoats? That's the official line isn't it?' he asked, looking the Inspector straight in the eye. 'That's the norm now.'

'Careful, son,' advised the Inspector, though he felt defeated.

'I'll be careful,' said Hilary. 'I'll be careful to write all the details to my MP and to the newspapers. You murdered my Gerwyn and now you want to brand him a killer. You. Your system. Your prejudices...your indifference...your callousness....'

'Mrs Freeman. Please go home. I shall interview PC Davies, but I'm not promising anything.  Please go until you're feeling better,' he said gently.

Hilary burst into tears. 'I'll go home,' she sobbed. 'What you must realise is that I'm controlling myself now. You'll not know what hit you when I'm feeling better. Come on, children. Let's find PC Davies to start with. I want him to see us. Then we'll start writing some letters.

Ken James

# Twenty Eight

Byron was sitting in his chair by the fireplace where the dying embers reflected his spirit. He was morose and silent and had uttered few words to his wife since coming in from the pub. At eleven o'clock the landlord had closed the curtains on the front windows, put the towels over the pumps, told the non-regular punters it was closing and locked the door. Byron and his mates were privileged to have a few drinks after time. He'd bought them extras hoping he'd motivate a jovial atmosphere that would blank out the new and depressing image he had of himself. But his drinking pals couldn't make him out.

Normally, he was outspoken and easy to understand; abrupt, perhaps, but open and they knew where they stood with him. But he'd been over generous and looking for compliments; telling them he wasn't such a bad guy really. They put the reason on too much drink. They couldn't know why he was so full of diplomacy and innuendo. They didn't realise that Byron suddenly didn't like himself, so they just humoured him not understanding. Nor were they told why he appeared to be a changed man. They eventually drifted from the enigma one by one and he'd been left alone.

The landlord was in no mood to accommodate the slurring of Byron, and as he was the last in the pub, the landlord advised him to call it a night. So he walked home in the drizzling rain with dripping beard, entered the house shouldering the sides of the passage and slumped in his easy chair, staring at the fire and holding his hands to the remnants of heat. His wife had shown a cursory acknowledgement, for her attention was wrapped in the last minutes of the television programme she had been watching.

When he did find some words to say to his wife, they were unusually soft in tone and with tender eyes. She said little. The tear-jerker film she was watching had taken all her concentration until the credits began to roll. She sniffed, and then flicked her eyelids with her finger. The sentiment had brought a little colour to her normally pallid face as she turned to her husband. It was the same each time he came in from the pub; she would leave him to himself and go to bed when her programme finished. But first she would say the customary good night.

'I enjoyed that.' she said as her hand searched her dressing gown pocket for a handkerchief.'

'If you say so, love. It looked a rubbish to me,' he slurred. 'Those programmes are rarely true to life.'

'You only saw the end.--What's the matter, Byron?' she asked, seeing his glum face. 'This horrible business in work still depressing you?'

'It's not exactly a cheerful time, is it?'

'No, I suppose not. Still, it's nothing to do with you, and there's nothing you can do about it.'

'You should have seen the family at the funeral today. His wife was on the verge of collapsing. His kids looked lost. David, his eldest, was holding his mother up. Oh God!'

'I thought you weren't all that fussy on Gerwyn. You said he was a wimp.'

'No, he was alright. Too quiet. Let people walk all over him.'

'They say you've got to watch the quiet ones. It was right enough in his case.'

'What'd you mean?'

'Well, little Gerwyn killing Pallet. I was shocked when I heard he had done away with himself, but when I heard he had murdered Pallet, that really made me think. You've got to be careful who you upset these days. There's no telling who you

236

may be talking to.'

'They only suspect him. They haven't proved anything.'

'I feel sorry for his wife and children. They've got to live with that stigma all their lives.'

'I'll see to it that we'll have another collection at the factory for his family. It will help them out until they get over it.'

'You make the collection? I thought you left that sort of thing to Steve. Besides, I don't think a collection is going to be a great help. It won't make a lot of difference.'

'I didn't say it would be a great help, but it's something, isn't it? It's better than nothing. At least they'll know we haven't forgotten them.'

'I suppose so. Oh well, I'm going to bed.'

'Yea, you go on up. I'll be up later.'

His wife went to the downstairs bathroom. He, sitting as though in a dream, looked blankly at the television screen, not seeing or hearing what was on. He sat there in a trance until his wife returned. She came in carrying a small brown plastic bottle.

'Do you know, I'm sure I had six Valium left in this bottle a couple of nights ago. Now there are only three.'

'What? What Valium?'

'My tablets, I thought sure I had six left.'

'You must have taken them.'

'I don't take them all that often. A month's prescription last me six months. That's why I felt sure I had more than this.'

'You must have miscounted.'

'I don't think so, I'm careful with my Valium. As you know, I only take them when I think I'm not going to sleep well.'

'I hope you're not going to make a fuss over a couple of bloody tablets!' he snapped. 'I'm not in the mood to listen to your neurotic ravings tonight. I'll go down the doctors tomorrow and get you a bottle of fifty.'

'Alright, alright, I was only making an observation. So you'll put my prescription in tomorrow, will you?'

'Yes, yes. Just go to bed.'

'Judging by the state of your nerves you need one yourself.'

'Will you please go to bed?'

'Alright I'm going,' she said finally, as she bent over and gave him a peck on the cheek.'

'Goodnight,' he said softly.

His wife closed the door quietly behind her so that the sleeping children would not be disturbed. Byron leaned forward and switched the television off, but continued to watch it as though he were projecting his own pictures on the screen. His eyes were wild and agitated; his fists clenched making his knuckles white. His shoulders began to rock back and fore. Then he gave a loud grunt, fell back in the chair and closed his eyes tightly. It could have been the drink giving him a premature hangover, or maybe the thought of the nightshift he had to face tomorrow night. But it wasn't. It was a series of images that kept passing through his mind:

The funeral and those innocent white faces, and that little guy who used to tilt his head every time his nerves got the better of him. The shop steward who knew the truth. Worse of all was that misty scene when he confronted his boss on roof. He only wanted to frighten him. He wanted to tell him that he had a list of his misdemeanours; his trips to town for hours when he should have been in work, his going home on weekends and booking the time in work. It was fraudulent. He wouldn't tell Fred because that would be a waste of time. No, he'd go to Area Office about it. If Pallet ever thought of sacking him he'd let the cat out of the bag.

So when he looked out of his bedroom window that morning and saw the fog, he thought what an opportunity for some plain talking with no witnesses. He rang Steve in work, insisted that there would be big trouble if the roof-top job wasn`t sorted. He knew Pallet would go up and find something to be of advantage. But it all went wrong when Pallet suddenly saw him come out of the morning fog from behind a big cowling; He regretted wearing a black balaclava. That was too much. He didn't realise Pallet would panic, nor did he know how close he was to the edge of the office block roof. The unexpected ghostly apparition sent fear through Jonathan's heart. So painful that it had caused him to lose his balance. Byron's instinct was to grab him to save him falling. But Jonathan, believing he was going to be pushed, gave a quick evasive movement which took him nearer the edge. The sudden surge of confusion ended with Byron attempting to hold his boss from falling, but in spite of his attempt to grab him, he actually ended by pushing, and Jonathan fell to his death.

He couldn't admit it. They would never believe he was trying to save Pallet. He could hear him cry out even now; that was the image that was going to haunt him.

In a disguised voice he'd rang the switchboard and reported a man falling off the roof; hoping that the paramedics would come in time to save him. But a greater sin which he could not forgive himself was the fact he was letting his mate take the blame. And he thought of Pallet and Sidney and how they took every opportunity to take advantage of Gerwyn. And Byron knew it was he who was taking the biggest liberty of all; stealing three of his wife's Valium and placing them where the police could find them sealing the blame on Gerwyn.

It revealed the true character of his inner self, and he didn't like it. And he knew he would never forget it.


The End

Ken James